Uncomp

The Earl of Ro... blackmailing, sch... Miss Philippa Mayhew did have a surprising degree of spirit and charm.

For her part, Philippa had to allow that for an insufferably arrogant, unbearably self-important, and odiously self-righteous aristocrat, Roxbury might have a certain appeal for a woman weaker than Philippa most certainly was.

But whatever secret doubts these two angry antagonists had about each other, neither would do anything to interfere with their war of wits, wills, and wiles . . .

. . . especially not anything as unmentionable and unthinkable as love. . . .

DAWN LINDSEY

NOTORIOUS LADY

A SIGNET BOOK

NEW AMERICAN LIBRARY

NAL BOOKS ARE AVAILABLE AT QUANTITY DISCOUNTS
WHEN USED TO PROMOTE PRODUCTS OR SERVICES.
FOR INFORMATION PLEASE WRITE TO PREMIUM MARKETING DIVISION,
NEW AMERICAN LIBRARY, 1633 BROADWAY,
NEW YORK, NEW YORK 10019.

SIGNET TRADEMARK REG. U.S. PAT. OFF. AND FOREIGN COUNTRIES
REGISTERED TRADEMARK—MARCA REGISTRADA
HECHO EN CHICAGO, U.S.A.

SIGNET, SIGNET CLASSIC, MENTOR, ONYX, PLUME, MERIDIAN
and NAL BOOKS are published by NAL PENGUIN INC.,
1633 Broadway, New York, New York 10019

First Printing, June, 1987

1 2 3 4 5 6 7 8 9

PRINTED IN THE UNITED STATES OF AMERICA

1

WHEN INFORMED that the Earl of Roxbury was still at breakfast, the fashionable caller did not hesitate, but swept past her brother's butler, leaving a wake of expensive French perfume. "Good! I was hoping to catch him before he went out," she said in her determined way. "You needn't announce me, Firth. Be so good as to inform my coachman I shall be wanting him again in exactly half an hour!"

His lordship's butler, well aware that brother and sister, both of a forceful nature, seldom met without quarreling, did not obey this peremptory dismissal, but insisted upon sedately conducting her ladyship to the breakfast room, opening the door to announce warningly, "My Lady Holyoke, my lord!"

The earl, who had been out of town for some days and had only returned the evening before, received this news with no noticeable evidence of joy. "Good God, Theresa! What the devil brings you out at such an hour? I thought you never stirred before noon."

His sister, a well-preserved matron on the shady side of forty, observed the large breakfast his lordship was consuming with something like a shudder, and answered irritably, "If you had taken the trouble to inform me you meant to go out of town, I need not have. I have written no fewer than three times in the past week requesting you to call upon me on a matter of some urgency. It was only

5

the merest accident I learned from Julian this morning that you had been out of town for more than a week."

The earl, a tall, powerful figure some ten years younger than his sister, possessed a harsh countenance and exceedingly hard gray eyes. He unerringly picked several unopened letters, written on a distinctive blue hot-pressed paper, out of the pile beside his plate, and said unpleasantly, "If you wish me to read your letters, Theresa, I would recommend you not to drench them with scent. Now, what's to do? I have an appointment in half an hour."

Her lips tightened at this unsubtle reminder, but since the matter was of some urgency, she swallowed her resentment and accepted a seat, though she declined anything to eat. "I never eat anything more than tea and thin bread and butter at this hour, as you very well know. Where have you been, anyway—or need I ask? To inspect some vulgar factory or another, I have no doubt. I will never understand what you find to fascinate you in a pile of dirty smokestacks. Or credit that a brother of mine could be interested in anything so middle-class as business."

But he merely looked amused at this feeble sally. "And I have no intention of trying to explain it to you yet again, especially at such an hour. Cut bait, Theresa. If you want my help—as I must suppose, since I doubt you have interrupted me at this hour for the sake of my conversation—I would advise you to let me have it without any further roundamatoud. What can it be? Is that young fool Julian up to some mischief? I can't think of any other reason you would seek my advice."

Her bosom swelled at this unjust accusation, for she was convinced that no more satisfactory son than her own could be found. Young Lord Holyoke was a charming, obedient youth who had not given his widowed mama one moment of heartache all through his long minority, and displayed only a slight inclination, now that he was a young adult, of setting himself up in opposition to her autocratic will.

For this latter she had no doubt at all where to lay the blame, of course. It had never ceased to gall her that her late husband had appointed her brother in joint guardianship with her, leaving him in complete control of the noble minor's fortune. That the earl's unfashionable bent for business had increased Julian's inheritance several times over, so that now it might be reckoned a very pretty fortune, made very little difference. She had always resented his influence over her son, and never given up trying to detach the impressionable youth from one whose example no sensible mother could help but deplore.

In that she had been only moderately successful, for though she could not accuse her brother, whom she believed completely selfish, of encouraging Julian or paying any noticeable attention to his fatherless nephew, Julian seemed to have developed a marked predilection for his uncle's company. Fortunately, at least he had never shown any particular aptitude for his uncle's unnatural interests as well, which had been her chief fear for many years. But now that he was grown, he also betrayed as little interest in the social world, which made up his mama's chief interest and upon which all her ambitions were centered.

And she knew exactly whom to blame for that. Too many years separated brother and sister for them to be particularly close, but she had also never ceased to lament her brother's wasted potential. At thirty-five he was well-born, immensely wealthy—thanks to his unnatural talent for unlikely investments—and possessed of a countenance that was, in her opinion, too saturnine to be considered handsome, but in the wealthy Earl of Roxbury might be considered no handicap. He might have looked as high as he pleased for a bride, had his manners been more conciliating or his business interests less unorthodox.

His sister was perfectly aware of the number of highly flattering lures that had been thrown out to him over the years by ambitious young beauties, and she herself had spared no effort to present to his notice the most eligible of each new Season's crop of young heiresses. He had succumbed to none of them, and she was beginning to resign herself to the fact that he would never marry. He had certainly carried on several discreet affairs over the years with mature, usually married beauties, but when in desperation she had introduced several charming widows to his notice in hope that he might appreciate their more mature charms, it had not helped. She was in fact beginning to believe him a confirmed misogynist.

Aside from every other consideration, it annoyed her that such an immense fortune should go to waste. Roxbury had managed to increase the depleted fortune he had inherited from his extravagant father several times over by his shrewd investments. He owned outright several plants in Birmingham, near where his principal seat was located; he had an interest in a number of others; and he was as likely to hobnob with vulgar merchants and factory owners as with the set he had been born into. Nor could she even console herself that her own son might someday inherit his uncle's fortune. That would go to some distant cousin, the mere thought of which was almost enough to make her scream with vexation.

No, she had no doubt at all where to place the blame for this current disaster, and said bitterly, "Not that I should be at all surprised, I suppose. You have wasted little effort in encouraging my son to thwart me, for what reason I can only guess. I only hope you will be happy when he has contracted an impossible marriage as a result of your influence."

The earl betrayed the first faint sign of interest at that. "I am unlikely to have gone to so much effort, even to thwart you, my dear Theresa," he remarked unkindly. "But is Julian about to contract an impossible marriage? I wasn't aware he had even started in the petticoat line yet. Who is she?"

He showed so little natural feeling for her news that she said even more resentfully, "Yes, I might have expected you to take it that way. But I wonder how you will look when you find him wed to the niece of a notorious actress."

"I don't doubt I shall look exceedingly surprised. Good God, Theresa, try not to be quite so buffleheaded," he said contemptuously. "If that is why you have disturbed me at breakfast, you might have spared both of us the trouble. He may very well have fallen in love with an actress. In fact, nothing is more certain. But if so, you may take my word for it it's not marriage he has in mind."

She flushed unbecomingly. "I hope I am not a complete fool," she retorted scathingly. "That is what I supposed when I first heard of it. But I tell you that when I confronted him with it, he informed me he means to wed the creature."

The earl looked even more sardonic. "Yes, I suspected it must have been something like that. I won't ask how you came by your information. One of your network of spies, no doubt. I only marvel at your absurdity in confronting him with such a tale. What else was he supposed to say?"

"Since it appears the affair was common knowledge in Tunbridge Wells, where he met her, he should scarcely be surprised I came to hear of it. I never approved of his going there in the first place to stay with that friend, as you know. But you are always so convinced I mean to keep him on leading strings that I relented. And now we see what comes of it."

"You are a constant source of wonder to me, Theresa," he remarked in amusement. "If you came for my advice, which seems improbable, I would advise you to allow the whole to blow over. You may be sure it will, especially if the young lady in question resides in Tunbridge Wells."

"That's just it," she cried quickly. "She doesn't! It seems she lives in London and has lost little time in following him here. I make no doubt the hussy meant to have her toils in him from the beginning."

"Nevertheless, my advice stands. You never would believe that no good could come of tying the boy to your apron strings. I warned you he would revolt sooner or later."

He sounded bored, and her bosom swelled resentfully. "I don't need you to advise me how to raise my son."

He shrugged, threw down his napkin, and went to open the door for her. "In that case, you might have spared both of us a wasted morning. Now, I have an appointment as I told you, for which I'm late already. You must excuse me."

"Is that *all* you have to say?" she cried in disbelief.

"That's all."

She stiffened and played her trump card. "You surprise me. I doubted even you would welcome into the family the niece of Isabella Monteith."

"What?" he demanded incredulously.

She smiled thinly, gratified that she had at last managed to shake him. "Yes, I thought that might make you change your tune. I have little doubt the aunt is behind it all. She has no reason to be fond of our family, as you know. And if the niece is anything like the aunt, it is no wonder my poor boy has been bewitched."

But the earl had turned away impatiently again. "Don't be absurd! Julian may be captivated, but it is unlikely he is thinking of marriage. He's not such a fool."

"Our father was," she pointed out dryly.

"But then I have a great deal more respect for Julian's good sense than our late father's. Whatever happened to her, by the way? The aunt, I mean. I have heard nothing of her in years."

"She did manage to trap some besotted fool into marrying her in the end. Edgar Mayhew, whom you may not remember, for he died some years ago. Evidently it was not a particularly successful marriage, as you might imagine. I understand when he died he left her heavily in debt, which is no doubt why she means to mend her fortunes by entrapping my poor boy."

He once more recommended her rather shortly not to be such a fool. But after she had left in a cold fury, hoping sarcastically that he was prepared to welcome the niece of such a woman into the family if he meant to do nothing to prevent it, he stood frowning down into his empty fireplace for some moments, then straightened and abruptly changed his plans for the morning.

When he ordered his chestnuts brought 'round, neither his groom nor his butler was surprised, for they had been kept idle during his brief absence, and were one of his chief extravagances, outside of buying up factories. But his groom was rather surprised when he turned, not toward

Richmond as he had been expecting, but in the direction of Piccadilly.

Halfway down St. James's Street he was evidently rewarded, however, for his groom caught sight of his lordship's young nephew walking with a party of friends.

The earl pulled up immediately, and Lord Holyoke, catching sight of him, hurried over, betraying no sign of embarrassment at sight of his relative. "Marcus," he cried with every appearance of pleasure. "So you are back! I meant to walk 'round this afternoon to see if you had returned, and because I had something in particular I wanted to talk to you about. How was your trip? Did you buy any new factories, or whatever it was ﹔ ᴐu went to look at?"

He was a handsome, fair youth with an open countenance and a great deal of unconscious charm. The earl could detect no difference in his manner, but frowned a little at the news he had something he wanted to talk over with him, and invited abruptly, "Then come with me, unless you have something more pressing to do. I am on my way to Richmond to exercise my chestnuts. Fobbing noticed a slight falling off of my leader while I was gone."

The younger man seemed to hesitate only an instant, which reassured his uncle even more. "Nothing that won't keep," he said readily. "Just let me tell the others. I won't keep you standing above a moment."

He was as good as his word and soon swung up into the racing curricle beside his uncle. He looked a little surprised when the earl left his groom behind, sending him to run an errand for him, but made no comment and said merely, as they threaded their way through the traffic, "Did you have a successful journey? But then, I suppose I needn't ask. What was it this time? Coke foundries?"

"Canals," responded the earl calmly, controlling his leader's tendency to resent the presence of a handcart by the side of the road.

"C-canals?" repeated Julian, rather startled. "I never know when you are serious or not, Marcus. What on earth is there to look at in a canal?"

"Very little. But I am thinking of investing in the construction of one to move iron directly to London. And don't pretend you're interested. What did you want to see me about?"

Thus directly confronted, Julian flushed a little. "As it happens, I . . . Well, the truth is I am thinking of getting married, Marcus," he said in a rush. "I wanted you to know before . . . Well, I just wanted you to hear it from me, is all."

Roxbury's heart sank, but he said merely, "This is somewhat sudden, isn't it? I had no notion you had any such intention two weeks ago when I left."

Julian flushed still more. "No. Well, I hadn't meant to tell anyone just yet, but then some cat wrote and told Mama all about it. Not that I mean I'm ashamed of it or anything, but . . . Well, you know what Mama is."

"None better," said the earl dryly. "Is there any reason you should be ashamed of the match?"

"No, none whatsoever," said Julian a shade too defiantly. "I . . . Well, I will admit it is not a particularly brilliant match, but you know I have never had any desire for that kind of marriage. I'm sorry to disappoint Mama, but she never would understand that I never shared her ambitions in that direction. And she is perfectly respectable."

The earl had to bite back an instinctive retort and after a moment said merely, "Where did you meet her?"

"In Tunbridge Wells. You remember I went there a few months ago to visit an old friend of mine. In point of fact, I was beginning to regret having accepted his invitation, for the place is full of nothing but valetudinarians and crochety old ladies, and I discovered I had less in common with my friend than I had remembered. But then I met Diana and everything changed in a flash," answered Julian naïvely.

"I'm not surprised you found it flat. I have never cared for it either, on architectural or medicinal grounds. But go on. I take it she was an acquaintance of your, er, old friend?"

Julian flushed once more, looking uncharacteristically defiant. "Well, actually, no. We met quite by accident, but I hope you don't mean to make something absurd out of it, as Mama has. It had come on to rain one afternoon when I'd gone out without an umbrella. Normally I wouldn't have cared, of course, but as luck would have it, I had promised to visit an old friend of Mama's who had latched on to me. I can tell you I was dreading it, but afterward I could only be thankful, for otherwise I might never have met Diana at all. She . . . You'll have gathered she was sheltering from the storm as well. And I know our meeting was unconventional, but it's not what you're thinking, for she is so sweet and shy, Marcus. She—she didn't want to let me walk her home, once the rain stopped, for we hadn't been properly introduced, of course, but I was able to overcome her scruples. And I—I know it sounds silly, but I think I fell in love with her from that first moment. I tell you she is nothing like the gorgons Mama is always trying to interest me in. You will see what I mean once you've met her, Marcus.''

The earl abruptly let his hands drop and passed a cart on a dangerous curve, clearing it only by inches. Julian, momentarily distracted, cried admiringly as soon as they were past, "Oh, well done! I made sure you would have to wait until the straight. What a complete hand you are, Marcus.''

Roxbury, his brief spurt of anger at the chit's cleverness controlled now, said dryly, "Then that is a moment we will both have to look forward to. Do take it this attraction was mutual?''

Julian glanced at him, as if suspecting for the first time that his uncle was not being quite as sympathetic as he had hoped. "Yes, and you needn't say it like that. I know our meeting was unconventional, but it was perfectly respectable, and if you are insinuating that she is a fortune-hunter, as Mama did, let me assure you she didn't even know who I was until I told her. At any rate, my fortune is hardly large enough to tempt the sort of female you are imagining.''

"I imagine it is quite large enough to tempt a great many women. But never mind. I will attempt to restrain my natural cynicism.''

Julian glanced at him again, apparently reassured. "Thank you, for the truth is, I am relying upon you to help bring Mama round. She . . . Well, Diana's birth is as good as mine, but both her parents are dead, so she has no portion, or at least a very small one—not that I care a fig for that, of course. Thanks to you, my fortune will be quite princely when I come into it. But . . . The thing I haven't told you, but which Mama's spies took great care to inform her, is that Diana's aunt—the one she lives with—used to be a rather notorious actress. She married quite respectably after that, and at any rate, it was all a great many years ago, but you know what a snob Mama is. And that's why I'm relying on you to help me make her see reason," he added with naïve trust.

Roxbury had to once more bite back the impulse to utter some choice words against such an obvious harpy, but merely said dryly, "I fear you flatter me. I suspect that is beyond anyone's power. But do you value my advice, Julian?"

"Good Lord, you know I do."

The other smiled faintly and without humor. "Then I would advise you to do nothing hastily. On your own admission your mother has every reason for disliking the match, and you have, after all, known the young woman only a short time."

"Naturally I mean to do nothing hasty," said Julian a little sullenly.

"You relieve my mind. I take it the aunt approves of the match?"

His tone was again dry, and Julian flushed a little. "I haven't applied to her formally yet. But I have no reason to believe she will object to it. Why should she?"

"Why, indeed? I should imagine she will leap at it. Never mind! Don't ride rusty, you young gull-groper! I have only one more thing to say, and you had better listen well to it: I am fond of you, as I think you know, but I will not hesitate to exercise my responsibilities in terms of your fortune if I discover you have fallen into the clutches of some practiced harridan. No, don't bother to annihilate me. You will not succeed and will only do violence to your own feelings. If you are right about your Diana, what I said need not concern you. And if you aren't, nothing you can say will make me change my mind. Now let us speak of it no more. I am traveling to Sussex at the end of the week. Do you care to come with me?''

Julian seemed inclined to argue the matter for a moment, but then accepted the change of subject and said a little stiffly, "Do you go to visit Grandmother?''

"I mean to bring her back with me. She writes that she is bored with your Great-aunt Hatty's company and longing for some liveliness.''

"Grandmother's a great gun," Julian said more naturally. "With all her failing health, she never complains. But if you're bringing her back, I think I won't, if you don't mind. I—I have several engagements in town.''

They both knew what those engagements no doubt were, but Roxbury said merely, "Then dine with me tomorrow evening, if you can spare the time.''

Julian more happily agreed to that, and the rest of the drive passed pleasantly enough. In fact, Julian, who had been fearing that his mother would get to his uncle first and poison his mind against the match, emerged from it with considerable relief, convinced that his faith in his favorite uncle had not been misplaced.

Julian would have been less reassured had he been privileged to read his uncle's thoughts when the earl gained the privacy of his own study once more. He was fond of his nephew, as he had said, and had been uninclined to give credence to his sister's fears. But after talking with Julian he was obliged to acknowledge that the affair was more serious than he had supposed. Despite Julian's faith in him, he had his own reasons for despising the sort of amoral female likely to try to lure so innocent a youth into marriage, and as his sister had foreseen, the fact that she should turn out to be the niece of Isabella Monteith only made it ten times worse.

Well, he had seen no point in alienating Julian just yet, and so had said no more, but for once he was obliged to own that his sister had not exaggerated the danger. The chit—or her aunt—had been very clever so far, but she would find she had him to reckon with now. And he thought he would stop at nothing to wrest his young relative from the clutches of such harpies.

Abruptly he looked down to discover he had crushed the thin gold snuff box he held in his hand. He laughed unpleasantly and tossed it on a table, then went belatedly to keep his appointment.

2

FOR ONCE, however, the earl's mind was not on business, and he soon dismissed his man of affairs and for the second time that day abruptly changed his plans. A quick look in the city directory revealed that a Mrs. Isabella Mayhew lived in Green Street, and he determined to pay her a visit without further delay. Whether she would appreciate that visit was another matter entirely.

He was obliged to own that the address was respectable enough, but it was immediately apparent to his practiced eye when he reached it that Number 59 showed subtle signs of neglect. It could have used a new coat of paint, and a window at the top of the house was cracked. Roxbury's mouth tightened grimly and he plied the knocker with unnecessary force.

The door was opened to him by an extremely youthful housemaid, who gaped at him rather stupidly, but revealed when asked that her mistress was away from home and she didn't know when she was expected back. Roxbury swore to himself, then on impulse demanded to see Miss Mayhew.

The maid looked even more startled, but admitted that Miss was up in the small parlor. "Very well," he said curtly. "Be so good as to take my card up to her and request the favor of fifteen minutes of her time."

She curtsied doubtfully and left him standing in the hall while she went to obey this request. He noticed contemptuously that the inside of the house showed further unmistakable signs of poverty. The wallpaper was faded, the stairs uncarpeted, and the brocade curtains at the window neatly darned. The latter surprised him, given the nature of the inhabitants, and he further noticed with a frown that despite its shabbiness everything was swept and well-polished and there was a bowl of flowers on a table in the hall.

His brows rose, but then he shrugged and abruptly followed the maid up the stairs.

He was in excellent time to hear a well-modulated voice from a room off the first landing exclaim in consternation, "Lord Roxbury! Good God, are you sure he asked for me?"

"Oh, yes, miss!" exclaimed the maid breathlessly. "He asked for the mistress first, but I explained as she was out, so then he asked for you."

"Oh, bother," said the first voice. "I have been dreading something of the sort, and I would have to be in my oldest dress and with my hair no doubt coming down. Tell him I can't see him . . . . No, I suppose I must. But for heaven's sake delay him until I have had a chance to tidy up."

His lordship smiled grimly and stepped into the room. "That won't be necessary, Miss Mayhew. I promise my business won't take long," he said unpleasantly.

She started violently, but though she was undoubtedly mortified at having been caught in such a position, he was bound to admit she recovered quickly. She hesitated only a moment before rising from her desk, where she appeared to have been doing accounts, and coming forward, with just a hint of becoming color in her cheeks. "Lord Roxbury?" she asked with unexpected dignity. "You wished to see me?"

He looked her over critically, obliged to admit that in appearance at least she was better than he had anticipated. She had certainly not been expecting visitors, for she was attired in an outmoded gown that had seen better days, but even that she carried off with an unexpected aplomb. In addition she was both older and not the out-and-out beauty he had been expecting. She possessed a tall, decidedly elegant figure, and her hair was a luxuriant shade of chestnut, worn in a surprisingly demure braided coronet that somehow suited her, but her face was not conventionally beautiful by any standards. It was not a fact, he realized with growing grimness, that one long noticed, for she possessed an unusual vividness, her dark eyes animated and glowing with an unexpected intelligence, and her generous mouth looking as if it were made for laughter—or to be kissed.

In fact, he was bound to admit that he would not have credited his young nephew with so much taste. But for some reason the thought of this ripe, oddly assured woman with his nephew annoyed him more than it should have, as if a sleek lioness had chosen to toy with a cub for sport.

His lips parted in an unpleasant smile, and he said insultingly, looking her up and down, "Yes, ma'am! I just wanted to see you. But I must confess you are not what I was expecting."

She looked startled, and since the unpleasantness of his tone was unmistakable, her eyes began to flash a little, but after a moment she said evenly, "If it comes to that, you are hardly what I was expecting either, my lord. But I will confess I have been half-expecting this visit."

"I can well imagine, ma'am. Or did you really believe that my nephew's family would welcome with open arms the niece of such a woman?"

This time the flash of anger in her eyes was unmistakable, but once more she seemed to control her temper with an effort. "Insulting me will accomplish nothing, my lord. I am fond of your nephew, but I have no desire to—"

He interrupted her with a crack of rude laughter. "Fond! As a cobra is of its prey, no doubt. I would have thought the difference in your ages would have dissuaded you, if nothing else."

This time she looked even more startled. "Difference in our . . . What on earth has that to do with anything?"

"I would presume everything. How old are you?" he demanded rudely.

"I am five-and-twenty. Hardly in my dotage!"

"But scarcely a match for three-and-twenty, wouldn't

you say? And by looking at you, I would say the difference in experience is even greater."

"Difference in . . . Oh, good God," she exclaimed in sudden understanding. "You think . . . I'm afraid there has been some mistake, my lord. You asked for Miss Mayhew, and I am the eldest. I am Philippa Mayhew. I believe it is my sister Diana you wish to speak with."

He had frowned swiftly, thrown off his stride for the first time. "Good God! Don't tell me there are two of you?"

She flushed again with temper, but said steadily, "As it happens, I am not sorry for this mixup, for I have long thought it might be helpful if we were to meet. If you can forget your prejudices for five minutes, we might be able to settle this matter. Pray sit down."

"No, thank you. Whatever we have to say to each other can be said standing," he said rudely, recovering himself.

She evidently chose to ignore that. "Very well. You have made it more than plain that you dislike the relationship between your nephew and my sister. I am far from approving of your reasons, but it might surprise you to learn that I am little more in favor of it."

He gave a crack of unamused laughter. "It would!"

Once more she ignored him, though her remarkable eyes began to flash a little dangerously. "Odd as it may seem, I have little more liking for such misalliances than you do. My aunt made just such a marriage, and it was a most unhappy one. You may try to provoke me into quarreling as much as you like, but it seems to me we would be far better occupied in trying to prevent both of our relatives being made unhappy."

He had leaned his shoulder against the doorframe and was regarding her with open contempt. "And what do you suggest, Miss Mayhew?"

"And what do you suggest, Lord Roxbury?" she countered angrily. "To forbid your nephew to see my sister ever again? I would remind you that they are both of age. All that will accomplish will be to drive them into the very thing we both hope to avoid."

"Is that a threat, Miss Mayhew?" he inquired unpleasantly.

"No, it is not! It is merely a warning. Obviously you do not choose to credit it, but my sister and your nephew are—or believe they are—very much in love. Whatever we may think on the subject matters very little."

He laughed again and removed his shoulders from the doorframe. "I've no doubt your sister has taken pains to see to that, Miss Mayhew. But you are mistaken if you think my opinion doesn't matter. My nephew may be of age, as you say, but you have overlooked one vital fact. But then it is always best to make sure of an investment first, I have found."

She flushed furiously. "Investment?"

He came farther into the room, and she betrayed her nervousness for the first time by instinctively backing before him. "Very wise, Miss Mayhew," he remarked sardonically. "I am not known for my amiable temper, and I will confess I would take great pleasure in strangling you at the moment. If I had my way, women like you would be whipped at the cart tail."

"Women like me?" she repeated in a strangled voice.

"I don't know whether your aunt put you and your sister up to this, or it was mere coincidence that my nephew fell into your orbit. I don't even know whether you actually hoped to fool him into marriage, or merely meant to force me into buying you off. Neither matters, for, as I said, you have miscalculated badly this time. My nephew's entire fortune is tied up in a trust that I alone control until he is thirty, or until I choose to end it. And you may be sure that if he were to marry your sister, I would refuse to wind it up a day before his thirtieth birthday."

She seemed to have stiffened and two bright spots of color stained her cheeks. "You—you—"

"Cat got your tongue, Miss Mayhew?" he inquired nastily. "I thought that would come as an unwelcome surprise to you. As you can see, you have not a hope of seeing a penny of my nephew's fortune for a number of years. And I doubt you are willing to wait quite that long for a return on this particular investment. My nephew at present has nothing but a modest quarterly allowance, and you may be sure I will not increase that either, so long as he is likely to throw it away on your immoral sister.''

She was no longer even attempting to control her temper. ''The only unwelcome surprise is that Lord Holyoke could possess so unpleasant a relative,'' she cried scathingly. ''I had hoped to make you listen to reason, but it is plain you are incapable of it. But at least I had expected better of you than empty threats.''

''If your sister cares to call my bluff, she will soon learn how empty they are.''

''You think you are so clever! Of course it has not occurred to you that they might actually choose to defy you and forgo Julian's fortune?''

''I must confess it has not. But I meant what I said. If Julian marries your sister, he will not see a penny more than his present allowance until the day he turns thirty.''

''Good God! I am beginning to believe you would actually do that, even though your nephew would be the one to suffer most.''

''You would be wise to believe it. I am beginning to think there is nothing I would not do to prevent my nephew's alliance with such harpies,'' he said deliberately.

She flushed up with rage. ''You may insult me as much as you like, but all your blustering and threats will avail nothing if Julian chooses to defy you.''

''I think it would be impossible to insult you, Miss Mayhew. But I doubt your sister will care to put it to the test. A wise businessman always knows when to cut his losses.''

''We shall see, my lord,'' she said furiously. ''You have issued your challenge, but in point of fact there is nothing you can do to prevent the marriage. You would not believe me, but I was almost as opposed to it as you were. But now I think there is nothing I would not do to force you to eat your words.''

Before he could reply there was an unexpected interruption. The door had remained open, and a youth of perhaps sixteen, bearing a strong resemblance to her, looked in the open doorway, saying a little self-consciously, ''Is everything all right, Philippa? I thought I heard raised voices.''

The earl was astonished, but Miss Mayhew seemed to make an effort to gain control of herself. "Yes, of course," she answered hurriedly. "Lord Roxbury and I were merely having a slight difference of opinion, that's all. Pray go back to your books."

The youth hesitated, looking between them uncertainly. He plainly did not believe her, but lacked the assurance to press the issue. "Very well," he said reluctantly. "But I'll be in the next room if you should need me."

His meaning was clear, and Roxbury had to hide a sudden smile at the thought of so slight a youth attempting to evict him.

Miss Mayhew did not seem to find it amusing, however, for she said again, in something like exasperation, "No, no! Don't be absurd. Now go away, please. You are interrupting us, you know."

He flushed and with another look at his lordship reluctantly obeyed her.

"Who the devil was that?" demanded the earl, making no apology for his language.

"My brother, Darius," she answered coldly.

"What did you call him?"

"Darius. And I see no point in prolonging this interview any further. You obviously have no intention of seeing reason, and I have had more than enough of your insults."

"Then I fear you will have to call back your brother to evict me, Miss Mayhew, for I am far from being finished yet," he retorted sardonically.

She flushed furiously, but short of calling back her brother, was plainly helpless, as they both knew. "Very well, Miss Mayhew," he said, his tone hardening again. "I have only one more thing to say and you would do well to listen. If you or your sister chooses to defy me, you will soon learn your mistake. Not only will I keep my word about my nephew's fortune, but I can also promise you I will take great pleasure in exposing and ruining all of you, your aunt included. Have I made myself perfectly clear?"

"Perfectly," she retorted contemptuously. "Now let me make myself equally clear. I will make you regret you dared to threaten us, if it is the last thing I ever do. Diana shall marry your nephew, and there's not a thing you can do about it. If you try to withhold his fortune, it is you, not we, who will be made to look the villain in the eyes of the world. And if you try to ruin us, you will effectively ruin your nephew as well.''

He straightened, his expression harsh. "It little matters, since he will be effectively ruined the day he weds into such a family. I can only advise you to be very careful before choosing to make an enemy of me. I am no callow youth, and I will stop at nothing to protect my nephew from such conscienceless jades.''

She flushed up furiously at the insult and made no answer as he bowed mockingly and strolled out.

Once more on the pavement he hesitated, then shrugged and turned toward his sister's house in Brook Street.

He found her undergoing a fitting, but though she looked far from gratified to see him, she abruptly dismissed her dresser. "Very well, Jurby! That will be all. Ring for some tea as you go.''

"None for me, thank you. My business won't take me that long.''

She waved her maid away in some irritation. "Very well, that will be all, then. Now, what do you want?'' she demanded ungraciously as soon as her maid was out of the room. "I have a thousand and one things to do this afternoon.''

"In that case I am sorry to disturb you, but I thought you would like to know at once that your son is no longer in danger of that particular entanglement,'' he observed sardonically.

Her expression changed on the instant, and she almost fell on his neck. "Marcus! Oh, thank God! Did you see that hussy? Is she still as beautiful as ever?''

"If by that hussy you mean Isabella Monteith, no, I did not. Nor did I see Julian's Diana, who seems to be the younger sister, as a matter of fact.''

"Good God! Don't tell me there are two of them.''

"There seems also to be a sixteen-year-old youth in the house, which I confess I was not expecting. They must find him a considerable handicap in their chosen profession.''

"Never mind that. Were you forced to buy them off?"

"I was not. I merely pointed out to the sister—she calls herself Philippa, by the way—that Julian does not come into full possession of his fortune until the age of thirty, or until I consent to wind up the trust. She was extremely annoyed, as you might expect, and issued a great many threats, but you may be sure she will not care to waste her time on so unpromising an investment. On his present income Julian would prove more of a liability than an asset, and I think I convinced her I would not consent either to wind up the trust or even to increase his allowance a day before necessary if he is so foolish as to wed her sister."

Lady Holyoke stared at him, torn between relief and resentment. "I might have known you would reduce everything to terms of profit and loss. But I must confess I never thought to be grateful for that dreadful trust. Of course you would not do it, but she does not know that."

"You are mistaken."

He spoke so harshly that she eyed him a little uncertainly. "I own that almost anything would be preferable to marriage to such a creature, but you must know Julian would never forgive you. Not that that would be such a very bad thing, for I've always disliked your influence over him. I know well whom I have to blame for this present situation, in fact."

"You are again mistaken," he said mockingly. "I have not, I believe, shown any inclination to fall victim to beautiful fortune-hunters, nor have I encouraged Julian to do so."

"No, but that is scarcely to your recommendation," she grumbled, losing sight for the moment of the main point. "Sometimes I wonder if you possess a heart. At least my poor Julian is not a—a walking ledger book, as you seem to be."

He bowed mockingly. "I thank you for the compliment, sister dear. But if so, you will have cause to be grateful to me, for you may be sure if Julian weds Miss Mayhew I will not hesitate to invoke the full terms of the trust. Even to spite me you will scarcely wish your son to wed such a harpy."

She forgot her resentment instantly. "Good God! Are they as bad as that?"

He seemed to consider the matter for a moment, a slight frown between his eyes. "If you mean, was she vulgar or obvious, I would have to say no. In fact, the sister, at least, played her role very well. She was by no means a beauty, but she is certainly one of the most striking women I have ever seen. In looks alone she would do very well, I must confess."

Lady Holyoke was staring at him in some astonishment. "Good God! This is praise indeed, coming from you. Take care you don't fall victim to their wiles," she added waspishly.

"I am not likely to. I am hardly an impressionable youth. At any rate, I said in looks alone. In all else, they are the harpies I called them. I have little doubt they set out to lure Julian in—or some other fool like him—just as you said. You were also right to say Mayhew left his wife without a feather to fly with. The evidence of poverty is everywhere. But Miss Philippa Mayhew now knows she has chosen her victim unwisely this time."

"I can't be sorry you did it, of course, but I own I feel for my poor duped boy," said his sister irrationally. "Will you break the news to him?"

He laughed unpleasantly. "You wanted the foul deed done, but you don't wish to appear the villain in the piece, is that it? You needn't worry, however. It will be unnecessary for either of us to tell him. I believe we may safely rely upon Miss Mayhew to do that."

"Well, I hope you may be right. But I have a dreadful suspicion she will not give up a fortune so easily. You should have bought her off and been done with it."

He smiled sardonically and strode toward the door. "I almost hope she does. Even if Isabella Monteith weren't their aunt, I confess it would give me great pleasure to ruin so conscienceless a group of doxies."

Once more she stared at him, but wisely said no more.

3

IN THE meantime Miss Philippa Mayhew was still standing where the earl had left her when her aunt returned from her shopping expedition and found her there.

As Isabella Monteith she may once have been a reigning toast, but she had grown sadly stout over the years, and even the climb up the stairs left her a little breathless. "Oh, there you are, dear," she gasped, sinking onto a sofa and fanning herself. "I swear those stairs get steeper every day."

She was still pretty in a brassy fashion, though the gold in her curls owed more to artifice than nature, and she continued to make free use of rouge and powder, despite her altered position in life. That change in position had been as much source for unhappiness as good fortune, but she was of a cheerful disposition and so seldom bothered to repine over wasted chances.

She added now, once she had caught her breath, "But never mind that! What is this Betsy has been telling me? Roxbury has been here? Did he . . ." Then, as she saw her niece's stormy face for the first time, her countenance fell ludicrously. "Oh, dear," she said pitifully. "I was afraid of that. He doesn't approve . . ."

She was obliged to break off, however, for her voice had penetrated into the next room, where her lap dog had been napping during her absence. He came in now to demand instant attention from her, uttering a series of shrill yaps and wheezes that made all conversation impossible.

She picked him up, complaining, "I vow Caesar is growing as stout as I am. Hush, you absurd creature! I can't imagine why I put up with you. I fear frustrated old women who resort to keeping pugs are positively disgusting."

Caesar, his paroxysms of welcome finished, sneezed, shook himself, then settled contentedly into her lap.

"Now, what were we saying?" said her distracted aunt. "Oh, yes! I could get no more from that stupid girl than that Lord Roxbury had called. It was Julian's uncle, I presume? What did he say? Did he disapprove the marriage as you feared he would?"

Philippa gave a harsh laugh. "You will be surprised to learn, ma'am, that women such as I should be whipped at the cart tail."

Her aunt's jaw dropped. "Dearest, he never said so? Is the man mad? I have heard he is very proud, but he can't be serious."

"You are mistaken, Aunt. He was good enough to inform me that if Diana marries his precious nephew, he shall take great pleasure in ruining us all."

"Well, that at least is no threat," pointed out her aunt philosophically. "I'm sure I have been on the brink of ruin for years. But what can he be thinking of? You always suspected Julian's family would not like the match, but I daresay the Mayhews are as old a family as the Darroughs."

"But you are forgetting our handicap in the eyes of the world, Aunt," said Philippa contemptuously. "Apparently it was enough for him that we were living with the notorious Isabella Monteith. It was obvious he cared to learn nothing about the family, or even to meet Diana and judge for himself. It is bigotry such as that that I most despise." She had begun to stride up and down the room in her rage.

Her aunt watched her for a moment, then sighed. "Yes, but, my love, you always knew Julian's family would be opposed to the match."

"Opposed, yes! But not—not wholly unreasonable. Oh, I can't remember when I have been so angry. If Diana marries Julian, it is to ruin him, so I am given to understand.''

"Well, my dear, I have no wish to defend him," said her aunt reasonably. "But there were a great many people who refused to receive your uncle after he married me, you know. And while I'm sure I have never regretted inviting you to live with me, we both knew this was bound to come up.''

"If my uncle was snubbed, ma'am, it is probably because he was invariably foxed in his later years and had developed the unpleasant habit of attempting to borrow money from whomever he met," retorted Philippa. "And if we hadn't come to live with you, I have no doubt we would all have starved long since, which is hardly any more of a social recommendation. At any rate, don't attempt to be rational. You cannot know the violence of the language he used, or the studied nature of his insults. I tell you I have never met anyone I disliked more.''

"Yes, my love, so I can see," said her aunt, frankly removing one of her shoes and massaging a plump foot. "I swear I must have walked miles today in search of new shoes for Genia. But I don't see that this visit, unpleasant as it must have been, really changes anything. You know you have always been against the match as well, for what reason I can only guess. I must confess I have considered her meeting him in the light of a godsend myself. You know we have worried how we are to establish Diana creditably. And there's no denying that Julian's fortune is quite respectable and heaven knows he's nutty upon her.''

"I have never been against the match," Philippa said self-consciously. "If his family would agree and if their fortunes weren't so different, you know there is nothing I would like better! But you made just such an unequal match, Aunt Bella, and were treated abominably. I have no desire to see Diana make the same mistake. Or at least I hadn't! Now I am so angry I think I would do almost anything to thwart so unpleasant a man.''

"Well, my love, they are both of age, as you know," pointed out her aunt. "In truth, I suspect it is out of both of your hands.''

But at that Philippa's eyes flashed her contempt. "You are mistaken, Aunt. Lord Roxbury was at considerable pains to inform me that Julian's entire fortune is tied up in a trust administered solely by him until Julian turns thirty. If Julian is so unwise as to wed over his objections, he will not hesitate to invoke the full terms of the trust and keep Julian tied to his purse strings until the very day of his thirtieth birthday."

"What?" exclaimed her aunt, moved to strong emotion for the first time. "I've never heard of anything so barbaric. Tied up until he is thirty? I always knew his father was a cautious man, but that is carrying things too far."

Philippa was momentarily diverted. "Good God, Aunt Bella, you never mentioned that you knew Julian's father."

"My dear, in my line of work one didn't go about boasting of the gentlemen one knew," replied her aunt dryly. "But there were few men of wealth or importance I didn't know. Lord Holyoke wasn't one of my particular court, I remember, but certainly I knew him. I remember one evening backstage . . . But never mind," she added hastily. "There is nothing more boring than other people's reminiscences, after all. But if Julian's fortune is indeed tied up until he is thirty, obviously there's no more to be said. I'm sorry for it, for aside from every other consideration I fear poor Diana will be hurt. But heaven knows a penniless husband is worse than no husband at all, as I should know."

"Good God, Aunt Bella, surely you don't think I intend to submit so tamely to such blackmail?"

Aunt Bella's jaw dropped at this volte-face, and she demanded uneasily, "Now, Philippa, what are you up to? I own I have never approved of such arrangements, but if Julian's fortune is really tied up as he says, it is as well to be practical. I'm sure I'm very fond of Julian, but God knows we don't need another liability."

Philippa knelt by her aunt's chair and took her hands, her expressive eyes beginning to sparkle with sudden mischief. "Dearest Aunt Bella, we both know you have never been practical in your life. And you must admit that, if nothing else, it would certainly infuriate Lord Roxbury more than anything else we might do, to know that his nephew was a pensioner of the notorious actress Isabella Monteith.''

"No, Philippa! I warn you now: I won't house Julian, however fond I may be of him," declared her distracted aunt with sudden stubbornness. "It is all very well to infuriate Roxbury, but not when we seldom know where next month's food is coming from." She stopped as a new thought occurred to her, and she added more thoughtfully, "Unless, of course, you think to force his hand with a runaway marriage? I own the thought had already occurred to me."

Philippa flushed guiltily. "No," she said, revolted at the thought. "Good God, that would make me as bad as Roxbury believes. At any rate, you don't know him if you think he would be forced to change his mind, even by public opinion. I think he would let them starve before he would back down.''

Mrs. Mayhew was far from understanding these unnecessary scruples and said so, but Philippa repeated quickly, "No, no, you know you don't mean that, Aunt Bella. And at any rate, I hope you know I wasn't serious. I would never saddle you with any further responsibilities. We have been a dreadful charge on you already, I fear.''

"Don't be absurd, my love. I'm sure I wouldn't know what to do with myself if I didn't owe anyone anything. When your uncle was alive, we were used to have bailiffs upon us half the time, and if I can endure that, I can endure anything. I own I wish we had not that mortgage hanging over our heads, but I try not to think about it more than once or twice a day. And if it weren't for Darius' fees, and Iphigenia forever outgrowing her shoes, I'm sure I would not have a care in the world.''

Philippa had to laugh. "In fact, we have been a positive blessing, I have no doubt. But I promise you I don't mean to foist anyone else on you. Or trap poor Julian in a runaway marriage. But there has to be a way we could force the odious earl to release Julian's fortune. Then there could be no thought of entrapment, for he could marry Diana or not, without any outside influence.''

Her aunt was in agreement, but far from hopeful. "If he is as bad as you say, ten to one he will even forbid Julian to see poor Diana again," she said gloomily.

Philippa said confidently, her eyes snapping once more, "He won't do that, at least. You may be sure he is relying upon us to put an end to the connection. He meant to scare me off by revealing the way Julian's fortune is tied up. It is obvious he hopes never to have to appear as the villain in the piece. I am tempted to tell Julian exactly what has occurred and see how he likes it."

Aunt Bella thought that an excellent notion, but knowing her niece, she was not even very surprised when Philippa's inconvenient conscience intervened once more.

"No, no, I didn't really mean it. I own I'm tempted, but apart from every other consideration, I have no wish to have anyone, particularly Julian, know how vilely we have been insulted. At any rate, that would be to take unfair advantage of poor Julian, for he is too besotted at the moment to react sensibly. No, I tell you I am determined to find some way to outwit Roxbury without having to resort to making Julian unhappy."

Aunt Bella, used to her niece, made no reply to that, but said merely, a curious half-smile playing about her mouth, "I am half-sorry I wasn't here to meet him myself. What was he like, my love?"

"You might have had my place for the asking," replied her niece roundly. "I tell you he is the rudest, most detestable man I have ever met. His habitual expression seems to be a sneer, his manners are nonexistent, and everything he says is a studied insult."

"No, no, I meant to look at, girl," grumbled Aunt Bella.

Philippa surprised her by blushing, which was unlike her. "Good God, what difference does that make? If you must know, I was favorably impressed at first, for he is not just in the common mode. He dresses with a lack of ostentation I particularly liked, since he boasts none of the absurdities of the current dandy set. Nor does he affect that bland, foolish look so much in fashion these days and which I find so irritating. In fact, until he opens his mouth, he looks like a sensible man. He is not precisely hand-some, for his eyes are too hard and his manner too abrupt, but I was pleasantly surprised in him. That was before he said anything, of course. Then even his insults were uttered in so bored a tone that I soon was longing to hit him. In fact, I wish I had! I can't remember when I have disliked anyone so much.''

"Yes, my love, that is obvious. Still, it seems very odd. His father, you know, was considered one of the most charming men of his day. Even when in his cups he was renowned for his address. One could seldom tell when he had been drinking, as a matter of fact, for he never lost one whit of his polish. He was a true gentleman.''

But Philippa, suddenly alert, almost pounced on her aunt. "Dearest Aunt Bella, don't tell me you actually knew Roxbury's father as well? That would be too good to be true.''

Her aunt's cheeks took on quite unaccustomed and natural color for once. "Good God, it was all a very long time ago. Nor do I wish to recall it, for, if you must know, it was the only time I ever came close to making a fool of myself. Except when I married your uncle, of course, which is a very different thing.''

"Aunt,'' demanded Philippa in something like awe, "he wasn't actually in love with you, was he?''

"I'm sure I don't know why you should say it like that,'' retorted her aunt, bristling a little. "If I say it who shouldn't, I'm sure half the men in London were in love with me at the time. But if you are thinking there was anything more to it than that, then you are mistaken. He was married already, of course, and in the end I married your uncle, which just goes to show. If I had run away with him as he wanted, I could scarcely have been any worse off, but unfortunately hindsight is always a very different thing, as I've discovered. And I'm sure I was wedded to the god of respectability in those days, little though you may believe it.''

"Oh, Aunt, don't you see?'' cried Philippa in high glee. "We have him now! How dare he behave so when his own father was ready to run off with you? I wonder if he can know? Surely he can't, and still behave so hypocritically.''

"You would be amazed at how hypocritical men can be,'' pointed out her aunt cynically. "But ten to one he didn't, for he could have been little more than a boy then. But I fail to see how a twenty-year-old love affair is likely to help.''

"You just leave it to me. If nothing else, he will hate having it pointed out to him that his own father was so weak as to fall in love with you. But we both know you never threw anything away in your life, dearest Aunt! Only tell me you still have some love letters his father wrote you, and I promise you Julian shall have his fortune tomorrow. The wicked earl would never stand still for having them published to the world.''

"Philippa,'' cried her aunt in genuine alarm, "you wouldn't! I would never consent to such a thing.''

"Good God, of course I wouldn't. He doesn't know that, however. He already thinks us the type of hussies willing to entrap a boy for his fortune, so he will be quite willing to believe it.''

"Well, that is what you are doing when you talk of forcing him to countenance the match,'' pointed out her aunt irritably.

Philippa had the grace to blush a little, but insisted stoutly, "No such thing! I am merely forcing him to release a fortune he has no right—no moral right, anyway—to withhold. We both know Diana did nothing to entrap his precious nephew. If they have fallen in love and are determined to marry, there is nothing he or anyone else can do about it. I merely intend to see that the odious Lord Roxbury refrains from blackmailing poor Julian with a little judicious blackmail of my own.''

4

HER AUNT was far from acknowledging the fineness of the distinction, but she was prevented from saying anything more by the return of the subject of their conversation. Diana had gone out for a walk with her younger sister, and both could be heard in the hall below.

Philippa just had time before they came upstairs to say hurriedly, "Whatever happens, Aunt Bella, don't, for heaven's sake, tell Diana about the odious earl's visit. If I am successful, I have no wish for her to know anything of the matter. And if I am not, well, she will learn of it soon enough, I fear."

Diana Mayhew proved to be shorter and fairer than her elder sister, with a quantity of pale curls and a soft mouth that at the moment was drooping unhappily. She was dressed becomingly in a walking dress cut down from one of her aunt's old costumes, and if she lacked her elder sister's animation, or her intelligence, she was more conventionally pretty, in a style very much in vogue at the moment.

Philippa saw at once that she was in low spirits, but said cheerfully, "Hello, love. Did you and Genia have a good walk today?"

"Yes, we went to the Green Park," answered the other in a gentle, dispirited voice. "I like it much better than Hyde Park, with all its fashionable quizzes and the men who try to stare you out of countenance. Besides, it reminds me a little of home.''

This sounded melancholy indeed, but the youngest member of the group soon explained it by adding cynically, "It also has the advantage of letting her enjoy a tête-à-tête with Lord Holyoke away from prying eyes." She plopped ungracefully onto a sofa, disturbing her aunt's dog, who woke with a snort, then jumped down and left the room with obviously ruffled dignity. The youngest member of the Mayhew clan was a thin child of some twelve summers with a deep rent in one of her stockings and a precocious air of maturity that sat ill on her freckled countenance.

Diana, who was standing nearest the door, was obliged to open it for her aunt's dog, but said, blushing hotly, "That's not true! At any rate, Genia was there the whole time, so it's not as if there was anything clandestine about the meeting." Then abruptly her lip began to tremble. "Oh, Philippa! Julian's mama has found out about us. That is what he had to tell me today. And she will manage to separate us, I know she will," she cried tragically.

Her sister handed her a handkerchief, but asked practically, "And what does Julian say?"

Diana blew her small nose and lifted her damp, tragic eyes to her sister's face. "He says he m-means to marry me regardless. Oh, but, Philippa, how can I marry him knowing it must c-cut him off from his family?''

"Goodness, Diana! I don't mean to be unsympathetic, but I warned you how it must be from the beginning," said Philippa in some exasperation. "You always knew Julian's family was unlikely to approve the match.''

"I know," wailed Diana. "I ought to give him up, I know that too. But I don't think I can bear to. Oh, Philippa, what am I going to do? I am so unhappy.''

Philippa and her aunt exchanged glances, and the latter threw up her hands, knowing when she was defeated. Unfortunately Iphigenia, who was addicted to all the more lurid forms of novels to be obtained from the lending library and had followed her sister's star-crossed romance with great interest, said critically, "Yes, but if you did renounce him, it would be very romantic. Probably his family would be forced to relent in the end, too, for Julian would no doubt go into a decline. Only when he was on his deathbed would they send for you, but by then it would be too late. You would arrive just as he died, with your name on his lips, and his family would be forced to see how unjust they had been.''

Diana did not seem to find this romantic picture in the least appealing, but Aunt Bella, evidently resigned to her fate, replaced her shoe with some difficulty and rose. "Very affecting! I once played a scene something like that, and there wasn't a dry eye in the house. Unfortunately life is very seldom like the theater. In my experience he is as likely to forget all about Diana and marry someone else within six months. But that would be nearly as great a shame, in my opinion, for I've always liked Julian.'' She added resignedly, "And I suppose even another mouth to feed is preferable to having to endure *Romeo and Juliet* enacted around me from morning to night.''

Diana was looking bewildered by now, but Philippa said firmly, "Never mind that! Only tell me, Diana, were you aware that Lord Holyoke's fortune was tied up in such a way that he must have his uncle's permission to wed?''

"Yes, of course," answered Diana innocently. "Julian told me all about that. But he says it's not his uncle we have to worry about, but only his mother.''

It was all Philippa could do to keep from choking, but Iphigenia, pursuing her own romantic weavings, said with unexpected acumen, "I bet you're wrong about the uncle, though. In all the novels it's always the wicked uncle who plots to thwart the young lovers. Either he saw Diana once and fell madly in love with her, or he means to have Julian's fortune for himself.''

Darius had wandered in in time to hear this, however, and said scornfully, "Stuff! Julian told me himself that his uncle's as rich as Croesus. He would hardly need to steal from Julian.'' He cast Philippa a curious glance, but to her relief made no mention of Roxbury having called there that day.

"That's what he wishes everyone to think," announced Genia triumphantly. "In truth he's probably lost his entire fortune on 'Change, and doesn't want the world—particularly his debtors—to discover it.''

"Don't mention the word 'debtor' in my hearing,'' objected Aunt Bella with a strong shudder. "I can almost feel the walls of prison closing around me now.''

But she was evidently resigned to her fate and made no more objection to turning over her letters to Philippa later, or even to inviting Julian to dine with them to demonstrate to his uncle that they had no intention of knuckling under to his threats.

"I daresay we will all be clapped up in prison over this,'' Aunt Bella complained gloomily. "But it will almost be worth it to be revenged upon Julian's mama. She once snubbed me in the establishment of a fashionable modiste, I remember, and I have never forgiven her for it. I wonder how she will like having me as her son's aunt-in-law?''

It was plain the notion had done much to reconcile her to the loss of her letters, for she had brightened considerably and even appeared more than usually cheerful at dinner that evening, apparently relishing her victory over such an old enemy.

The first warning the Earl of Roxbury had that his gauntlet was being picked up by the Mayhews was when his nephew dropped by the next morning to beg off dining with him that evening.

Julian betrayed none of the symptoms of a youth who had just had his engagement broken, but on the contrary seemed to be in excellent spirits, which roused his uncle's suspicions immediately.

"I'm sorry to interrupt you, for I know how busy you are,'' he said ingenuously, having found his uncle at his desk, surrounded by papers. "I won't take up but a minute of your time. I just dropped by to tell you—to ask if I may beg off dining with you tonight? I'm sorry for the short notice, but I know you won't care a rap for that. The truth is, I have been invited to dine with Diana's family instead, and well . . . You understand!''

The earl's head had snapped up, his black brows drawing together rather dangerously. He was unused to having his challenges picked up with quite such alacrity, and did not much relish the experience. "Oh, you have, have you?" he inquired grimly. "A sudden invitation, I gather?"

"Yes. That is, well—the truth is, I never have been permitted to dine there before, as a matter of fact," admitted Julian in a burst of confidence. "Miss Mayhew—Diana's sister, you know—felt it wouldn't look right as long as my family was ignorant of our attachment. In fact, I never thought to be grateful to whatever busybody took it upon herself to warn Mama, which just goes to show, doesn't it?"

"Do I take it Miss Mayhew has now withdrawn her objection?" demanded the earl in growing wrath.

"Well, it was never really an objection, you understand. She thought—and I had to agree with her—that as long as Mama was ignorant of our relationship, it would be wrong of her to encourage me. But we had a long talk this morning and I explained to her that I never had any intention of allowing Mama to dictate my marriage. Good God, what a fellow I would be if I were to do so! Not that I blame her, for she must naturally wish to protect Diana. But when I explained, and . . . Well, the long and the short of it is that she has said she has no objection to our engagement. Naturally I told her of the terms of my trust, but that that should be no problem, and she said that once I had your approval, the announcement could be made immediately. I am so happy, Marcus. I feel as if I am walking on air."

The earl, closing his teeth on his instinctive retort, discovered he would like to have Miss Philippa Mayhew's neck between his hands at that moment. She had not wasted any time in issuing her own challenge, it seemed. He had no doubt she meant merely to force him into buying her off, for he did not believe her foolish enough to risk an actual marriage. But he began to suspect he had underestimated her, which was not a thing that often happened.

Well, he would be damned before he would enrich such

a harpy by so much as a penny. And she would soon learn her mistake if she chose to cross swords with him.

Nevertheless he managed to hide his growing wrath from Julian, who was far too happy to be particularly observant at the moment, in any case, and soon went off to order some flowers for his hostess. But under the circumstances Roxbury was not surprised to receive a second visit from his sister later that same day.

The earl had retired to his library with a glass of brandy after dinner when Lady Holyoke burst in on a cloud of rustling silk, indicating that she had stopped off on her way to an evening engagement.

"I thought you said you had frightened the creature off," she accused angrily, wasting no time in launching the attack. "Instead, Julian is dining there this very evening."

He had risen at her entrance, though his harsh countenance robbed the gesture of any gallantry. "I am aware of it," he said shortly. "Julian was to have dined with me this evening and begged off at the last minute. Miss Mayhew has wasted little time in launching her counterattack, it seems."

"How can you take it so calmly?" she cried furiously. "I warned you she would be a fool to give him up so easily. You should have bought her off from the beginning."

He shrugged and poured himself another glass of brandy. "If you choose to do so, I cannot stop you. But I warn you, it will be without my help—nor will I advance one penny of Julian's principal for the purpose."

She was startled and furious, and demanded unkindly, "Good God, she has gotten under your skin, hasn't she?" Then she hunched a pettish shoulder. "Oh, very well! I am sure I have no desire to enrich such creatures. But nor do I have any more desire to admit them into the family. What do you mean to do, then, or may I ask?" she added sarcastically.

He ignored her sarcasm. "Don't worry. Rest assured I will do whatever necessary to deliver Julian from the clutches of such notorious harpies," he added grimly.

His harsh tone seemed to reassure her, however, for after a moment she sat down, irritably throwing off her evening wrap. "I could kill Julian for this, positively I could. I have no doubt that dreadful creature is enjoying being revenged upon us after all these years."

He showed his teeth briefly. "If you mean Isabella Monteith, I have yet to detect the aunt's fine hand in this. Unless I am very much mistaken, it is the elder sister who calls the tune, and seems to be a worthy successor to her aunt. But she will learn her mistake if she tries to match wits with me."

His sister regarded him, torn between curiosity at his obvious fury and continued annoyance. "Well, for God's sake, don't take her in such dislike you lose sight of the main point, which is to rescue poor Julian from their clutches. Which reminds me, Julian tells me you are going to bring Mama back with you. I hope while you are in the vicinity you mean to look in on Louisa. I am more than annoyed with her. Heaven knows I know what it is to be widowed, but I have warned her repeatedly she would do better to overcome her grief and move about in the world a little bit more, if only for Lucinda's sake."

"Louisa is a damned nuisance," the earl said roundly, not mincing matters. "If she doesn't take care, she will have that minx of hers in total rebellion. How old is she? Sixteen? Seventeen?"

"Seventeen, which you would know if you paid the least attention to your responsibilities."

"She is no responsibility of mine, I thank God! I am far from approving her father-in-law being left in control of everything, for he strikes me as being nearly as great a fool as Louisa. But it is not my concern. Though if you had devoted less of your time to amusing yourself and trying to keep Julian tied to your apron strings, and taken Lucinda to live with you instead, as I recommended, you might both be the better for it."

But that, at least, fell on deaf ears, for Lady Holyoke said with perfect truth that Louisa would never have consented to be separated from her only daughter. And since there seemed no more to be said, she rose and drew on her gloves again, saying merely, "Well, give Mama my love. And I will wait to hear from you on that other matter. I can't help thinking if it might not be wiser to send Julian out of town for a few weeks, in the hope that the whole will have blown over."

"My dear Theresa, Julian is a grown man. I doubt if he would go," retorted her brother. "At any rate, I have said you may safely leave Miss Philippa Mayhew to me."

5

PHILIPPA, MEANWHILE, wasted little time in furthering her challenge by calling the next morning on the hateful earl, armed with one of her aunt's letters.

She took a hansom for the occasion, which was an unaccustomed luxury, but she had no desire to arrive on his doorstep hot and windblown. Once in Grosvenor Place, where she had discovered the earl lived, she requested it to wait for her, since she did not believe her business would take much time.

She had also taken the precaution of wearing her most becoming hat and walking dress, having no intention of giving the earl the same advantage he had enjoyed before, when he had found her in one of her oldest gowns and her hair no doubt tumbling down. That the gown was five years old and the hat refurbished with feathers from one of her aunt's old hats, no one need know, for she thought if she did not look precisely in the vanguard of fashion, she looked presentable and assured, which was all she demanded. She was therefore able to sound the knocker with at least a semblance of confidence and confront the earl's forbidding butler with bravado, requesting a brief word with his lordship.

For a moment, however, she thought he meant to refuse even to carry her message to his master. He looked her up and down with frank astonishment, but since the glossy feathers so close to her face were vastly becoming, as was the high color in her cheeks, caused by nervousness, which her scrutiny in her mirror had failed to tell her, he at last condescended to confer with his lordship and allowed her to step into the hall.

There an unexpected sight met her, for she found it piled high with baggage. It was impossible to tell whether someone was just arriving or departing, but since it did not concern her, she merely followed the butler's disapproving back into a small salon on the ground floor.

Once left alone there, she clasped her hands a little nervously, annoyed to find she was by no means as assured as she would liked to have been, and she made herself look about the room. It was furnished in the height of elegance, but gave little hint of its owner.

She had gone to straighten her hat before the mirror over the marble mantelpiece, beginning to wonder if Roxbury meant to refuse to see her, when there was at last a firm tread outside the door, and it opened without warning to admit the earl.

She whirled, furious to be found in so betraying an act, but said coldly, "Lord Roxbury. I was beginning to think you meant to refuse to see me."

He looked her over with an ill-concealed contempt that instantly vanquished any remaining nervousness she might have been feeling. "On the contrary. I have been expecting this visit," he said unpleasantly. "But I said everything I had to say on the subject yesterday, I believe. If you imagine you will make me change my mind by your recent demonstrations, you are mistaken."

"You may have said all you had to say on the subject, my lord, but I have not," she said deliberately.

His expression grew even more unpleasant, if possible, and he did not invite her to sit down. Her wrath grew, but she controlled it with an effort and added with a touch of triumph in her tone, "In fact, I warned you, did I not, that I would do anything in my power to further my sister's marriage to your nephew?"

He went to lean his shoulders against the mantel, his very attitude an insult. "You may have done so, Miss Mayhew, but in fact, we both know there is nothing you can do, short of an elopement," he said harshly. "And I think you are beginning to know me well enough by now to know that I meant what I said. If your sister marries my nephew, you and your aunt may support them both, for he will see not one penny more than his present modest allowance. More, I will take delight in exposing you as the blood-sucking arch-doxies you are. And if you were hoping to force me into buying you off by your recent actions, as I must suppose, I will see you in hell first."

She gasped before this onslaught, suddenly so angry she was trembling. She thought she had never hated anyone in her life as she hated this insulting, arrogant man, and any doubts she may have been feeling at her choice of weapons died in that instant. She would positively enjoy using whatever it took to defeat him. She pulled the letter from her reticule, her hand shaking a little with her fury. "You believe you hold all the cards, don't you, my lord?" she demanded contemptuously. "I think this might interest you, however."

He scowled, but abruptly accepted the paper she held out to him. He unfolded it and glanced indifferently down, and she thought he stiffened. But his face betrayed no expression other than his habitual unpleasantness, as he rapidly scanned it, then looked up again. "Well?" he demanded harshly. "Have you read this by the way, Miss Mayhew?"

"No, of course not," she denied indignantly.

His sneer indicated he did not believe her, but he handed it back. "Very wise. It is a little early in the day for such nauseating pap. How many more of these remarkable effusions do you possess?"

"Some half a dozen, my lord," she answered steadily.

"Very well! How much do you want for them?"

"They are not for sale, my lord," she said contemptuously. "That is your answer to everything, isn't it? I will deliver them into your hands on the day you relinquish all hold on your nephew's fortune."

His sneer was even more pronounced, if possible. "On the contrary, not only are they for sale, you set a high price, indeed, it seems. And if I refuse to pay it?"

"I don't think you will, my lord. I think you are too proud a man to wish to see your father's letters published, especially addressed to such a woman."

It was only then that she realized exactly how furious he was, for a little muscle was jumping in his lean cheek. It even occurred to her to be a little afraid of him, and to wonder if she had been unwise to come alone. Her body might be found in the river that night, for in his present mood she thought him capable of anything.

"You think you know me very well, don't you, ma'am?" he demanded insultingly.

"I know you well enough to realize nothing will infuriate you more than to be obliged to admit you have been paid back in your own coin. But so you have, my lord. You came—you dared to come to insult me yesterday and issue your threats. Now the tables are turned, and we see how you like it."

"I said it before and I'll say it again, ma'am: nothing I could say could possibly insult such a harpy as you. If I had any doubts before, you have erased them. And if I had my way, you and every highly expensive and unprincipled doxy like you would be burned at the stake for the witches you are."

Her fists doubled up inside her gloves, and she had to fight the impulse to strike the sneer from that insufferable face. He seemed to realize it, for he added sardonically, "I wouldn't advise it. At the moment I would like nothing better than to strangle you, Miss Mayhew, so don't tempt me."

"You—you had no doubts from the first," she cried furiously. "It was enough that we were the nieces of a notorious actress. You were convinced we were the sort of scheming hussies to entrap your nephew and nothing we could say or do would convince you otherwise."

"Very affecting! You will forgive me for thinking that is exactly what you are doing by this unsavory little attempt at blackmail."

She flushed and once more had to restrain the longing to hit him. "Not at all. Julian is free to marry whomever he pleases. Which is more than you are prepared to grant him."

He laughed nastily. "I must confess I fail to see the distinction. And suppose I tell Julian of the lengths you are prepared to go to gain his fortune?"

"Suppose I tell him the lengths you are prepared to go to prevent his marriage? It is obvious he has no notion. It would serve you right if I told him the truth and unmasked you for the hypocrite you are."

He looked vaguely curious. "Why haven't you, as a matter of fact? I expected that to be your first move."

"Because I possess some scruples, if you do not," she cried, goaded into unwise retort. Then, as his brows drew together in a sudden frown, she added, "Oh, there is obviously no talking to you. I have given you your choice: release your nephew's fortune, or have your father's letters published to the world. Which is it to be?"

"I have no intention of giving you my answer now, Miss Mayhew," he answered shortly. "I am on the point of leaving town and won't be back for a fortnight. You may have my decision then, and not before."

She was dismayed and had trouble concealing the fact. "A fortnight? That is the merest stalling, and we both know it. And if I choose not to wait?"

He smiled unpleasantly. "If you choose to publish the letters before that time, I can't prevent you. But you will do so at your own peril, believe me."

She shivered a little, for she had no doubt he would make a dangerous enemy, but was by then too reckless to care. Even so, she had no choice but to accept his ultimatum, as he no doubt knew. "Very well, then," she conceded ungraciously. "But I warn you that if I have not heard from you within exactly two weeks from today, I will assume that is my answer and proceed accordingly. I hope you will not be so foolish as to force me into something we will both regret."

"I am beginning to think there is nothing you would regret, Miss Mayhew," he said nastily. "Julian's mother, by the way, believes it is your aunt behind this scheme, but we know better, don't we? Your aunt, for all her reputation, is innocent compared to you. I predict you will easily surpass even her immoral career by the time you're through.''

"Nothing you can say will make any difference, my lord," she countered angrily. "You are bested, and we both know it."

He showed his teeth in a dangerous smile. "We shall see who is bested, Miss Mayhew. And now, you will forgive me for not prolonging this pleasant interview, but I am late setting out already. And if you take my advice, you will guard those letters in your possession carefully. If they should get out—by any means!—I will not hesitate to hold you personally responsible."

He bowed once, sardonically, and left her there.

Philippa, left alone at last, required some moments to calm herself so that she could face his servants again without disgracing herself. She thought she had never met a man she despised more, and in that moment she would happily have stopped at nothing, even murder, to be even with him. In her present mood, if he called her bluff, she thought she would quite willingly publish his father's letters. And she had to forcefully remind herself that that, at least, was beneath her, even to be revenged upon him.

But it would be unnecessary, anyway. His very anger had told her that she had won, and the delay was no more than a face-saving gesture. It was annoying, but she could wait two weeks for the privilege of seeing him eat his words.

6

BUT EVEN so, the enforced delay was nerve-racking, especially since Aunt Bella, when she received a report of the unpleasant interview with his lordship, did not help by saying pessimistically, "I only hope he may not be planning some new revenge upon us! If he doesn't have us clapped up, he will very likely kidnap his nephew, or have us both murdered, or something dreadful. I feel it in my bones."

"Oh, pooh," said Philippa. "There is nothing he can do without revealing the very thing he wishes to hide, and he knows it. In fact, I am sorry now I allowed him to put me off, for it was the merest stalling, and we both knew it. Well, there is no help for it now, but if he doesn't return within two weeks, I am almost tempted to publish the wretched letters. It would serve him right for being such a hypocrite."

Aunt Bella naturally cried out against that, and Philippa was forced to back down. "No, of course I don't mean to," she said grumblingly. "That would make me as bad as he believes me to be. Worse, it would hardly help Diana's chances, for then I would no longer have any hold over him. But the temptation is almost irresistible, for no one more deserves being taken down a peg or two."

But in fact she was soon to have another reason for not publishing the letters, and one that despite all her anger made her almost regret the method she had chosen to be revenged upon the odious earl.

For this belated attack of conscience Julian was unwittingly responsible. Since that first time he had been allowed to dine with them, he had almost haunted the place and seemed to have no suspicion of his uncle's disapproval of the match. He seemed, in fact, to take his forthcoming marriage as a settled thing and showed no diminution in his devotion to the radiant Diana. His mother still disapproved, it was true, but he seemed convinced his uncle would soon bring her around, and as far as he was concerned, no other bar stood between them and happiness.

Philippa, despising the earl, was tempted to disabuse him of that naïve belief. But she could hardly do so without revealing her own part in the affair, which she was naturally loath to do, and so was obliged to bite her tongue whenever Julian spoke of his uncle in plainly affectionate terms.

But if she had suspected Roxbury's journey had merely been an excuse, Julian inadvertently confirmed its authenticity, though in a way that gave both Philippa and her aunt an unpleasant start. For according to Julian, his uncle had gone to Bath to fetch his mother to town.

Aunt Bella nearly choked on her soup at this news and had to be pounded on the back by Darius.

Philippa cast her a warning glance, but was by no means pleased at this information herself, and asked carefully, "I—we were not aware that your grandmother was still alive, Julian. Is this your maternal grandmother?"

"Oh, Lord, yes," said Julian cheerfuly. "She's a great gun. Regrettably she doesn't get around much now, for her health is not the best, but I'm very fond of her. More to the point, Marcus is too. Mama says Grandmama is the only female he has ever had a fondness for, in fact."

Aunt Bella choked again, but this time Philippa deliberately did not meet her aunt's eyes. She herself was aware of a foolish dismay, for it had somehow never occurred to her that anyone might be hurt by what she was doing—other than the wicked earl, of course, who deserved it.

Of course she had no actual intention of publishing her

aunt's letters. Still, she could not prevent herself asking unwillingly, somehow knowing the answer before she did so, "I take it your grandmother lives very quietly then while in London?"

"Oh, no! She is something of an invalid, of course, but by no means a recluse. She has a great many friends whom she sees, and even gets out for some shopping now and then," said Julian, blithely unaware he was striking dismay into the hearts of at least two of his listeners.

Aunt Bella said weakly, "I gather that your uncle is not noted for his amiable temper, Julian?"

Julian laughed. "No, I believe he's considered quite dangerous, in fact, to those who have tried to cross him. But I have always been fond of him, though I'll confess I have sometimes wished myself invisible, when I was younger and he caught me out in some misdeed. I wouldn't like to cheat him in a business deal, if it comes to that, for I don't doubt he can be ruthless. My cousin is afraid of him, and I think even my mama is a little, though she refuses to admit it. But that makes him sound terrible, and I don't mean to. It's only that he has little patience for weakness, you see, and certainly no tolerance for underhandedness. As I said, I wouldn't like to make him genuinely angry with me. But I have always found him very fair."

Aunt Bella closed her eyes and waved away the turbot, her appetite quite gone.

But Julian seemed to find it a very good joke when Genia insisted upon propounding her theory about his noble trustee, and promised he meant to repeat it to his uncle.

"For the truth of the matter is, he would just as soon not have had the responsibility, I suspect," he said frankly. "In fact, he has increased my fortune considerably during his care, a fact that makes Mama livid, I fear. Not that she disapproves of having my principal increased, of course. But she never approved of the trust in the first place, and has never forgiven Marcus for it, though I daresay he had nothing to do with it and has frequently had reason to wish me at Jericho. Compared to his fortune, mine is negligible, I'm afraid."

"Even so, it is rather an unusual arrangement," remarked Philippa carefully, trying to keep her tone neutral.

"Yes, but I've never minded it, particularly since I can hardly complain of the results. I think Papa did it to ensure I didn't waste my fortune before I turned responsible, for he seems to have had some absurd fear of that. But then, perhaps it was not so absurd, for by all accounts that's just what my grandfather—my maternal grandfather—did. I know very few of the details, for of course no one likes to talk of it, but I do know Marcus had the devil . . . I beg your pardon, Mrs. Mayhew. I meant a deuced hard time when he first succeeded to the title, for the estate was heavily mortgaged and even the interest on the debts was crippling, I understand. Evidently Grandfather was something of a philanderer as well, but I gather Marcus found some way to rein him in before he died. I gather it was unethical, or at least not the done thing, for I know Mama has never quite forgiven him for it. But then she seems to have been very fond of her father, and it seems fairly safe to say the family would have been completely ruined otherwise. Marcus, on the other hand, was the youngest and seems to have been overly protective of Grandmother all his life, which may explain why Mama and he have never gotten along."

Philippa was far from welcoming these intimate revelations, but Aunt Bella, who had forgotten her main concern in fascination at these details of people she once had known, if only from a distance, said curiously, "And what of your other aunt? There were two sisters, as I remember."

"Yes, my Aunt Louisa. She seldom comes to town, for she has been recently widowed and doesn't enjoy very good health, either. Marcus says she merely enjoys the attention she gets by being ill, but I don't know. My poor cousin—she's a minx, by the way! I know you will like her, Diana—leads something of a dog's life, I fear, for she is exceedingly lively and hates being immured in the country all the time."

"Yes, of course, I remember now," said Aunt Bella. "She married Tom Minton, didn't she? It was reported at the time that they had champagne flowing from indoor fountains at Roxbury House at her wedding, and the number of invited guests was so great half a dozen women fainted in the crush on the stairway.''

"Good God," said Julian, laughing. "I've never heard that, but I'm not surprised. No wonder Marcus was confronted by so many debts, for my grandfather died soon after that, I do know. Certainly neither my mama nor my aunt has any notion of economy, so perhaps it is fortunate my fortune was tied up as it was. Mama has her jointure, of course, but it always seems inadequate, I know."

Philippa, annoyed with the subject and afraid of what her irrepressible aunt might reveal of her knowledge of Julian's family, soon steered the conversation into safer channels. But when she stopped by her aunt's bedchamber later that evening, she could not help saying a little ruefully, "I own I wish I hadn't known about Julian's grandmother. Good heavens, Aunt, how could you have done such a thing as to almost run off with her husband?"

Bereft of the elaborate wig she wore to cover her own graying locks, and without the rouge she continued to wear, in defiance of current custom, Aunt Bella looked oddly colorless and vulnerable. She finished tying her nightcap under her chin and said a little irritably, "I told you it all happened many years ago, my love. Certainly he was the only man I ever came close to making a fool of myself over. I can't explain it, for usually they just amused me, but he—ah, he was so very handsome! And charming! You cannot conceive, for it was a different age, and no one has manners anymore, how charming he could be. I daresay he was weak, but I wasn't interested in seeing it at the time. And it was common knowledge that his wife was an invalid and seldom came to town."

Philippa thought that scarcely excused either of them, but she wisely did not say so. But as if aware of it, Aunt Bella went on defensively, "At any rate, he meant to set me up in an *hôtel* in Paris, so his wife need never have known anything about it. I have often wondered what would have happened if I had chosen differently, as a matter of fact. Ah, well. I daresay he was nearly ruined even then, if I had only known it, so it's probably just as well. I do know he seemed to retrench after that, and he died a few years later. Dear me. How it takes me back.''

Philippa went away, trying not to think her aunt sounded unattractively callous. It did no good to blame her, but she was almost sorry to have stirred up such old coals. It was Roxbury's fault, of course, for starting it all, but at the moment even that knowledge did not help very much

Once more she wondered if Roxbury could possibly have known of that old affair, and she could not make up her mind. On the one hand, it would certainly explain his bitterness. But then she disliked him enough to believe he needed no such excuse for his prejudice. What was it he had dared to call them? Harpies! Well, he should find that even harpies could best him if sufficiently angry.

With that decision she jumped into bed herself, but did not go immediately to sleep. Instead, she sat up against her pillows with her knees drawn up, weaving pleasant fantasies in her mind. It was unfortunate about the dowager, but no real harm need be done. Once Roxbury had been forced into releasing Julian's fortune, he would soon discover how unfounded were his prejudices. She had little doubt that Diana would make his nephew an excellent wife, and if Julian cared nothing for more worldly considerations, why should he?

Furthermore, if Roxbury feared that he would find himself forced to hobnob with Diana's family, he would soon learn his mistake. Once the wedding was safely over, she had no intention of jeopardizing her sister's happiness by forcing themselves on the newlyweds. Doubtless Roxbury feared, in his unpleasant way, that they meant to hang on Julian's sleeve, but nothing could be further from the truth. She had no intention of foisting her responsibilities off onto Julian.

It was pleasant to envision the odious earl forced to acknowledge how unjust were his suspicions, but in the back of her mind lurked the unwelcome suspicion that in so doing she was engaging in the sort of sophistry her father had most despised. It might serve to lull her own conscience, but Papa would undoubtedly have reminded her that unscrupulous methods seldom paid off, and no good ever came from evil means.

But then her father was dead and had left her with the future of her brother and sisters to provide for. Iphigenia was young enough so that she could safely dismiss her for the moment, and Darius, too, would be secure enough. His fees at Cambridge were a worry, but they would be paid even if it meant breaking into Mama's small legacy, which she had hoped would provide for her own old age, once the children were off her hands. Well, that was some years away, and if necessary, she would find employment somewhere after the children were grown. Perhaps abroad, as she had always wanted to visit the Continent.

Aunt Bella, of course, insisted she would always be welcome with her. But she also spoke occasionally of selling off this barrack of a house and retiring into the country to live with an old friend of hers. In either case, Philippa could not quite see herself growing old alongside one much less two fading beauties. They, at least, had their memories to sustain them, but it sometimes occurred gloomily to her that she had never really lived at all.

But it did no good to think of that, for nothing would change until the children were grown, and by then she would probably be too old to care any longer. Far more important was to settle Diana well, her chief concern for several years now. Diana had taken their papa's death five years ago harder, perhaps, than any of the others, for Genia had been too young, Darius away at school most of the time, and Philippa herself too numbed and worried over her sudden responsibilities to have much time to grieve. At any rate, Diana had always been the protected one, adored and petted by their father, whereas Philippa had been required to more or less take on the raising of the younger children when their mother had died some years before.

It did even less good to remember that she herself had been engaged at the time of their father's death, and only a few months away from her own wedding. Unfortunately it had not taken her long to make the painful discovery that few men were eager to embrace a bride with a ready-made family to suport, no matter how close the wedding day. Certainly John Hornbeck had not been. But then at this late date she supposed she could not even really blame him. He had had his own future to make, and though he had not been particularly romantic, even he must have hoped for something more than setting up a new household with three children under the age of sixteen as chaperones.

At any rate, she could no longer even recall with any certainty what he had looked like, so obviously her heart had not been broken. And in the end they had come to live with Aunt Bella, which at the time had seemed to be their only choice. It was a choice she could not regret, for Aunt Bella had proven to be amazingly kind and generous, despite her checkered background. But it was also true, as she was guiltily aware, that Roxbury would never dared to have behaved so had they not been living with a notorious actress.

Well, that did not excuse him, but it was why she was so determined Diana should not be made to pay for her own decision. That she herself had been made to pay for circumstances equally outside her control only strengthened her determination to protect her sister if she could.

Thus reassured, she resolutely blew out her candle and went to sleep, determinedly closing her mind to any further doubts.

7

TRUE TO his word, Philippa heard nothing from the Earl of Roxbury for almost a fortnight.

It had also occurred belatedly to her troublesome conscience to wonder whether she were being fair to Julian by her unwarranted interference, but to her relief, Julian showed no hint of regretting his engagement in that time.

Even when she gingerly broached the subject, wanting to make sure he would not come to regret Diana's unfortunate aunt, or begin to feel himself coerced in any way, he took her delicate questioning in a very different way.

He flushed and said, looking unexpectedly mature, "I realize you have some reason to doubt me, Miss Mayhew, but I assure you I always meant to make Diana my wife, with or without my mother's blessing. I would prefer to have it, of course, but if it leads to a breach between us, there is nothing I can do."

He sounded so sure of himself that she was reassured. For once they were alone, Diana having gone up to find a book she wished to loan Julian and none of the other children present. Philippa said truthfully, glad to have the subject broached, "I don't blame your mother. She naturally wished you to make an advantageous marriage. I wish only to make sure you will not come to regret later that my aunt was used to be on the stage, or to feel that we have taken advantage of you in any way. I think I need not tell you that my aunt made just such an unequal marriage and was very unhappy. I don't wish Diana to make the same mistake."

He flushed, but said forthrightly, with a sincerity she could not doubt, "Good God, I am not such a snob. Since we are being frank, I won't say it's a connection I'm delighted with, but Diana has made me see you had little choice in coming to live with her after your father died, and I honor Mrs. Mayhew for her kindness to you all. At any rate, I lack my mama's social ambitions, I fear. Most of the eligible heiresses she introduced me to scared me to death. Once Diana and I are married and I am in possession of my full inheritance, I mean to live in Somerset most of the year, if you must know. I have an ambition to see if I can't succeed as a gentleman farmer. My grandfather—my paternal grandfather, that is—did so, and despite my uncle's passion for business, I must confess I've always preferred country living myself. Fortunately Diana seems to as well, for she tells me she has never been completely happy in London."

"Yes, though in fairness I think she would have been happier had circumstances been more fortunate. But never mind that. It is true that she hated leaving home more than the rest of us, I think. And I won't deny you have relieved my mind more than a little. I am sorry for your mother, but my first concern must be for my sister's happiness."

It was his turn to hesitate. "My fortune is not large, by many standards, but once I am in full possession of it, it should allow us a comfortable and even a moderately luxurious life. And I wanted you to know that I am prepared to help Diana's family in any way I can. She thinks you will not care to live with us, at least at first, but I want you to know you are always welcome. And if there is anything I can do, once we are married, in the way of Darius' school fees, or whatever, I—I hope you will let me help."

She was touched, but said frankly, "The last thing you and Diana need to start off your married life is to have new in-laws hanging on your sleeve. As for the other, I hope you do not think I have countenanced the match merely in hopes of making my own life more comfortable. I'm sure Diana has told you we are by no means rich, but we have always managed to get by—at least once Aunt Bell paid off the last of my uncle's debts. I have no intention of becoming your pensioner, but I am touched by the offer and thank you for it. At any rate," she added dryly, "if he is as shrewd a businessman as you say, I suspect your uncle would have something to say about that if I were so conscienceless as to accept your kind offer."

He denied it, but not very convincingly, and since Diana returned then, they parted in mutual esteem, each having developed a better respect for the other. For her part, Philippa might be growing uncomfortable over her own compromising position, but she had few doubts that her interference was unwarranted. Whether or not she succeeded in freeing Julian's fortune, she thought he had made it plain he meant to wed Diana. And if so, it would be far better for their future happiness if he were in possession of his fortune, for his sake as much as Diana's. Nothing was more fatal to love than debts, as her aunt was fond of pointing out.

Even so, as the two weeks drew to a close, she found herself unexpectedly irritable. She blamed it on the earl, of course, and both longed for and dreaded his long-delayed return. And when Darius waylaid her one afternoon, obviously with something on his mind, it was all she could do to make herself say cheerfully, "What is it? Don't tell me you need another increase in your allowance already?"

He was a strange, conscientious boy, and she had begun to suspect lately that he was in need of a lasting male figure in his life. Perhaps Julian would fill that role, but she somehow doubted it. Darius was more intense and more intelligent than the easygoing Julian, and the latter was only seven years older and often seemed younger, for his life to date had always been relatively easy. To be sure, he had lost his father too, but he had had his uncle to step into the role, and she suspected he had never taken things as seriously as Darius.

He flushed now and said baldly, "No. And I hope you know if I did I would never think of coming to you. I have begun to think we none of us have appreciated all that you have done for us—or help you enough, for that matter.''

She was surprised and rather touched, but said readily, ''It is absurd to talk of appreciation, but if you want to help me more, I would be delighted if you would take over the marketing today. Cook is down in her back again, and Diana was to have done it, but has gone out with Julian, so we are likely to be without any supper tonight. But what has brought on this sudden burst of conscience?''

He gave her an unexpectedly mature look. ''It hasn't escaped my notice that Diana is seldom around to help with the chores lately,'' he said sarcastically. ''I almost wish she would hurry up and marry Julian, so then at least we might have some peace around here.''

Philippa was beginning to agree with that sentiment, but said fairly, ''Well, it's only natural that she should wish to spend as much time with him as possible. And we must get used to doing without her help, for it won't be long before she is gone, I fear. Don't you like Julian, Darius?''

He hunched a shoulder and answered indifferently, ''He's all right, I guess. Anyway, he should suit Diana. Which reminds me, I've been wondering why you've never told them of Lord Roxbury's visit that day? Is it because he does disapprove of the marriage as Genia suspects?'' he asked with unexpected shrewdness.

It was the last subject she wanted to discuss with him, and she felt herself blushing betrayingly. She covered it by asking vaguely, ''Haven't I? It must have slipped my mind. At any rate, you needn't worry. I assure you Lord Roxbury will have no objection to the match.''

She spoke more crisply than she had intended, and he looked a little doubtful, but said awkwardly, ''Well, that's all right, then. I just wondered if it had anything to do with Aunt Bella. That's why Julian's mother is opposed to the match, isn't it?'' he added, flushing a little and regarding her searchingly.

He had once more managed to surprise her, for she had never discussed the matter of Aunt Bella with him. She was forced to hold on to her patience with an effort, for she had no desire to do so now, either. ''If so, it need not concern you. Now, if that is all, I really must go. I have a hundred things to do today.''

He colored hotly at the obvious dismissal, and she regretted her tone almost at once. But he said with new resentment, ''It does concern me! I know you think I'm a child, but I'm not, and you have no right to—to take all the burden on yourself. Nor am I as naïve as you obviously believe. I know, for instance, that Aunt Bella used to be something of a—well, a scandal.''

Philippa made herself realize that he was indeed growing up and likely to begin to resent her control over him. She said more kindly, ''If so, it was a very long time ago. I will admit that it is not the very best recommendation for Diana, and that I have worried what was to become of her. But you see that Julian at least cares nothing about Aunt Bella's past, and that is all that matters. As for Lord Roxbury, you may safely leave him to me.''

''And what of your own future?'' he demanded stubbornly. ''Was it because of us that you didn't marry John Hornbeck? I've often wondered.''

He seemed full of unpleasant surprises that morning. ''Good God! I'm surprised you even remember that. If it was, you needn't worry about it. Oddly enough, I have far too much pride to wish to marry a man whose attachment can't withstand the existence of my brother and sisters. Nor have I thought of him in years, I promise you.''

He started to say something more, then abruptly shrugged his thin shoulders and walked away, obviously giving it up.

She looked after him, a faint frown between her brows. She suspected she had hurt his feelings, but in her present mood it was beyond her capabilities to go after him and smooth his ruffled feathers.

Even so, she must remember that he was growing up and try to be more careful of his sensibilities. It seemed she had been so long concerned with Diana that she had not paid enough attention to the other children, which made her feel guilty. She promised herself that as soon as Diana was safely wed, she would devote more time to him and to Genia, who was becoming uncomfortably pert.

Once more she wished Roxbury would return. But when Betty brought up his card that very same afternoon, she discovered she was in no mood to cope with him, after all, on top of everything else.

Fortunately Diana had gone out driving with Julian that morning, and Darius seemed to have been serious about helping more, for in addition to doing the shopping, he had unexpectedly volunteered to take Genia to Astley's Amphitheater as a special treat that afternoon.

Philippa's mind instinctively ran over the state of the house, grateful she and Betty had turned out the drawing room that morning, and said a little blankly, at last, "Oh, dear! I suppose I had better see him. Tell him I'll be right down."

She stopped off in her bedchamber first to inspect herself in her glass, however. Her gown was by no means new, but there was no time to change, and it would have to do. She smoothed her hair, wondering as she did so how Roxbury could possibly believe her an expensive high-flier. The first time they had met she had been dressed far from becomingly, and she had a lowering suspicion she looked now exactly what she was: an aging and harried spinster.

Then she straightened her shoulders and steeled herself to go down and face him.

She found him impatiently turning over the pages of a book that Darius had left on the table. When he heard her enter, he swung around and remarked sardonically, "Your brother's, I suppose? I would have thought the presence in the house of a sixteen-year-old boy would somewhat cramp your style."

Instantly she stiffened, once more swamped with the anger he seemed effortlessly to provoke. But then, since every word he uttered was an insult, it was perhaps not so surprising, after all. She made herself remember that she had the upper hand now and was resolved not to let him pierce her armor again, and said merely, "He may, but I have discovered few people are interested in taking him off my hands. But you have not come to discuss my brother, I'm sure. Have you reached a decision?"

He smiled unpleasantly. "I have. Kindly take a look at this. I believe you will find it as interesting as I found the document you once handed me."

She was instantly suspicious, but unwillingly accepted the heavy document he handed her. "Why should I? What is it?"

"I think it is sufficiently self-explanatory."

She glared at him, but then glanced down at the document, mystified. At first look it appeared to be some sort of legal document, and she frowned, fearing he indeed meant to sue her or charge her with blackmail over his father's letters. Then, as her eyes rapidly skimmed down the first page, they widened in shock, and she began to stiffen alarmingly. "Where did you get this?" she demanded furiously at last.

"It little matters. You may be sure it is genuine. As you may see for yourself, it bears your aunt's signature on the last page. It is, as it appears, a mortgage signed by your aunt, with this house pledged as security. But by all means call your aunt in if you doubt its authenticity."

She did not even grace that with a reply, for she did not doubt its authenticity. She merely inquired scornfully, "And what do you intend to do with this? Evict us? I must congratulate you. Your nephew should indeed be proud to know the lengths to which you are prepared to go to protect him."

"But then I warned you, did I not, that it would be unwise to cross me, Miss Mayhew? You were the one to resort to unscrupulous means first. But I think you will agree the situation has now altered somewhat. You once did me the honor of proposing a business transaction. I am merely altering the terms somewhat. I will hand you this mortgage in return for my father's letters."

"I told you they were not for sale," she cried.

He smiled even more unpleasntly. "As you once reminded me, you have very little choice, and you know it. I assure you I would not hesitate to call in the mortgage if it should become necessary."

He seemed to be enjoying her impotent rage and added mockingly, "Come, come! You are lucky, in fact, to emerge so well from the affair, for if I had given in to my first inclination, I would have seen you deported. And since the face value of the mortgage is somewhat in excess of five thousand pounds, you can hardly complain of your bargain. Such a sum may not compare with the amount you hoped to bleed from my nephew, over the years, but then that was always a risky undertaking, as you must have realized. After all, your sister might have died, or my nephew grown wise to you.''

She was almost speechless with rage and chagrin, and without another word turned and left the room.

When she returned, some five minutes later, she had a slender packet of letters in her hand. ''You had better count them,'' she said contemptuously. ''You will, of course, have to trust me that there are no more. Unless you would like to search the house?''

He glanced briefly through them, then bestowed the packet in an inner pocket. ''I would not trust you to tell me whether it were raining outside, Miss Mayhew,'' he said pleasantly. ''But I doubt even you would try this game on the same victim twice. I need hardly remind you that this transaction leaves us exactly where we started. If your sister is so unwise as to marry my nephew, I will not hesitate to withhold his fortune for as long as possible. I will also take great pleasure in exposing this charming little blackmail scheme of yours, regardless of the consequences. Do I make myself clear? Yes, I thought I did. In that case, I will bid you good day.''

At the door he halted. ''I almost forgot. You will be wanting this, of course,'' he said mockingly, and held out her aunt's mortgage to her.

She made no move to take it. ''I told you my aunt's letters were not for sale.''

''On the contrary, you have made an excellent profit on them, in fact. Five thousand pounds is nothing to sneeze at, even to one as grasping as you.''

When she still made no move to take the mortgage, he shrugged and tossed it onto the table. ''What's the matter, Miss Mayhew? You don't like having the tables turned on you? You must learn to bear your losses, as I am doing.

This little escapade has cost me five thousand pounds, remember. You should be flattered. Few women can boast they got as much from me. Particularly for so little pleasure in return."

"You think you have won, don't you?" she cried furiously. "I was beginning to regret my actions, but I promise you now I will make you sorry if it is the last thing I ever do."

He laughed and walked out.

8

AUNT BELLA, startled by the sound of something breaking, reached the drawing room just in time to find Philippa standing wrathfully over a vase she had just willfully smashed in the fireplace.

"Don't tell me," said that lady fatalistically, taking in all the signs of wrath in her niece's expressive countenance. "Roxbury means to have us all transported. I knew it from the beginning."

Philippa turned, careful to keep rigid control over herself, for she feared what she would do if she gave full vent to her rage. "Don't talk to me just yet, Aunt Bella," she warned. "I fear I am not safe yet. He—*he* . . . Oh, I have never met anyone I dislike so much. For the first time in my life I understand what drives people to murder. If I had had a sword in my hand, I think I would have run him through."

"Then thank God you had not," exclaimed her aunt fervently, sinking onto a sofa and weakly fanning herself. "It is bad enough wondering when we shall have the Bow Street runners at the door, without having his body to dispose of as well. Which reminds me, I never understood why writers are always littering the stage with bodies in plays, by the way," she added, for the first time considering the matter. "It seems to me it would be next to impossible to get rid of them in reality, especially in town."

"That would present no problem to me at all," cried Philippa bloodthirstily. "I would dump his body in the river and think no more about it than if it were a sack of refuse."

"Don't be absurd, my love. How on earth would we get it there?" she demanded reasonably. "And it is no good suggesting we put it in the cellar, for Flurry tells me there is not room for another thing down there. At any rate, he is not worth going to jail for, which you may be sure you would if you murdered him."

"Even that would almost be worth it, Aunt, if it meant I need never see him again."

"Believe me, if you had the slightest experience of prison, you wouldn't say so," said her aunt frankly. "Members of the company were forever being clapped up for debt, and I vow I shudder even now to think of the horrors they endured. But never mind that! Tell me at once what has happened before I go off into a strong apoplexy. When Betty told me who had called, I feared he had murdered you when I heard that crash."

Philippa's lips curled contemptuously. "I daresay he would have liked to. He seems to dislike me as intensely as I dislike him. But even I had not thought him capable of this. Read that, Aunt Bella."

Aunt Bella bewilderedly accepted the document she handed her and took one glance at it, then put it resolutely away. "If I am to go mad, which I daresay I shall from all that is happening lately, it will not be from reading such gibberish. It is no use asking me to read it, anyway, for it appears to be some sort of legal document, and you know I never understood one word in ten of such things. Nor am I in any mood for riddles."

"You should understand that legal document, Aunt Bella, for you signed it. It is the mortgage you took out on this house. Who held it, by the way?"

"Good God, what does that matter? An old friend of mine, which is just as well, for he has never pressed me for payment. And you needn't look like that, for it was all very legal, and I pay him the interest whenever I can.

Certainly he is in no need of it. I daresay he has forgotten it by now.''

"Well, he has obviously remembered it, or else come into sudden need of some money, for he has sold it to Roxbury. I only hope he may have gouged him unmercifully.''

"Sold it to Roxbury?" repeated her aunt, sitting up a little straighter, two very natural spots of color joining the rouge on her cheeks. "Well, I have never heard anything so base! If he had need of the money, he had only to tell me so, for I always meant to repay him. Heaven knows where I would have put my hands on such a sum, but to sell it out from under me without a word of warning like that . . . I would never have expected it of . . . Well, never mind. You wouldn't know him anyway, for he has been retired from London for many years. But he was always a perfect gentleman in the past. I can't understand his doing such a thing at all.''

"Oh, what does that matter? It is Roxbury I am furious with! How dare he? How on earth could he have learned of it, anyway?''

"Gracious, anyone who knows me knows I have never had a feather to fly with, my love," said her aunt distractedly. "That is no mystery. The only mystery is why Roxbury should buy up a worthless piece of paper, for there is no knowing when I shall be able to pay it off, if ever.''

"He doesn't expect you to, Aunt," said Philippa scornfully. "He bought it to exchange for his father's letters. Oh, he has been exceedingly clever, I'll grant you. He knew I would be forced to give them to him, for I have not the least doubt he wouldn't have hesitated to throw us out in the street if I had refused. How I wish they had not outlawed medieval torture. Boiling in oil is too good for him.''

But Aunt Bella, far from being as incensed as she ought to have been at such perfidy, was looking almost relieved. "Good gracious, is that what all this is about? I wish you had said so at once, instead of letting me fear the worse. I know you are angry, my love, but for myself I can't be sorry. I never did feel right about using those letters for such a purpose. In fact, I am almost glad he has made you give them up.''

Philippa nearly goggled at her. ''Aunt Bella, do you understand what I'm saying? Without those letters I have no hope of making Roxbury release Julian's fortune. Apart from every other consideration, how dare he think he can buy us off with five thousand pounds.''

''Well, I own it does seem paltry, when I have it on reliable authority that Julian's fortune is worth something in the neighborhood of ten thousand a year. But I daresay it is better than nothing.''

''That has nothing to do with it,'' cried Philippa furiously. ''How dare he think I would sell your letters to him at any price! And if you dare to say again that it was the same thing, I warn you I am likely to smash another vase. If you cannot see the difference between using them to—to force him into relinquishing Julian's fortune, when he had no right to withhold it in the first place, and selling them to him for five thousand pounds, then there is no use talking to you. Oh, I thought there was nothing worse he could do to insult me, but I was mistaken. I would like to . . . I cannot think of anything bad enough.''

''Well, since you cannot boil him in oil, or even run him through, I see no point in talking about it,'' pointed out her aunt philosophically. ''You had far better be thinking how we are to break the news to Diana. And just when I was beginning to think, with Julian's help, we might soon have been in the way of being completely comfortable.''

But at that Philippa had the grace to look slightly ashamed. ''Good God, you cannot think I meant to become Julian's pensioner, Aunt Bella? That would make me as detestable as the odious earl thinks me! And as for telling Diana, I am more determined than ever to beat him at his own game, even if it means supporting them for the rest of our lives.''

''Now I am sure I shall go mad,'' complained her aunt. ''Dearest, I am sure no one is more sympathetic than I am, but one must occasionally be practical, after all. And aside from every other consideration, I don't see how that will make Roxbury sorry.''

"At the very least, it will make him look ridiculous. How will it look to the world when it is discovered his precious nephew is obliged to live on his wife's family because his own fortune is unscrupulously tied up? Let us see how Roxbury likes that to get around."

"I'll tell you how it will look. As if we are the fools, not Roxbury," retorted her aunt tartly. "I sometimes wonder, in fact, what I have done to deserve all that has happened to me."

Philippa made an effort to control her temper. "Dearest Aunt Bella, you know you would never turn them away," she said coaxingly. "And we will get by, you know we will. We always have, haven't we?" Then her face hardened slightly. "At any rate, I think even starving would be worth it if it showed him up for the hypocrite he is! I warned him that I would make him sorry if it's the last thing I ever do, and I will. He thought he could be rid of us for a mere five thousand pounds, but he shall soon learn his mistake. How I hate him!"

But at the mention of the five thousand pounds Aunt Bella had brightened somewhat. "Well, at least there is still that," she conceded. "And I own it will be a blessing not to have that dratted mortgage hanging over our heads any longer. Especially if we are to have Julian living here as well now."

Philippa regarded her aunt almost pityingly. "Poor Aunt Bella," she said contritely. "I am sorry to be such a charge on you, but you cannot think I would let Roxbury buy us off for such a sum, or even five times that amount? I'm afraid that, far from being better off, we are even worse off, for now we must repay the wretched mortgage as soon as possible. I will not be in his debt one second longer than I have to."

As her aunt moaned weakly, she added indignantly, "And you needn't moan like that, Aunt Bella. You know we always intended to pay off the mortgage. But not by accepting handouts from Julian, or bribes from the odious Earl of Roxbury, either!"

It was too much to expect Aunt Bella to agree to that,

but to her outrage Philippa insisted upon bundling up the mortgage and sending it straight back to the Earl of Roxbury.

The note that accompanied it gave her a great deal of pleasure to write, for in it she icily informed Roxbury that her aunt's letters had never been for sale, as she had told him. If he had been foolish enough to purchase a mortgage belonging to them, he would be obliged to give them time to raise the money to redeem it. But he might be sure it would be redeemed at the earliest possible moment, for even that tenuous a connection with him was wholly repugnant to her aunt.

She signed it with a flourish and went out to post it herself before she could change her mind, or her aunt, wholly overcome by the thought of so improvident an act, could renew the argument.

9

PHILIPPA HAD hoped her letter would give the hateful earl pause, but in fact he did not read it for several days, owing to the hectic pace set by the Dowager Countess of Roxbury, visiting from Bath, where she made her home.

The dowager had not been to town for many months and insisted upon her son escorting her to all her favorite places and driving her out to visit a number of old friends in the country.

She was a handsome woman with a surprisingly youthful countenance, though she possessed grown grandchildren and was well over sixty. She had been widowed for nearly fifteen years and was in ill health, but neither fact had managed to dim her frank enjoyment of life.

A riding accident in her thirties had left her a partial invalid, and she walked only with great difficulty. She had never allowed it, however, to prevent her from doing exactly what she wanted, or to sour her outlook on life, and few people realized that she was the victim of almost constant pain.

Her son certainly was aware of the fact, but he had long since given up trying to restrain her or even question her about her health. To all inquiries she answered cheerfully that she was very well, and changed the subject.

Her only concession to her health was to reside in Bath, where the waters gave her some relief from the pain. She had an elder sister living with her who was devoted, but inclined to be gruff and overprotective, and the dowager said frankly that she came to London to escape the dangers of complete provincialism and to get up to date on the latest scandals.

She had naturally heard all about her grandson's unfortunate attachment, not from her son but from Theresa, her eldest daughter. She had been more amused than alarmed by the affair, but her son had been uninclined to discuss the matter with her. "It need not concern you, Mama," he said shortly. "I am sorry Theresa told you anything about it. But you may rest assured I have put a stop to the affair already."

She looked at him rather curiously, but said merely, "Poor Julian! I own I feel a little sorry for him. Is she really so bad?"

She was seated in his curricle, a becoming new parasol shading her face from the afternoon sun, being driven through the park at the fashionable hour—or lionizing, as she called it, for it was necessary to remind all her old friends from time to time that she was still alive. Nor did she consider it did her son any harm to be obliged to escort her on her infrequent appearances, for he was, as she also added frankly, in danger of becoming a complete hermit.

She now turned to bow to a slightly startled acquaintance, and added inconsequently, "Dear me, Lady Boscastle looks as if she had seen a ghost. I really must come to London more often. Still, it seems very odd of Julian to have fallen in love with the niece of such a creature. He has always seemed such a steady young man. But then, if his Diana is anything like the aunt, perhaps it is not so remarkable. She was a dazzling creature in her youth, I remember, though I daresay you are too young ever to have seen her, my dear."

"You are mistaken," he said briefly. "I did see her once."

"Did you? Then you will understand what I'm talking about. I once saw her in a comedy of some sort—I've long since forgotten the play, and it little mattered anyway, for she was the only thing worth watching in it. She wasn't even a particularly good actress, as I recall, but she still somehow managed to hold every eye. They attributed several duels and at least one suicide to her, I seem to remember.''

Her son seldom showed her the curt manner he showed the rest of the world, but he had no desire to pursue this particular topic with her, and said even more shortly, ''The niece is one by marriage only, so she can scarcely be expected to have inherited her aunt's fatal fascination.''

''Oh, yes. I do remember she married Edgar Mayhew in the end. Poor creature! I almost felt sorry for her, for she no doubt thought that she was bettering herself. It turned out sadly otherwise, as a great many people could have warned her. He was sadly unstable, you know, and had done his best to run through what I believe to have been a respectable fortune long before he met her. It was rumored she ended up selling all her jewels to support them, which I know some people thought poetic justice, but I have always thought particularly ironic. But if the niece is from that side of the family, it cannot be as objectionable as you say, surely? I believe the Mayhews are respectable enough.''

''You will forgive me for finding little to recommend in a man who would live off the sale of jewels his wife received from other men,'' he said grimly. ''As for the niece, she is a harpy.''

''Oh, dear! Theresa said so, but of course she would. I don't know why I'm defending Isabella Monteith, either, except that I have always had a sneaking sympathy for any woman caught in her predicament. Still, I suppose it wouldn't do, whatever my sympathies. Theresa wishes poor Julian to make a brilliant match, I know, but I had not expected you to care one way or the other. Do you?'' she asked, looking at him curiously.

''Not in the least. He may marry whomever he wishes, but I will not hand over his fortune to be squandered by a grasping little wanton.''

He spoke more harshly than he usually did to her, and she looked at him again curiously, but then she espied an old friend and abruptly abandoned the topic. ''Oh, there is poor Polly Rutherford! Pull up, dearest, for I must speak to her. I haven't seen her in years. Theresa tells me she is reduced to living as her son's pensioner, which is an abominable thing, I'm sure.''

He obligingly did so, and if his mother had any inkling he was glad of the interruption, she did not reveal it, too taken up with greeting an old friend to renew the discussion, even after they had driven on.

But the next morning, over a leisurely breakfast, her curiosity was once more aroused by her son's reaction to something in his morning's post.

The dowager had kindly declared that she had taken enough of her son's time and meant to receive visits from old friends anyway, that day, so he was free to pursue his own interests. Since he had neglected his affairs for some days, she even made no objection to his going through his post over the breakfast table, though it made him a less-than-attentive companion.

But she was surprised when he exclaimed involuntarily after opening a particularly thick parcel, ''What the devil! Now what does this mean?''

She glanced up, curious as to what had so aroused him. ''What does what mean, dear?'' she inquired interestedly.

But the earl had had time to recall her presence by then and to regret his outburst. ''Nothing. Just something that surprised me.''

But his eyes had run rapidly down the short letter accompanying the packet even as he spoke, and he was scowling slightly. As Firth came into the room to bring a fresh pot of tea, he demanded abruptly, ''When did this arrive, Firth?''

The butler seemed unrattled by the barked question, though he could scarcely be expected to know what ''this'' referred to. He glanced impassively at the packet his lordship held and answered woodenly, ''Two days ago, my lord. As it came by the medium of the penny post, I did not believe it required your urgent attention.'' HIs disdain was obvious.

Lady Roxbury was by now alive with curiosity, but too acquainted with her son to show it. ''What is it, dear? Not bad news, I hope.''

Abruptly the earl folded the letter and laid it aside. "No. Merely something I must attend to later," he said dismissingly.

"Well, you may do so at your leisure, for I am beginning to feel guilty at keeping you tied to my skirts for so many days. Not that it doesn't do you good to be obliged to remember your social duties now and then. And you needn't bother to scowl at me, for, unlike Theresa, I have long since given up trying to reform you. In fact, you may occupy yourself with inspecting factories, or whatever it is you do, for the next several days, for I must refurbish my wardrobe."

"There are of course no shops in Bath worth your patronage? But if you mean to go out, take Theresa with you. She may make herself useful for once."

"Good God, no!" said his mother in amusement. "I dislike being either hurried or treated like an invalid, and Theresa does both. Besides, I shall have Sidbury with me, which is all I require. As for Bath, I am reliably informed by Theresa that I am beginning to look positively provincial. I must do something about that, for I may choose to withdraw from the world, but I am determined not to grow as bad as old Mrs. Presteigne, one of the Bath quizzes. She boasts of not having had a new hat in forty years and deplores any fashion since eighteen hundred."

The earl seldom showed his mother the face he showed the world, and Philippa, for one, would have been more than surprised to know he was capable of behaving normally and even teasing her a little. "From everything I have been able to tell, Bath has as many gossips and scandals going on as London, and nearly as hectic a social round. Don't try to gammon me with talk of provincialism."

The dowager laughed. "At least in Bath I may go or not as I wish, and I have developed a good circle of friends. And when I decided to move there, after much soul searching, you know I had determined to rejoin the world, if even so minor a one. I haven't regretted it. One may look inside too long and grow positively hermitlike, and I was very much in danger of doing so, I fear."

His expression sobered and he reached out to clasp her

hand, an unexpectedly warm gesture from so abrupt a man. "You were never that, and if so, you had good reason, Mama. But I'm glad you're happy."

She turned her hand over to strongly return the pressure, but there was a hint of concern along with the deep affection in her eyes. But all she said was, "Now run away to your business, and George shall help me into the drawing room. I am expecting visitors soon. And you needn't think you must stay in to dinner tonight on my account, for an old friend has promised to dine with me, and I must tell you you will be very much in the way, for we are dying to catch up on several years of old gossip."

He smiled, raised her hand to his lips, and took his leave. She looked after him for a moment, her expression unexpectedly pensive, then sighed and rang the bell for the footman.

Once away from his mother, however, the earl hesitated, a heavy frown between his brows, then abruptly sent for his curricle.

For the third time he drove himself to Green Street, this time in a thoughtful mood. The return of the mortgage and Philippa's note had startled him more than a little, for it did not fit in with his preconceptions of her.

She might merely be playing some deep game, of course, but if so, he could see no immediate gain to her from such a course. She must know by now that he would stop at nothing to prevent her sister from marrying his nephew, and whatever she might be intending to do, the spurning of her aunt's mortgage made no sense.

It did not occur to him to go so far as to wonder if he might not have been mistaken in her, after all, but he admitted he was curious to know what she was up to.

Nor, if the truth be known, was he at all averse to having an excuse to see Miss Philippa Mayhew again.

The door was again opened to him by the same youthful maid, who seemed even more flustered than usual. She gaped at him, looking slightly scared and more than a little disheveled, but before he could inquire for her mistress, Philippa herself appeared in the hallway behind her, looking even more harassed.

"Betty, send whoever it is away and then go and find
. . . Oh, no!" She came to a standstill as she caught sight
of his lordship, and added distractedly, "Oh, go away! I
don't have time to quarrel with you today."

Roxbury was amused despite himself and had furthermore had ample time to discover that Miss Mayhew was
looking even more untidy than her housemaid. There was
a black smudge, as of grease, across one flushed cheek,
and the hem of her dress, for some astonishing reason, was
wet halfway up her skirt.

"Astonishingly enough, I have not come to quarrel with
you today, Miss Mayhew," he said in some amusement.
"But you appear to be in the midst of some domestic
crisis. What is it? Perhaps I may be of some help."

"You?" Her opinion of him was obvious, and he was
once more reluctantly amused.

"Why not? Stranger things have happened."

She hesitated, then, as shrill sounds of agitation reached
them from the nether regions of the house, said impatiently, "If you must know, the kitchen pump seems to be
broken, and there's water everywhere. If you can do anything to stop it, then for God's sake do it. I am in no
situation to be choosy at the moment."

She did not even wait for him to answer but disappeared
toward the back of the house. After a moment he shrugged
and followed her slender figure, wondering if he was
losing his mind.

10

WITHOUT HESITATION she led him straight through the baize door that separated the front of the house from the back, and down the kitchen steps, picking up her skirts as she reached the bottom. With good reason, he saw. The flagged kitchen floor was several inches deep in water.

The players on this remarkable scene were far too occupied to notice his arrival, and Philippa herself seemed to have forgotten him already, for without hesitation she lifted her skirts even higher and waded through the deluged floor, saying distractedly, "Good God, we shall have the water up to the ground floor if we don't get it off soon. I have sent Betty to try to find someone to help, but we may all be drowned before she gets back."

The youth he had seen once before had his coat off and was futilely trying to stop the flow of water with rags, his face even more smeared than his sister's, and his expression harried. Beside him, and doing more to hamper operations than help, by the look of it, stood a stout woman with a red face he took to be the cook. She was wringing her hands and lamenting the ruin of her clean kitchen and generally making a nuisance of herself.

As if aware of it, Philippa said sharply, "If you can't be quiet, Mrs. Huff, I wish you would go away, for you are helping no one. Darius, try turning it again. There must be some way to stop the flood."

"Have you tried turning the water off at the source?" inquired the earl calmly, enjoying the scene.

The results of his words were dramatic. Darius looked up and was so startled at sight of the earl that he abruptly released his hold and was soaked by a fresh burst of water. And after a brief moment Philippa said awfully, "Don't tell me you can turn it off? I don't know whether to scream or go off into a strong apoplexy. Where do you turn it off, for God's sake?"

He said sardonically, "Yes, of course you can. But by all means, allow me." And he disappeared out the kitchen door.

When he returned, some few moments later, the water had slowed to a trickle, and Darius was sheepishly unwinding his rags. "I thank you, sir," he said. "I should have known that myself."

"I doubt you can have had reason to need that particular piece of information," pointed out Roxbury, looking over the scene of destruction with amusement.

"Well, at least the wretched thing is off," said Philippa. "We can get someone in to fix it later."

"If you have a few tools, there is no need. I can probably do it for you," said Roxbury, surprising even himself. "I doubt if it's anything very serious."

This time her astonishment would have been insulting if it weren't so amusing, for just so might she have looked if a pet dog had volunteered to talk—or a poisonous snake to help her. "You?" she said again, even more unflatteringly.

As if aware of the inadequacy of her response, the youth said quickly, "C-can you, sir? We would be awfully grateful. But I'm afraid it's covered in grease, as I discovered for myself."

"I imagine I will manage to survive. Have you a wrench in the house? Good. Fetch it, and a hammer too, if you have one. The fitting is probably stuck."

Darius willingly went to do as he was bid, returning in a moment to hand him the required articles. He watched as the earl stripped off his coat and laid it on the table, then rolled up his sleeves and waded through the water to the leaky pump. As Roxbury began deftly to try to loosen the pipe fitting, Darius asked curiously, "How is it you know about such things, sir?"

Roxbury glanced up from his work briefly. "Because I am interested in anything mechanical. This is a primitive apparatus, I will grant you, but the principle is basically the same."

"A-are you, sir?" inquired Darius doubtfully.

"An unfashionable interest, I know, but one that is going to change the shape of civilization as we know it, in the next twenty years. As I said, I am more interested in factory machines and steam engines, but I don't despise technology in any guise. There, that should do it. The fitting had come loose, is all, as I suspected. Let me turn on the water again, and we shall see."

When he had returned from doing that and made sure he had stopped the leak, Darius said shyly, "Th-thank you, sir. Here's your coat. Do you really know all about steam engines? I must admit I'm impressed. I thought only radical geniuses understood such things."

"The men who invent them are no longer radicals, nor are the men who invest in them. I have no patience with people who are afraid of the future." The earl wiped his hands on a cloth the youth handed him, then rolled down his sleeves and allowed him to help him into his coat again. "For instance, you have no doubt heard that gas lighting is highly dangerous, and the work of the devil besides, but I have had it installed in several factories I own in the north, and in my own home in the country as well. Neither of my sisters will visit me there, for fear they will be blown up while under my roof, but I have yet to be blown up, as you can see, and the workers find the light vastly superior for working, believe me."

Darius seemed fascinated by these revelations, but Roxbury, reminded of where he was, said then, "But don't get me on my hobbyhorse. Where is your sister? I wanted . . . Oh, there you are! I came to have a word with you if I may, Miss Mayhew."

Philippa had retreated to the stairs, her unpleasantly wet skirts lifted away from her legs, and had been observing this scene with something like astonishment. If anyone had

ever told her she would find her arch-enemy not only in
her kitchen with his sleeves rolled up, repairing a leaking
pump, but being carelessly kind to an adolescent youth
while he did so, she would frankly have thought them
crazy. But she was reminded that she had thought him,
before all the bitterness started, a man, and not a painted
puppy.

As if aware of her thoughts, he regarded her mockingly,
and she was annoyed with herself for flushing revealingly.
"Y-yes, of course," she said, unusually flustered. "Darius, go up at once and get out of those wet clothes. I will
be down in a minute to help you clean up this mess, Mrs.
Huff."

Once more he followed her figure, this time up the stairs
and to the drawing room on the ground floor, but said
frowningly, as soon as the door was closed, "Have you
no one else to mop up the kitchen? That is hardly fitting
work for you."

'No, I have not," she retorted grumblingly. "Mrs. Huff
suffers from the gout as it is, and Betty is very little help.
Where do you turn the water off, by the way?"

"Where the main pipe comes in to the house. There's a
valve there that you turn," he said in renewed amusement.
"You should have a male servant to take care of such
emergencies."

"I should also have the moon on a plate and gold forks
to eat it with, no doubt," she retorted sarcastically.

"But then I don't doubt you will before you finish, at
the rate you're going," he added, fast returning to normal.

Instantly she flushed and said through her teeth, "I must
be grateful to you for fixing the leak, but if you have come
merely to insult me, as usual, I wish you would go away. I
find I am not in the mood today."

'No, I came to return this." He handed her the packet
containing the mortgage. "We had a bargain, or so I
understood, and I don't go back on my word."

She eyed the packet suspiciously, as if expecting some
new trick, but when she saw what it contained, she flushed
even more, with unmistakable wrath. "We had no bar-

gain, my lord. I told you my aunt's letters were not for sale, and I meant it.''

He frowned once more, eyeing her rather searchingly. Unless she were a better actress even than he believed, she was serious. It made no sense, but he said merely, "Whatever you call it, the mortgage is yours. And if you are hoping to impress me with this belated show of virtue, you are wasting your time. I meant every word I said about my nephew's fortune.''

"How I wish I were a man!" she cried furiously. "Then we would see if you dared to speak to me like that.''

She had removed the smear of grease on her cheek, but her face was flushed and glowing, her rich chestnut hair loosened and curling a little with the damp and her exertions, and her eyes brilliant with fury. She looked, in fact, so vital and beautiful that he said dryly, "If you were a man, Miss Mayhew, this conversation would hardly be taking place." He frowned, remembering the callow youth upstairs and added surprisingly, "Or even if you had a man to protect you. I must go. I am late for an appointment already.''

"If you dare to leave that here, I will merely send it back again," she threatened wildly.

For answer he picked it up, tore it across, then dropped it in the wastepaper basket and walked out.

But if Philippa was surprised by the earl's unexpected behavior, Aunt Bella, when she came to hear of it, was even more astonished. "Tore it up?" she gasped. "After you had been such a fool as to send it back to him? I am beginning to think you are both mad.''

"Don't be ridiculous. We are neither of us mad," snapped Philippa, annoyed for some reason. "But it makes little difference. He may tear it up a dozen times, and I shall still repay him, if it takes the rest of my life.''

"Repay him, when I daresay he is so rich he will not even notice such a sum? Don't tell me you're not mad, for you clearly should be locked up in Bedlam. Especially when heaven knows how we are to get by if costs keep rising as they have been doing, because of this wretched war. And that's saying nothing of Darius' fees at Cambridge. I tell you it is absolutely sacrilegious to fly in the face of providence as you are suggesting, for when you sent it back the first time, I despaired of ever seeing it again. If he is so crazy as to return it, you cannot mean still to pay him?''

"Of course I do! He thinks—he believes us exactly the sort of females to do such a despicable thing as to sell his father's letters for a price," said Philippa in an oddly strangled voice. "Oh, how can I make you see? When I did what I did, it was out of desperation—and because he had made me furiously angry, I admit it. I am not particularly proud of it now, if you must know. But this: to accept money for your letters! No! Every feeling must be revolted. If nothing else, I would not give him the satisfaction of thinking he was right about us from the beginning.''

If her aunt thought this extremely inconsistent piece of logic unlike her usually levelheaded niece, she did not trouble to point it out. "Never mind. I have given up trying to understand any of it. Least of all that Roxbury has been here fixing the pump. I am beginning to wonder if I have not been mistaken in him, and he is not nearly so bad as you have led me to expect, in fact. Really, if it weren't for Diana, I would be quite in charity with him, for you can't deny his behavior has been more generous than we deserve, under the circumstances.''

"Of course I can deny it! I will own I must be grateful to him for this afternoon, for Cook would do nothing but stand and wring her hands, and I was little more use, I fear. But I daresay any man could have done the same," said Philippa stubbornly. "At any rate, I dislike him far too much to give him credit for anything.''

"That, at least, you need not have told me," retorted her long-suffering aunt. "For my part, I am far angrier with Alder . . . Well, never mind! But a party who shall remain nameless. I have half a mind to write and tell him off, for I never expected him to behave so shabbily. If he had no intention of holding my mortgage, he had no business lending me the money in the first place.''

"How long ago was it signed, ma'am?" asked Philippa curiously, gratefully abandoning the topic of Roxbury.

"Good God, how am I expected to remember that? It must be all of ten years ago by now. I only remember I was particularly desperate at the time, for your uncle had just died and I had no notion how I was to pay off all the money I owed. I thought of selling the house, but somehow I couldn't bear to, but then Alder—well, never mind—but then my friend suggested I should take out a mortgage on it, which answered almost as well. Not that I was able to settle all my debts by any means, but then I have never been one to chase after miracles."

But Philippa's face had softened. "Poor Aunt Bella," she said ruefully. "My uncle used you shamefully, and so, I'm afraid, have I. But let us talk of something else, for we are unlikely to agree on this particular topic, and the odious earl has taken up quite enough of our time. However he may have behaved today, ten to one the next time I meet him he will be even more unpleasant to make up for it."

11

SHE WAS right, for the next time she saw Roxbury he was very angry indeed, and for a reason she could not at first even fathom.

She had gone out to run a few errands and to exchange her books at the lending library. Genia usually accompanied her on this mission, but she had had a slight sore throat that morning and had remained unwillingly at home, charging her strictly instead with several urgent commissions.

To find the particular books Genia wanted had taken more time than Philippa had expected, and she was just finishing up the lengthy transaction with the clerk when a handsome, older woman standing next to her at the bookstore counter said unexpectedly, "Forgive me, but I couldn't help overhearing your name, just now. You aren't by any chance Miss Diana Mayhew, are you?"

Philippa was startled, for she did not recognize the fashionable stranger, but answered with a shade of reserve that she was Diana Mayhew's older sister.

The other woman looked her over with a thoroughness that would have been insulting had there not been such a kindly twinkle in her eyes. "Then I think you and I had better get acquainted," she said even more surprisingly, "for you are not at all what I had been led to expect. But forgive me. My son says I rattle on like a magpie, and I fear it's true. I am Julian's grandmother, you know."

Philippa nearly dropped her parcel of books, cursing the

coincidence that should have led her to meet the Dowager Countess of Roxbury, of all people. She had little doubt what the dowager had been led to expect of her and Diana, if her son was her source of information. But though it was extremely tempting to expose Roxbury's unreasoning prejudices, she could not help but feel that a meeting between them was unwise, under the circumstances.

Nor was the dowager countess what she herself had pictured, from Julian's descriptions. This lady was certainly leaning rather heavily on two canes, but she looked absurdly youthful to be the grandmother of a grown man, and her eyes twinkled so infectiously that it was even harder to picture her the mother of Lord Roxbury.

In fact, under different circumstances the dowager would have appealed strongly to her, for she looked extremely kind and as if she possessed a sense of humor. But that merely made matters worse, for Philippa could not help recalling with sudden guilt that Aunt Bella had once nearly run off with this woman's husband, and worse, that she herself had threatened to make his letters public.

The dowager, unfortunately, did not seem to share her hesitation, for she said cheerfully, "But we can't talk here. I fear I have overextended myself this afternoon, for you will have noticed that I cannot stand for hours without suffering the consequences of my folly. But my carriage should be just outside the door, by now. Perhaps I might drop you somewhere, and we could have a comfortable chat on the way."

The last thing Philippa wanted to do was enjoy a comfortable chat with the Dowager Countess of Roxbury, but it seemed churlish to refuse. She contented herself with saying that she had some other errands to run, but the dowager could drop her in Bond Street, if she were going that way.

The dowager readily agreed, but Philippa saw now that she was indeed looking a trifle strained under her cheerful mask. A middle-aged woman Philippa took to be her maid was hovering anxiously at her elbow, and said now in the scolding voice of a very old servant, "I will see to them books, my lady, as I should have from the beginning. And here is Jacob, just when he's wanted. You go along now and get off your feet.''

Jacob proved to be a particularly large and muscular young footman, who insisted upon taking Philippa's parcel from her and then helped her ladyship out to a carriage with a crest upon the door waiting at the curbside. The reason for his size was soon apparent, for without ceremony he lifted his mistress and deposited her on the vehicle's velvet squabs, then held the door respectfully for Philippa.

The dowager survived this ungraceful operation with unimpaired dignity, merely saying ruefully, as Philippa unwillingly took her place beside her, ''I apologize, my dear. But I learned long ago not to be self-conscious about my infirmity, or else I would have had to become a total recluse.''

''You are fortunate to have such devoted servants, ma'am,'' said Philippa politely.

''Indeed, yes!'' The dowager's eyes twinkled in their infectious way. ''But what you mean, I suspect, is that if I were poor, I would not be able to overcome my handicap quite so easily. It is a sad fact of life, I agree. But never mind that. I sensed you were somewhat unwilling to come with me, Miss Mayhew, so perhaps I should tell you from the outset that I am far from being the snob my eldest daughter is. And now that I have met you, I am even more convinced some mistake has been made.''

Philippa was beginning to regret the impulse of politeness that had made her accept this unexpected woman's offer, for it placed her in a completely untenable position. She could only assume—and devoutly hope—that Lady Roxbury knew nothing of Aunt Bella's affair with her husband, but that fact merely made things worse, for she had no right to accept her kindness, under the circumstances.

She said with sudden determination, blushing a little, ''Lady Roxbury, please stop the carriage and let me out. I—I am not ungrateful for your kindness, but I think this meeting unwise, as things stand. You must know your son and daughter both oppose my sister's marriage to your grandson, and though I am far from agreeing with their reasons, while that is so I fear we can have nothing to say to each other. I don't mean to be rude, but—"

"My dear, you will discover once you know me better that I make up my own mind on most things," interrupted the dowager, making no attempt to comply with this request. "Pray humor my curiosity for a few minutes longer. If you don't mind my asking, how is it you came to live with your aunt? It seems an unexpected arrangement, for I am told she is an aunt only by marriage."

"She offered us a home when my father died five years ago," said Philippa stiffly. "And I should warn you, ma'am, that whatever she used to be, I am excessively fond of her. More, we owe her a great deal, far more than we can ever repay, for she took us in when the alternative was that my sisters and brother and myself would almost certainly have had to be separated. She did so when she is, as you say, indeed merely an aunt by marriage, and had no great reason to be fond of my family, either. My uncle—"

Abruptly she broke off, regretting what she had been about to say. But the dowager said frankly, "Did not treat her as he should! Oh, don't look so surprised, my dear. It was common knowledge at the time, and I must confess I felt sorry for her when I heard she had married him."

Philippa was indeed surprised, but asked shortly, with a little curl to her lip, "Did you know my uncle, ma'am? Then I need say no more, except that he married her, I have always believed, merely to spite my grandpapa. Unfortunately, that is hardly grounds for marriage, and he was soon ashamed of her and treated her abominably. I think she was relieved when he died, and who can blame her. But when my own father, her brother-in-law, died, a few years later, she did not hesitate to offer us a home with her. It could not have been easy either, for my uncle had not only left her badly in debt, but wasted what she had been able to accumulate, and there were four of us. I was twenty, by then, but my youngest sister was scarcely eight years old. I think you will see why I have reason to be fond of her."

"Good God! That was indeed generous of her. I had no idea there were so many of you."

"Yes, ma'am," said Philippa dryly. "You may not believe me—your son certainly didn't!—but my aunt's experiences were why I initially opposed my sister's attachment to Ju—to Lord Holyoke. I had no wish to see her make the same mistakes my aunt did. But I have since come to believe him to be as sincerely in love with my sister as she is with him. Of course I am bound to say that, aren't I?" she added bitterly. "Lord Roxbury perhaps naturally believes we are interested only in Julian's fortune, and there is nothing I can say to convince you otherwise. And that is why this conversation is pointless. I can only warn you that I am determined to do everything in my power to further the match, even if it leads to a breach in Julian's family."

"Dear me," said the dowager mildly. "I am beginning to think it a good thing I came to town. I gather you don't like my son very much, Miss Mayhew?"

"He is, ma'am, the rudest, most insulting . . . But I have no wish to offend you any more than I have already done. Suffice it to say that he has threatened to withhold Julian's fortune until he is thirty if he marries my sister against his wishes. He has also promised to ruin my aunt and myself if we dare to defy him."

"Good God, that sounds unlike my son. If you had asked me before this, I would not have said he cared whom Julian married, particularly since he himself has categorically refused to make an eligible marriage himself," remarked the dowager thoughtfully, still looking vaguely amused for some reason.

"That is very different from wedding the niece of a notorious actress," Philippa said, her fine eyes betraying her scorn.

"And am I to understand your sister still intends to wed my grandson, Miss Mayhew, even in the face of my son's threats?"

Philippa flushed for some reason. "I told you my sister was never particularly interested in Julian's fortune, ma'am. But that is up to them. As yet, Julian has no suspicion that his uncle opposes the match as much as his mother does. Lord Roxbury has taken care not to alienate him by openly revealing his intent. It is very possible that once he discovers the truth, Julian may indeed draw back. But if he still wishes to wed Diana, knowing what Lord Roxbury intends to do, I have no doubt my sister will care very little for the loss of his fortune. And if worse comes to worst, my aunt and I are resolved they may live with us, for we have no intention of casting them off as Lord Roxbury threatens.''

Lady Roxbury was regarding her with a great deal of shrewd interest, though it was impossible to tell what she was thinking. But before she could reply, they drew to a stop, and she looked around her with something like surprise. ''Are we there already? Then I won't keep you, my dear. But I won't pretend I haven't found this conversation highly interesting, or that I am not glad to have met you. I fear I have very little influence in the matter, but for what it's worth—''

But Philippa was to wish that she had gotten out when she first intended, for before the dowager could finish, she was interrupted by the opening of the door. Both of them expected to see the footman standing there, but it was Lord Roxbury's voice that said, ''Good God, Mama, I thought you would have gone home hours ago! If I had known you meant to be so foolish, I would have insisted upon Theresa—''

But he had seen Philippa by then and broke off, his brows snapping together and his expression stiffening alarmingly. ''What the . . . ?''

''Hello, dear,'' said his mother calmly. ''Miss Mayhew is just getting out. Perhaps you will be so good as to escort her where she wishes to go.''

Philippa had initially started violently, as if caught out in some guilty act. Then she made her spine stiffen, annoyed with herself for allowing him to make her feel self-conscious for a meeting that had been none of her seeking. But at that she said hurriedly, ''Oh, no, th-thank you, ma'am! I am going only a step.''

But Roxbury had had time to recover himself as well, though Philippa had no doubt, by the hardness of his eyes as they rested on her, that he was very angry indeed. She was far from understanding the reason for it, however, except that his temper was always abominable. "Certainly, ma'am," he said with dangerous restraint. "I would like nothing better than to have a word with Miss Mayhew."

"Good," said the dowager comfortably. "Then that is settled. I have enjoyed our little chat, Miss Mayhew. I hope we will meet again someday—under happier circumstances."

Philippa was left with no choice but to accept Roxbury's hand to climb out, and wish the Dowager good-bye, conscious all the while as she did so of the furious earl standing with mocking attentiveness at her elbow.

12

AS SOON as the dowager drove off, Philippa would have left him without another word, had Roxbury not taken her elbow in a hard grasp and said unpleasantly, "Oh, no, Miss Mayhew! I have one or two things to say to you first."

She still knew no reason for his unexpected anger and could only read in it a dislike of having his mother exposed to the sort of woman he believed her to be. She knew a deep mortification as well as a burning anger of her own, and retorted coldly, "But I have nothing to say to you. Kindly let me go."

For answer he laughed harshly and drew her hand through his arm, beginning to walk her down the street, his tight grip preventing her escape. To passersby they must have looked like an ordinary couple, were it not for the harshness of his expression and the rising fury of her own. Only Philippa knew by the strength of his grip how exceedingly angry he was.

She tried to wrench her arm from his grasp, but his hand tightened cruelly so that she suspected she would find a bruise there tomorrow. "Oh, no," he said again, not slackening his pace. "I have a great deal to say to you, but not in so public a place. And I would not advise you to try to struggle, for you will only provoke a scene I think even you will find embarrassing to extricate yourself from, you beautiful treacherous little bitch."

She was now as bewildered as she was angry, for his fury seemed out of all proportion to the provocation. He had not liked her talking to his mother, that much was obvious, but surely his reaction was extreme, even for him? And it was absurd, for he could hardly expect to abduct her in broad daylight.

She said through her teeth, "If you don't let me go this instant, I promise you I will create a scene you will find far more embarrassing than I will."

They had fortunately reached a side street by then that was relatively empty, though she was beginning to wonder if that were indeed fortunate from her point of view. She thought she had never seen him so angry, and he had seldom been anything else in her presence. For answer he stopped with such suddenness that she nearly ran into him, and almost threw her arm away from him, as if he could no longer bear to touch her. "You needn't worry, Miss Mayhew. I have no desire to prolong this interview any longer than necessary."

She was once more taken aback by his unexpected scorn, but said hardily, refusing to give him the satisfaction of seeing her rub her bruised elbow, "As far as I am concerned it has already gone on longer than necessary. I am going now, and if you dare try to stop me, I shall send for a constable and tell him you are detaining me against my will."

He laughed harshly. "That is nothing to what I would like to do to you, Miss Mayhew. I would advise you not to tempt me. Tell me, did you enjoy wounding a woman who is an invalid and who has never done you any harm? Or are you so genuinely amoral you don't care whom you destroy to get back at me? I should have known you didn't need the letters to do your filthy work."

She had at first merely gaped under this unexpected tirade. Then, as his insulting meaning became all too clear, she paled and stiffened with outrage. "You think— you dare to think that I would . . . ?"

"That's rich, coming from you. I begin to think there is nothing you will not dare. And to think I was even fool enough to begin to wonder if perhaps I might not have misjudged you, after all. That's a laugh! The only thing I misjudged was your capacity for spite."

She was almost beyond words, she was so furious. "You—you—"

"Tell me, Miss Mayhew," he went on contemptuously, "is this a personal vendetta, or do you merely take pleasure in destroying whatever you come into contact with, like the harpy I once called you? Your aunt did her best to ruin my family twenty years ago, and now you are obviously bent on finishing the job."

She was beyond being afraid of him any longer, or even of rational thought, and struck out at him with all her strength.

She might have saved herself the effort, for he easily forestalled the blow, grabbing her wrist in a punishing grip that brought her unbearably close to him, her body bent back a little by the pressure he was exerting.

"Oh, no, Miss Mayhew," he said, exposing his teeth in a way that betrayed how near he was to losing all control. "I warned you not to tempt me, for at the moment I would like nothing better than to strangle you with my own hands for the lying, destructive arch-doxy you are."

She was as much in danger of losing what little restraint she possessed, for she had never in her life before been so angry she had been driven to attempt physical violence. Both of them seemed to have forgotten they were on a public street. His grip on her wrist was extremely painful, and she was thrown off balance by the force he was exerting. She could not break free, for he was far too strong, and so she did not hesitate, but stamped on his instep with all the power she could manage in an effort to make him release her.

He swore, then cruelly increased the pressure on her wrist, so that she was nearly bent double backward. As if goaded beyond control at last, before she could divine his intention, he had thrown his other arm tight around her and was kissing her, the very violence of his lips an indication of the fury he was feeling.

She struggled futilely, sick and humiliated, not making the mistake of taking his assault as anything but the insult it was meant to be. Her lips were ground back painfully against her teeth, and she could taste the warm saltiness of her own blood in her mouth. So violent were her emotions, and so confused, that her head seemed to whirl blackly, and for the first time in her life she was in actual danger of fainting.

After what seemed like an eternity he lifted his head, as if becoming at last aware of her immobility and the absence of any fight left in her. He, too, was panting a little by that time, whether from anger or something else she could not know. "If I cannot murder you, Miss Mayhew, I can at least purge you as one purges a particularly violent and unpleasant disease," he said oddly, and abruptly released her.

She thought for a humiliating moment she would fall without the support of his arms. Then she turned without another word and left him.

She had no notion of any destination, only of escape, for she felt more shaken by the violent encounter than she wanted him to know. In fact, the tears were burning hotly behind her eyes and at the back of her throat, and she feared at any moment she would totally disgrace herself by breaking down completely.

Certainly she had no thought of looking where she was going at the moment, or was even aware that she had stepped out into the street. There was a shout behind her, but she was too overcome for it to mean anything to her. She was totally oblivious to possible danger until jerked back to sudden consciousness by the realization she was almost directly in the path of a fast-moving coach and four that had just swept around the corner.

The coachman didn't at first see her, and in any event he was traveling too fast for him to be able to pull up his horses in time. Philippa stood frozen in the middle of the road as the team barreled down on her, knowing she was going to be run over but too shocked to go either backward or foreward.

Then, as if at the last possible moment, she was pushed violently from behind and half-propelled, half-carried forward out of harm's way.

This time she could hear the driver shouting and sawing

ineffectually at his reins, and she felt rather than saw as
the horses thundered past, missing her seemingly only by
inches. Then she stumbled and sprawled painfully and
inelegantly in the street.

For a moment after it was over she could only lie where
she had fallen, too stunned to pick herself up. The narrow-
ness of her escape, shock, and belated fear on top of the
previous scene she had endured, all combined to make her
limbs feel like water and her head to spin dizzily.

The next moment Roxbury was bending over her, saying
in a harsh voice she scarcely recognized, "Good God, you
little fool! Were you trying to kill yourself?"

She sat up shakily, to stare at him as if she had never
seen him before. "You—you saved my life," she said
foolishly.

He, at least, seemed to be fast returning to normal,
though his cheeks were suspiciously white, for he said
shortly, "A momentary aberration that I shall no doubt
come to regret. Can you stand?"

"I—I think so."

But when he helped her to her feet, she would have
fallen again if he had not caught her, for her left ankle
would not bear her weight and buckled painfully under
her.

She looked up and said breathlessly, biting her lip against
the pain in her ankle, "I'm sorry. I seem to have sprained
my ankle."

Then for the first time in her life she fainted dead away.

Afterward she was to be relieved she was thus spared
the ensuing scene. Roxbury swore and swept her up in his
arms just as the driver of the coach, who had managed
belatedly to halt his team, came running back, and since
they had gathered quite a crowd by then, for a few minutes
confusion reigned. The driver was trying to explain and
excuse himself, and most of the spectators felt it incum-
bent upon themselves to question or proffer advice, or
merely to exclaim at the closeness of the near tragedy.

Roxbury ignored it all to lay her carefully down and run
his hands expertly over Philippa's arms and legs. He determined with relief that she was not seriously hurt and had

merely fainted out of shock. Then he swung her up in his arms again and disposed of the crowd with one curt statement.

"The young lady has merely fainted, so you may all return to your own affairs. I would be obliged, however, if someone would call me a cab first. As for you, my good man," he added, swinging on the driver, whose excuses had centered on blaming the young lady for running out in the road in front of him, "I have heard more than enough from you. If you had not been driving too fast, you would have been able to pull up in time, which I will certainly point out to the proper authorities unless you take yourself off immediately."

Several in the crowd grumbled and the driver stiffened resentfully. But after a moment he obviously thought it wisest to follow this advice, and since a hansom cab had pulled up by this time, summoned by a helpful gentleman in a frock coat, the crowd soon dispersed, convinced the show was over.

Fortunately Philippa knew nothing of any of this, or even when Roxbury deposited her in the cab. She did not return to full consciousness until some time later, when she found herself in a swaying vehicle, her cheek resting, incongruously, against the waistcoat of the Earl of Roxbury and his arm tightly around her.

Her head was still swimming unpleasantly, and it took her a moment to remember what had happened, but when she did, she sat up with alacrity, hot color replacing the unnatural pallor in her cheeks. "Wha-what are you doing?" she cried breathlessly. "Where are you taking me?"

"I am not kidnapping you, if that is what you fear, Miss Mayhew," he remarked dryly. "Though I'll admit I have once or twice been tempted. You fainted. I am merely taking you home."

But she had had time by then for memory of the accident and her near escape to come pouring back. Even so, she said incredulously, "I fainted? You must be mistaken. I have never fainted in my life."

"Then you are a better actress than even I gave you credit for, for you gave an excellent imitation of it. You little fool, have you no more sense than to run out in front of an oncoming coach? Didn't you hear me shouting to you?''

She was aware of aches and bruises all over, her ankle was throbbing painfully, and she seemed to lack her normal defenses where he was concerned. Her hands were skinned, as were her knees from when she had fallen, and she had a horrible suspicion of what she must look like. Far worse, she was mortified to be placed in such a position before Roxbury, of all people.

''Did you shout?'' she asked foolishly, and managed to rally her spirits enough to add, ''But then, if you had not—not assaulted me, I would have had no need to escape from you.''

''Yes, I thought it would not be long before it was my fault. But I must confess I have had a great many responses to my kisses—not all of them favorable, by any means—but no one has ever before tried to kill herself,'' he remarked sardonically. ''I admit you are beginning to puzzle me, Miss Mayhew.''

13

SHE FLUSHED, but at least his anger seemed to have left him, for which she could only be grateful. "I fear I find you all too predictable," she retorted. "And I was not trying to commit suicide, as you well know. Merely to escape from your pawing!"

A slight flush crept up his cheeks, which surprised her even more. "For that, at least, I apologize," he said unexpectedly.

She was so surprised she nearly gaped at him, suspecting some trick. Then she said bitterly, "But not for anything else you have done or said to me, obviously."

"No, not for anything else," he agreed, his voice hardening again. "But I am trying to remember that you are shaken and not your usual self, and so I have no intention of discussing that with you at the moment. You still look very pale, in fact. Are you sure you're all right?"

"I have no need to be reminded of what I must look like," she complained even more bitterly. "But I should expect no better from you than to insult me even as you pretend solicitude."

To her surprise he smiled, for once without his usual unpleasantness. "It is obvious you are fast recovering, if you have begun to remember your appearance," he said dryly. "But you have no need to worry. Your dress is torn and filthy and you have a streak of dirt on one cheek, but I suspect you are very aware you still manage to look surprisingly beautiful.''

This time she could indeed only gape at him, for this was perilously close to being a compliment coming from him. Then, as his words sank in, she forgot that in horror of the appearance she must be presenting, and tried desperately to at least remove the mud from her cheek.

After a moment he took out his handkerchief and leaned forward to complete the task for her, taking her chin in his fingers.

The movement brought him perilously close, and the intimacy of his fingers on her chin and his face so near to her own filled her with sudden and unexpected confusion. She had to prevent herself from pulling sharply away from him, as if his fingers burned her. Instead, after a moment, she put up her own hand, saying foolishly, ''Th-thank you, but I am convinced it is a hopeless task.''

He regarded the high color in her cheeks as if she indeed puzzled him, then frowned abruptly and sat back. But as he did so, he caught sight of her hands for the first time, and his mood changed on the instant. Before she could prevent him, he had caught both of her wrists in his hard grip and turned them over, swearing at what he saw there.

She had been vaguely aware for some time of a painful burning on both palms, where she had skinned them on the cobbles, but she was surprised to see them bloody and raw and instinctively tried to close her hands over them. ''It doesn't matter,'' she said breathlessly, surprised at the harsh expression in his eyes. ''It is my own fault, after all, as you have already pointed out to me.''

His grip tightened on her wrists, further mangling the one he had already bruised earlier. ''You little fool! These must be hurting like hell.''

''My knees are also scraped,'' she retorted with some of her old spirit, managing to withdraw her hands at last and hide them in her lap. ''But I hope you don't propose to inspect them as well.''

Once more he looked genuinely, if reluctantly, amused, though the puzzlement did not leave the back of his eyes.

"Don't worry. I'll leave that to your aunt. But these should have ointment put on them as soon as possible."

Fortunately the cab pulled to a halt then, and she saw with relief that they had reached Green Street. She said hastily, beginning to gather her scattered belongings about her, which he had obviously picked up from the street and placed on the opposite seat, "Th-thank you. I . . . Despite my words, I am not ungrateful for your rescue. I fear I would have been killed or badly hurt if you had not pulled me out of the way. But there is no need for you to come in with me. I shall be perfectly all right now."

He eyed her with some of his old sardonicism. "And how are you proposing to get in, Miss Mayhew? I doubt you will be able to walk on that ankle, and your brother will scarcely be able to carry you."

She bit her lip, but was forced to acknowledge the truth of his words. She had no choice but to allow him to lift her out and carry her up the steps, feeling extremely foolish as he waited for Betty to answer the door, and more than a little shaken by the proximity of his harsh countenance and the strong arms that seemed to support her so effortlessly.

Betty naturally fell back a step or two when she opened the door to find her mistress being held in the arms of the Earl of Roxbury. She gave a faint scream and dropped the duster she was carrying. "Oh, miss! Has there been an accident?"

"I have merely sprained my ankle, Betty," said Philippa in acute embarrassment. "Is my aunt or sister at home?"

But her heart sank as Betty said anxiously, "Oh, no, miss! They've both gone out shopping."

Roxbury pushed past the maid and carried her into the hall, saying in his usual autocratic style, "That ankle should be attended to immediately. You, what's your name? Betty, is it? Fetch some bandages and a bowl of cold water up to Miss Mayhew's bedchamber immediately. And bring as well any soothing liniment you may have in the house."

Philippa was annoyed to feel herself blushing like any schoolgirl. "I assure you there is no need! At any rate, you need not carry me upstairs."

"And how do you propose to get up to bed later?" he

demanded impatiently. "I've seen ladies' boudoirs before, if that's what's worrying you. Now, where is your room?"

He had started up the stairs even as he spoke, and she had no choice but to direct him, having no doubt that he indeed had seen any number of ladies' boudoirs before. The thought was far from a pleasant one, for some reason.

Once he had deposited her on her narrow bed, however, she gathered what was left of her shattered dignity about her and said instantly, "Thank you, but I don't require any further help. In fact, I most definitely don't want yours. Now, go away, before I am in danger of forgetting how grateful I must be to you."

"Don't be absurd! Your ankle will swell to twice its normal size if it's not strapped up immediately. And this show of modesty is somewhat absurd under the circumstances, don't you think? We both know what you are."

The color invaded her cheeks, and she drew herself up furiously. "You may think what you like, but you are not going to strap up my ankle. At any rate, I was not aware that you were a physician, along with all your other qualities."

"It doesn't take a physician to know what will happen to that ankle if it's not seen to immediately," he replied rather impatiently. "And if you are about to ask me how I know that, my unlikely innocent, I can assure you that I have wrapped more than my share of horse's legs in my life, and the principle is much the same, believe me."

She was annoyed at the comparison, as he no doubt meant her to be, but at that moment a wide-eyed Betty reappeared, bearing a loaded tray. "Oh, miss," she said sympathetically, taking in her bedraggled appearance, "you look like some'at the cat drug in—begging your pardon. Would you like a nice cup of tea? Cook's out, but I can bring it up in a jiffy."

She was even more annoyed at Betty for the reminder, but Roxbury said instantly, "An excellent idea. It may even help to improve her temper. Go and make it at once."

Betty giggled and hurried out again, and Philippa said irritably, "My temper was perfectly amiable until I met you. And no one gave you leave to order my servants about.''

"Your temper is abominable," he answered roundly, not mincing matters. "Almost as bad as my own, in fact." He was looking around the room assessingly even as he spoke, and added dryly, "But if I had had to choose a setting for you, this would certainly not have been it."

She blushed and stiffened, suspecting another of his vile insults. "Thank you. I don't doubt I can imagine what you think my perfect setting is."

He looked momentarily amused. "I doubt it. I will confess you are beginning to puzzle me, but this monastic little cell is hardly what I expected. You are not as beautiful as your aunt was by any means, but you possess a vividness that she lacked, and from everything I've ever been able to tell, a great deal more intelligence. You deserve a more colorful setting."

"However unsuitable, it is my own, and I wish to be alone in it. Pray don't let me keep you," she cried furiously.

He ignored her as if she had not spoken, and advanced purposefully toward the bed. She regarded him in impotent fury, but short of engaging in an ungainly struggle, which she knew she was bound to lose, in the end had no choice but to submit to his ministrations.

Nor, to her surprise, did he attempt to take advantage of his victory as she might have expected. He explored her swollen ankle with unexpectedly cool, capable fingers and all the impersonality of a physician.

Even so, she could not help wincing once or twice as his fingers explored a particularly painful area. He glanced up at her, but said merely, after a moment, "I don't think there's anything broken, which is luckier than you deserve. But it should certainly be strapped at once, to keep the swelling down. Otherwise you may not be able to walk on it for some days. Take your stocking off."

She fairly goggled at him. "Take—? You must be joking. I may have had to endure being insulted and nearly run over today, but there is nothing you can do to make me remove my stocking."

"Isn't there?" he demanded with raised brows.

"You wouldn't dare!" She was almost rigid with outrage.

"I think you know by now I don't make idle threats. And I find this show of modesty less amusing even than your usual unpleasant behavior," he said with growing impatience.

She flushed furiously, but after a moment was obliged to agree with him. And since her ankle was in reality throbbing quite painfully by then, she gave in with ill grace. "Oh, very well! But turn around."

He frowned, then looked faintly amused again and obligingly turned around. She whisked her stocking off with record speed and stuffed it under her pillow, then rearranged her skirt so that just her swollen ankle was showing, before telling him stiffly that he could turn around again.

He eyed the prim picture she made with something like his old mockery, but made no other comment and sat down on the edge of her bed and began expertly to wrap her ankle.

He was tying his final knot when there was an unexpected sound at the doorway. "Philippa," cried her aunt in outrage.

Philippa was in no mood to deal with any more scenes, and said wearily, "Oh, go away, Aunt Bella. I have endured enough today already."

Far from going away, Aunt Bella advanced into the room with all the air of a lioness defending her cub. "I couldn't believe it when Betty told me . . . Are you all right?" she demanded, her meaning obvious.

Philippa blushed, but Roxbury calmly finished his task, then rose, giving Aunt Bella a swift, unfavorable scrutiny. "Are you Mrs. Mayhew?" he inquired, and added unnecessarily, "I am Roxbury."

"Well, that at least was obvious," grumbled Aunt Bella, forgetting herself for a moment. "I would have known you anywhere, in fact. You have more the look of your father than I was expecting. But if you think I am going to permit you to insult my niece in my home, you are mistaken," she added, rapidly recovering. "I am glad we have finally met—though not in my niece's bedchamber, which is a thing that would never have been permitted in my day, I can tell you, whatever you may think of me!—for I have a great deal to say to you. And if you are counting on my being grateful for having my mortgage returned to me—and I will admit I am, no matter what Philippa may say—then you don't know me very well.''

He had listened to this rather garbled speech with a sardonic expression, but at that he inquired curiously, ''And what does Philippa have to say?''

''Everything of the most violent! You don't need me to tell you she has taken you in dislike, for which I don't blame her. But if you have anything more of a disagreeable nature to say, you may say it to me, for I am the one your quarrel is with, not my nieces.''

But at that he straightened. ''You are mistaken, ma'am,'' he said unpleasantly. ''My objections may be based upon your past career, but since one of your nieces has tried to entrap my nephew into marriage and the other to blackmail me, I think you will agree I have some legitimate quarrel with them, as well.''

''Oh, dear,'' said poor Aunt Bella, forced against her will to acknowledge the truth of that. ''I confess I never approved of using those letters, but it is your own fault, after all. If you had allowed the marriage in the first place, none of this would have happened.''

''You must excuse me on that ground, ma'am. I will never consent to my nephew's marriage to so blatant a fortune-hunter.'' But he was again frowning unexpectedly. ''But what do you mean you never approved of using the letters?''

But Aunt Bella had once more stiffened. ''Fortune-hunter, is it?'' she demanded bitterly. ''I wish it might be so, when I am faced with supporting the pair of them. As for the rest, I've lost count of the number of offers I've had over the years to publish my memoirs. And you may be sure that would have been worth a great deal more than a paltry five thousand pounds. But I've accepted none of them, and I never will, for obvious reasons.''

''The reasons are indeed obvious, ma'am, if you possess many letters such as you sold me," he retorted with heavy irony.

"Oh—oh, go away! There is plainly no talking to you," grumbled Aunt Bella. "Philippa said you were very different than your father, and I don't mean that as a compliment, you may believe me. Your father may have been weak, but he would never have condemned my nieces for something that happened twenty years ago."

"I certainly am not as susceptible as my father, if that is what you mean, ma'am," said Roxbury grimly, his arms crossed over his chest as he leaned against the bedpost. "And I would have said you had profited enough from my family already. You forget I am aware of exactly how much my father squandered upon you, since most of the debts for your jewels and carriages were unfortunately passed on to me at his death."

Then he caught sight of Philippa's white face and said abruptly, "But I have no intention of discussing the matter with you here and now. You would be better advised to see to your niece's hands. And since my services are no longer required, I will bid you both good day."

As Aunt Bella stared after him, her mouth open in shock, Philippa closed her eyes and said wearily, "Good God, Aunt Bella, how much did his father squander on you? I begin to suspect he has good reason for hating us so."

14

ROXBURY, IN the meantime, returned home with a faint frown still between his brows, and his mood oddly abstracted. When informed by his butler that her ladyship was upstairs in the small saloon and requested his presence as soon as he should return to the house, he started, amazed to discover he had actually forgotten her.

Then his grim frown returned and he took the stairs two at a time.

He burst in on the dowager without knocking, startled and not best pleased by the knowledge he had allowed his growing and unwarranted preoccupation with Miss Philippa Mayhew to make him forget exactly what he owed to her.

To his complete amazement he found his mother calmly drinking tea.

She looked up as he came in and said cheerfully, "Oh, there you are, dearest. Just in time to have a cup of tea with me. Did you escort Miss Mayhew home?"

For one of the few times in his life he found himself totally at a loss. At this late date he had not expected that his mother would be shattered by the news her husband had had an affair before his death with a notorious actress, but nor had he expected her to behave exactly as if she had not spitefully been told of a liaison that was bound to wound her. He said, regarding her searchingly and feeling his way with care, "Yes. Are you all right, Mama?"

She smiled sunnily and handed him his tea. "Yes of

course I am. Why shouldn't I be? Oh, you think I overtired myself shopping this afternoon. I will admit I was a little tired and grateful enough to get into my carriage. That's why I offered to drop Miss Mayhew somewhere, since I wanted to have a little chat with her. And I'm glad I did, for I have seldom enjoyed a more interesting half-hour."

He was frowning heavily by now, more shaken than he liked to admit by her news. "Let me get this straight," he said harshly. "You wanted to have a chat with Miss Mayhew?"

She looked slightly mischievous. "Well, I must confess I was curious, after the things Theresa told me and the things you even more pointedly did not, so when I overheard the clerk in the bookstore address her by name, I couldn't resist. It was obvious she was by no means eager to accept my invitation, either. I liked her, as a matter of fact. Don't you?"

"Like Miss Mayhew?" he repeated in astonishment and loathing. "No, I do not! But I want to be perfectly sure I understand you, Mama. You invited Miss Mayhew to talk with you, and she was by no means anxious to oblige? You're not lying to me, or trying to protect her from some quixotic impulse of your own?"

Her answer was obvious in her raised brows. "No, dear, why should I? Why is it so important anyway?"

He turned away abruptly, unable to tell her—or indeed explain to himself—why it was so important. He was merely conscious of a burning urge to return at once to apologize to Philippa, which was as absurd as it was uncharacteristic.

He said at last, over his shoulder, "It doesn't matter. What did the two of you talk of?"

"Oh, this and that. Mostly Julian and her sister, of course. As I said, she was not particularly anxious to meet me, for which I can scarcely blame her, under the circumstances. She also defended her aunt to me, which I must confess I respected in her. Evidently Isabella Monteith took them in when their own father died without providing adequately for them, which you certainly will admit she had no obligation to do. In fact, she seems to be quite a remarkable woman, for it seems they are now prepared to support the newlyweds as well, if you persist in withholding Julian's fortune.''

He was still trying to adjust his ideas to this new and startling development, and was scarcely attending to her, but at that he turned incredulously. ''What did you say?''

''Yes, it startled me a little as well. But I think she was sincere. Have you really threatened to withhold Julian's fortune if he weds the poor child, my dear? That sounds unlike you, for you are not usually such a snob.''

He colored uncharacteristically. ''It has nothing to do with snobbery, nor do I intend to discuss it with you, Mama.''

''Doesn't it, my dear?'' she inquired blandly. ''How odd it is that we never recognize unpleasant traits in ourselves that we readily recognize in others. It took a great many years, for instance, for me to realize I was indeed turning into the recluse everyone accused me of being. As for you, of course you are a snob, dearest. Oh, not the social snob that Theresa is, but you are perhaps an even worse kind of snob, because you don't like anyone very much.''

His lip curled a little, and he put down his tea and went to stand looking down into the street, his hands behind his back. ''If so, I have good reason. I find very few likable people in the world. If that is a sin, I refuse to apologize for it.''

''No, it's no sin, but it's a little sad,'' she said unhappily. ''I blame myself very much.''

''Good God, it has nothing to do with you. You are certainly no misanthrope, Mama.''

''No, but I keep people at a distance, which is my greatest fault. And I never accused you of being a misanthrope, my dear. What you are is a misogynist, I fear, which is perhaps worse. I am well aware it is my sex for whom you reserve your greatest dislike and distrust.''

''If so, it has nothing to do with you, Mama,'' he said curtly. ''And whatever you think me, I would appreciate it if you will curtail your friendship for Miss Mayhew while you are in London. Whether or not I favor the match, you must be aware that Theresa will never accept the niece of such a woman into her home. Even you cannot wish to see Julian alienated from her completely.''

But when she had gone upstairs to lie down before dinner, he stood staring off into space, unpleasantly obliged to readjust his ideas and reevaluate the situation in light of the startling discoveries he had made. It seemed Philippa Mayhew had not only not sought out the meeting with his mother, but had unaccountably and against all logic or expectation refrained from taking advantage of it. If she had done so, it would have been without hope of gaining anything, but merely out of spite, in an attempt to be revenged upon him in the one way that would have been the most effective. But that she had not, made everything he had believed about her suddenly suspect.

In fact, the omission was wholly inexplicable, given her former behavior and her threats to make him sorry if it was the last thing she ever did. But he did not believe his mother a sufficient-enough actress to fool him on such a matter.

It was always possible he had interrupted her before she had a chance to do so, of course. But somehow he was no longer inclined to believe it. Which left him with a puzzle concerning Miss Philippa Mayhew that was as annoying as it was unwelcome.

But perhaps not so unexpected, after all, for once or twice he had caught a flash of such outrage in Miss Mayhew's fine eyes that he had been momentarily shaken, despite all he knew of her.

But then he must not forget she was an accomplished actress, or that the entire family had shown itself in its true colors time and again. Twenty years ago Isabella Monteith had tried to run off with his father, and now her nieces were following directly in her footsteps.

But now that he came to think of it, this was not the first time she had behaved inexplicably and in a way that seemed to be suspiciously close to being against her own advantage. There was the matter of the mortgage, for one thing, for he could not see what she had hoped to gain by returning it to him. And then there was the fact that she had yet to tell Julian of her dealings with his uncle, which he had expected to be one of her first retaliatory steps. She must know she had very little to lose, for in his present besotted state Julian could be relied upon to spring instantly to his beloved's defense against even his own family.

Well, she might be shrewd enough to guess that it would make little difference in the long run, for he had no intention of avoiding unpleasantness by weakly releasing control of Julian's fortune. But if her intention was, as she frequently stated, to be revenged upon him, she must have known it would be a highly effective way, as well as undermining at one blow any influence he might have over Julian for some appreciable time to come.

In fact, he was beginning to be very curious about the workings of Miss Philippa Mayhew's mind. There was as well the presence in the house of a sixteen-year-old youth, which he had always found surprising, and the apparent poverty of the establishment. If they were as unprincipled as he believed them, they had very little to show for it, for the house was shabby, and the only times he had seen Philippa she could hardly be said to have been dressed luxuriously.

That might merely be for his benefit, of course. In fact, for every doubt there was a guilty as well as an innocent explanation. But if she were not the unprincipled and highly skillful actress he believed her, his own behavior was thrown into an unflattering relief, and he was bound to own she had every reason for hating him as she appeared to do.

Then there was her behavior on the day he had fixed her pump, and this afternoon as well, after her accident. If he had not thought the notion absurd, he would almost have said she was shy of him and embarrassed to be caught in such a situation. The women of his acquaintance would not have hesitated to take every advantage, clinging helplessly to him and trying to arouse his protective instincts in a highly nauseating fashion.

Instead, Miss Philippa Mayhew had quarreled with him and tried to hide the extent of her injuries. She had not

succeeded, which might mean she was simply more skillful than most women at hiding her methods. But for the
first time, perhaps the oddest of Miss Mayhew's inexplicable omissions struck him. She had been furious, contemptuous, and even threatening in his presence, but at no
time had he seen any sign of coquettishness. And if Miss
Philippa Mayhew were anywhere near as intelligent as he
believed her to be, it must long ago have occurred to her
that he was a far richer prize than his nephew.

Few women he knew had been able to resist the lure of
his fortune, even when they obviously disliked him. But
Philippa, far from trying to attract him, had quarreled with
him on every occasion and wasted few opportunities to
make him dislike her. And that when, as he had discovered unpleasantly for himself this afternoon, he was far
from being as indifferent to her as he would like to be, as a
woman of her experience must be perfectly aware.

But then the absurd notion he had taken this afternoon—
that despite all expectation she had very little experience of
men—intruded once more, not to be so easily dismissed.
She was certainly no beauty, as her aunt had been, but he
was obliged to admit she had a vivacity and spirit that
would appeal to a great many tastes. And yet she seemed
to make no attempt to take advantage of her attractions.
On the several occasions on which they had met, she had
been modestly, even shabbily dressed. The way she coiled
her luxurious hair in that absurd braid, though oddly at-
tractive, was almost puritanical, and that monastic little
bedchamber of hers hardly supported his belief that she
and her sister were little better than straw damsels.

Oh, damn her for creating such absurd doubts in his
mind. Miss Philippa Mayhew was exactly what he believed her: a clever, unscrupulous little bitch. It merely
said more of her acting skills than her morals if she
succeeded in making anyone believe otherwise. Nor must
he forget the essential fact that she and her sister had
entrapped Julian in hopes of gaining a fortune, and when
that had been thwarted, had not hesitated to try to blackmail him in a most unpleasant and unsavory manner.
Those were hardly the acts of innocent damsels.

Nor could he make himself believe, as he admitted he was tempted, that their aunt was behind the whole. Isabella Monteith he had dismissed from the beginning, for he had thought her a flighty, shallow fool twenty years ago, and today's meeting had not changed that opinion. No, it was clearly her eldest niece who was directing operations and meant to mend her fortunes by whatever means at hand.

He turned away abruptly, annoyed with his own uncharacteristic soul-searching. Damn all women anyway. Even the best of them—and he was prepared to admit to very few of those—were seldom consistent or capable of preventing their emotions from overruling their heads, as his mother was doing. If Miss Philippa Mayhew was behaving inconsistently, it was merely because she was not nearly as clever as she believed herself. He would be a fool to allow himself to believe otherwise.

15

NEVERTHELESS HIS doubts, once aroused, were not so easily dismissed, and he had to fight the irrational impulse to return to Green Street the next day. He had to remind himself it was absurd to think he would be able to tell the truth just by seeing her again. As absurd as to think he could have been so mistaken in her.

But when, as he drove down Piccadilly later that morning, he saw a youth he recognized trudging along carrying a heavy parcel, he surprised himself very much by abruptly pulling up.

Young Mayhew seemed almost as surprised to recognize the earl, but after a moment accepted his offer of a lift. "I . . . Thanks," he said cheerfully. "I'll admit these books are heavier than I thought when I started out."

Roxbury regarded his awkward parcel with raised brows. "I can imagine. Why didn't you take a cab?"

The youth flushed, making Roxbury wonder suddenly if he could afford one, but he recovered quickly. "It didn't seem that far when I started out. Anyway, I suppose I must get used to carrying books."

"Yes, my nephew tells me you are going to Cambridge next year."

The youth flushed again, for some reason. "Yes," he said unexpansively, and abruptly changed the subject. "I'm glad to see you, sir, as it happens, for I wanted to thank you for bringing my sister home yesterday. In fact, she says you more or less saved her life.''

"She exaggerates. Did she happen to tell you what prompted the accident?'' he added curiously.

"No. Only that she walked out into the street without looking.'' He grinned then, looking suddenly much younger. "Which didn't surprise me, for she often jumps into things without looking. I often tease her about it.''

"In this case she was lucky she wasn't killed by her impulsiveness,'' said Roxbury. "How is her ankle?''

"Oh, I don't think it's badly sprained. At least she refused to stay in bed today. Aunt Bella found a cane for her to use, and she is able to hobble about pretty well.''

"Your aunt seems to have a great many useful items in those old trunks,'' remarked the earl rather grimly.

But the reference obviously went over young Mayhew's head. A brief silence fell, then he said abruptly, as if girding up his courage, "There is another reason I'm happy to see you, sir. You said the other day that you were interested in machinery and the like, and I wondered, if I—if a person wanted to go about getting a job in business, with some future in it, I mean, how would he go about doing it?''

It was the last thing the earl had expected, but he had not missed the almost desperate tone in the boy's voice. He turned his head to regard him a little searchingly, but said merely, "It depends upon how old and intelligent he is, and who he knows, for that matter. Are you referring to yourself? If so, I thought you were going to Cambridge next year?''

Darius flushed, but did not back down. "I . . . Please, will you just answer my question? Assuming someone of—of my age and—and average intelligence, what would be his chances, and how soon could he expect to make enough money to do any good?''

The earl's curiosity was definitely aroused now. He had stopped on impulse, hoping to lay to rest some of his new doubts, but several possibilities for this unexpected development presented themselves, none of them particularly palatable. The boy might be ashamed of his relations and wish to escape, or be no longer welcome there. Or the household could be so much in debt that even the meager wages he might earn had become necessary. He frowned, but instead of giving way to useless speculations, said bluntly, "It depends upon how much money you consider useful. Tell me, have you been accepted at Cambridge?"

Mayhew looked surprised at the question, but nodded shyly. "Yes, last week. What difference does that make?"

"Then I would say you are of above-average intelligence. And if so, you don't need me to point out that a university education would be exceedingly useful to you. Why do you feel the need to earn money immediately?"

"Not—not for the reasons you may be thinking," said Darius quickly. "At the very least I would be doing something to contribute, instead of spending three more years being a liability," he burst out, apparently unable to contain himself any longer. "Even if I didn't earn very much at first, it would be a help, whatever Philippa says."

"And what does Philippa say?" inquired the earl with a frown, unwilling to have his doubts of yesterday reinforced.

"She—she wants me to go to school, of course. She doesn't understand, but I won't have her make any more sacrifices for my sake. If it comes to that, I suppose *I* am the head of the family now, not her, and it's time I began to contribute, instead of being just another—another problem for Philippa to handle. It was all very well for her to take charge when I was still a child, but I no longer have that excuse."

"Even so, you will forgive me for pointing out that you are not very old yet," the earl said dryly. "What sacrifices has your sister made, by the way?"

Darius seemed not to find the question unusual, or else was too relieved to have someone to confide in to resent it. "She means to use her inheritance for my tuition, but I'm not going to let her do it. Aside from every other consideration, she needs that for her own security. I can't make her see reason, for she is determined I shall go to Cambridge like Father did, and I daresay his father before him, but what I say is, *What* difference does it make if I want to—to find a niche in business anyway? Why should I waste her money when I will end up the same place and could be earning something in the meantime? You must understand that, sir, for you seem to have a grasp of reality, instead of falling into the trap of doing what's always been done, just because it's traditional.''

The earl smiled slightly. "Thank you for the compliment, but I fear you flatter me. And I take it you have advanced these arguments to your sister and she wasn't impressed?''

"Dozens of times. She wants me to go into the Church, like Papa did. But I don't even particularly want to go into the Church, and anyway, heaven knows there's no money in that, as we should know.''

"Your father was a vicar?" demanded Roxbury in a stunned voice, thrown off his stride for the first time in this remarkable interview.

"Yes, and I daresay he meant me to follow in his footsteps, but I think it's foolish to feel bound by that. He couldn't know what was going to happen in the future, or even what kind of man I would be,'' persisted Darius stubbornly. "But Philippa thinks she's the only one to keep the family together or know what's best. I don't mean to complain, for she has, and against difficult odds, I know. But the thing is, it's time I started taking some responsibility, too.''

"Just exactly what did your sister do to keep your family together?" inquired the earl slowly, by no means certain he wanted to know the answer. He was cynical enough to know that being a clergyman was alone no guarantee of probity, but he was obliged to own that the news had come as an unpleasant shock to him.

"Well, she made the decision to come and live with Aunt Bella, of course. I understand why she did it, for the alternative seems to have been for us to be separated, which none of us would have liked. But, well, I'm not so certain now even that was such a good idea. Tell me, sir,'' he said abruptly, evidently determined to air all his doubts at once, "do you disapprove of my sister's marriage to your nephew?''

For one of the few times in his life the earl found

himself forced to equivocate, for he was oddly unwilling to hurt this odd, prickly youth's feelings. "Why do you ask?" he stalled, wishing he had never initiated this odd encounter.

"Well, I couldn't help overhearing, that day you first came. And whatever Philippa may say, you were both very angry, that much was obvious even to me. More, she has never told Diana that you came, which is highly suspicious, and she gets a funny look whenever your name is mentioned. But she only got angry when I asked her about it. She thinks I'm still a child, but I'm not as naïve as she thinks, and, well, something some of the fellows at school said once made me wonder if Aunt Bella's reputation is worse than I thought. Is it?" he asked bluntly, looking at the earl with his unsettlingly candid gaze.

Roxbury for some reason found himself far from immune to that gaze. "I think that is something you must discuss with your sister, not me," he said rather desperately.

"She will only say that Papa taught us not to judge people by their past, but by how kind they are," retorted Darius in obvious disgust. "And I can't deny Aunt Bella's been good to us, taking us in and all. But if my sisters' reputations are going to be ruined and no one will marry them, I think I have a right to know. And you needn't remind me that Julian is going to marry Diana, for he's so nutty upon her he probably doesn't even notice Aunt Bella, and I do know his mother disapproves of the match."

"Julian's mother is a snob," Roxbury said truthfully, wondering what on earth he was going to find to say to soothe this prickly young fool's cursed suspicions. "And has it never occurred to you that anyone, er, sufficiently nutty on one of your sisters, as you said, will be perfectly capable of overlooking your aunt's drawbacks?"

"John Hornbeck didn't," answered Darius with the blunt persistence of the very young. "At least, that was even before we came to live with Aunt Bella, but it seems pretty clear he was unprepared to take on a penniless bride hampered with three dependents. And if he wouldn't marry Philippa then, you can't tell me it's not far worse now, when we are living with my aunt."

Roxbury for some reason found himself by no means glad to be the recipient of the information that Philippa had once been engaged. But all he said was, "Then I suspect your sister was lucky to be rid of him."

"Yes, that's what she says. But even aside from all that, there's Iphigenia still to be thought of, and she shows no signs of developing either of my other two sisters' beauty. I can't help thinking that Philippa didn't consider all this when she agreed to come and live with Aunt Bella."

"Perhaps she didn't have the luxury of considering such future problems," said the earl dryly. Then he gave a start. "*What* did you call her?" he demanded incredulously.

Darius grinned momentarily, obviously used to the question. "Iphigenia. I know it's absurd, but my father would name us all the most outlandish names. My father's hobby was classical scholarship, I'm sorry to say, for he insisted on naming us all for classical heroes. In Greek mythology Iphigenia was—"

"I know who she was," interrupted the earl. "But are you saying there's still another sister I don't know about?"

"Oh, yes, though she's only twelve. She hates her name, of course, and I must admit Papa outdid himself by the time he got around to her. Diana is not so bad, for it's a normal name, you know, but my name is extremely embarrassing. And Philippa is very lucky Papa didn't get his way and name her Philippi, which Mama assured us he wanted to."

Roxbury was even less pleased at this image of normal home life his ingenuous companion was revealing, or the picture he was obtaining of Miss Philippa Mayhew, but he said, "I must agree with you. Do I take it your sister intends to provide for all of you until you are grown?"

"Yes, and that's why it's time I started taking more responsibility, don't you think? And it's no good Philippa telling me I will have time enough to worry when I'm grown. She says both the girls are her responsibility, not mine, but I—I think that's just an excuse. I'm the only male in the family, after all."

"Your concern does you honor, but your sister is right that you are a little young yet to be worrying how to support your family. Is money such a problem?'' asked the earl unwillingly. ''Your aunt must be expensive, I suspect, and that house wouldn't be cheap to maintain.''

Darius blushed, but said truthfully, ''It's not so much Aunt Bella is expensive, as that she has no notion of money. Philippa says we mustn't blame her, for she never has had the least notion how to handle it. It just seems to run through her fingers, even in the days she had plenty of it. Before we came, she was used to have executions in the house all the time, and live in dread of bill collectors. Since Philippa has been handling things, that has stopped, of course, but there is very little to spare for emergencies, which there always seem to be. Aunt Bella had a small income of her own, and there is ours from the trust Papa left, though it is very little. And that is why I am determined Philippa shall not spend her small nest egg on my education. She says it was left to her by our grandmother before the rest of us were born, and so rightly belongs to all of us, but I say that is a mere rationalization.''

''Perhaps your sister regards your education as an investment in her own future,'' pointed out the earl, wishing he had never embarked upon this conversation.

''I . . . Perhaps so, but that sounds like a rationalization too, if you ask me,'' said Darius unwillingly.

Abruptly Roxbury pulled his whole attention back to the troubled youth before him. He was obliged to own he liked Darius, despite his extreme youth, and it was obvious he was in strong need of some male guidance, even his own inexpert fumblings. ''Very well, you have asked for my advice, and so you are going to get it, even though you may not like what I am going to say. But if your goal is indeed to help your sisters, you would be far wiser to complete your education, however difficult you may find it to continue as a dependent. I am aware that is not what you wanted to hear, but your sister is right. You will be far more useful to all of them with a good education behind you.''

''But . . . Even if I plan to go into business?'' demanded Darius unhappily.

''Especially then. I own that there are a few self-made

men and that the world has little grasped the changes that are going to happen in the next fifty years as industrialization takes over more and more of our lives. Most of the coming opportunities will be taken by young men of vision and daring, able to see possibilities in that future that the rest of us either can't envision or will actively try to prevent. But don't get me on my favorite topic. If you mean to be one of those young men, you won't waste your time at university, believe me. Learn all you can about mathematics and science and technology, and even more about reading men, for that is just as important. You could learn all that on your own, of course, but you will do it a great deal faster in a formalized setting and may even make important connections that will serve you well in the future. You will find that those of the new breed who can understand the new world we're making and who still move comfortably among gentlemen will have an even greater advantage than the genius with no social polish, for that's still where the money lies at present.''

"Oh. I had never thought of it like that,'' said Darius slowly, his mind obviously grappling with this new viewpoint.

"Yes, I thought perhaps you hadn't. I am not saying, of course, that you couldn't achieve the same ends by leaving school immediately and finding a job with some prominent businessman. But at most you would be facing years of drudgery as a clerk or copy boy. Believe me you will find three years spent at university, among youths of your own age and class, far more enjoyable.''

"I . . . Well, that doesn't matter.''

The earl smiled. "Don't worry. If you are indeed ambitious and willing to work hard, it won't be all enjoyment, I assure you. And if you decide to take my advice, come and see me when you do finally graduate. I make you no promises, but we may be able to work something out to our mutual advantage. I am always interested in anyone who shares my ungentlemanly passion for making money.''

"Oh!'' said Darius, his earlier gloom completely forgotten. "Do you *mean* it? I . . . Thank you, sir. I will! I own I would like to finish my education, if you don't think it's

selfish of me? And—and I will repay Philippa every penny
she spends on my behalf. It's just that when I thought it
would be years and years before I would be any help, and
no sure promise of anything even then . . . But if you
think that's what I should do, then I needn't worry. And I
will take care of Philippa and the other girls, no matter
what happens, so it's not as if I were robbing her of her
inheritance. I'm glad we had this talk, sir,'' he added
naïvely.

Roxbury was by no means in agreement with him about
that, at least. But when he at last dropped him off in Green
Street, with a great many renewed thanks from Darius and
promises to apply himself unsparingly to his studies, he
drove away with a great deal to think over, none of it
particularly pleasant. And not the least was to wonder
whatever had possessed him to encourage such a youth,
however likable.

16

NEVERTHELESS THE earl found himself returning to Green Street the next day, uneasily aware he was behaving completely out of character. Darius' revelations the previous day had severely shaken him, coming on top of his own doubts, and he could not dismiss the superstitious and probably wholly false impression that he would be able to judge the truth only by seeing Philippa Mayhew again. Either she was indeed the unprincipled harpy he believed her, or else he must accept the fact that she was a woman of more than ordinary courage and spirit, with no more to apologize for than a strong sense of responsibility for her young family.

The latter was so unwelcome a thought that he was tempted to reject it out of hand, for a number of reasons he had no wish to delve into too closely. But it seemed he had jumped to far too many conclusions concerning Miss Mayhew, and he owed her at least the opportunity to explain herself, at long last.

But when he was ushered in to her, it was plain that explaining herself was the last thing she had any intention of doing. She was seated on a sofa in the small room he had first seen her in, and was occupied in the mundane and highly unglamorous task of mending a basketful of stockings. A cane was propped beside her and a footstool placed before her where he suspected she had been resting her injured foot until he had been announced.

She looked pale and thoroughly out of temper, for she had had ample time by now to remember his vile accusations. Absurdly, however, the fact seemed merely to verify the earl's growing suspicions.

"Am I to have no peace, even in my own home?" she complained as he came in, eyeing him with marked disfavor. "And if you have come merely to insult me further, as I must suppose, then I must warn you I will have no hesitation in sending for the watch."

"That won't be necessary," he said dryly. "I have not come to quarrel with you, for once. But should you be up so soon? And unless I am very much mistaken, you had your foot on that stool until I came. I wish you will put it back again, for I know it must be painful."

"And I wish you would go away. I think I preferred even your insults to your solicitude, for at least I found that mood a great deal more predictable."

He looked down at her for a moment, then demanded harshly, "Why did you refrain from telling my mother about your aunt's letters? You must have known that was the surest way to be revenged upon me, as has been your oft-stated desire."

She flushed up and put down her mending, her hands visibly trembling with the strength of her outrage. "Since you have made your opinion of me painfully clear, I should hardly be surprised that you think me capable of—of—" Then she broke off, as if regretting what she had been about to say.

But he finished the sentence for her, his voice grim, "Capable of harming a woman who has nothing to do with the quarrel between us? Isn't that what you were about to say, Miss Mayhew?"

"No!" she flashed back. "You were right, as a matter of fact, for I believe there is nothing I would not do to be revenged upon you. And my sister *will* marry your nephew, whatever you have to say on the matter or however unpleasant you become."

He was still looking down at her with a heavy frown. "And I begin to think I have been guilty of the rankest and most willful blindness where you are concerned. Did your brother tell you of our talk yesterday, by the way?"

She looked startled at the change of subject. "Yes. And it seems I am somewhat in your debt—for that at least," she acknowledged grudgingly. "I have been trying for months to convince him of the wisdom of finishing his education. You, however, seem to have had no difficulty in swaying him in half an hour where all my oratory had failed," she added bitterly.

He smiled automatically at that, not surprised to hear the resentment in her tone. "But then I have the novelty of being a stranger. I fear youth is always ready to accept words of wisdom from anyone else, so long as it's not a member of their own family."

"No, I am aware it was more than that, at least. He . . . Well, I will admit Darius is getting beyond me," she admitted honestly. "Perhaps I have been too preoccupied with Diana lately to give him the attention I should have. At any rate, I should hardly be surprised when he accepts the advice of a man, especially one experienced in the ways of the world, over mine."

"Yes, he is reaching the age where he needs a man's influence more than ever," he said a little harshly. "How old was he when your father died?"

"Eleven," she answered, obviously wondering where on earth all this was leading. "He remembers him, of course, but it was still a very young age to be left fatherless."

"And your fiancé at the time was plainly unwilling to assume the role. Why have you never married since, and supplied him with a father figure?" he demanded bluntly.

She had resumed her mending at last and now pricked her finger in astonishment. "I needn't ask who told you that, I suppose," she said bitterly, sticking the injured finger in her mouth. "Nor should I be surprised you would take delight in throwing it up to me."

"Yes, Darius told me. Was that really the reason?"

"Good God, you sound surprised. You should know from your own reaction how suspicious the world is of single women on their own, or how reluctant to assume the responsibility for other people's children.''

He did not attempt to answer that. "Were you in love with him?''

"No I was not,'' she retorted furiously. "But it still was no pleasant thing to be jilted. And this is even more absurd than what usually passes for conversation between us.''

"Yes, we seem to have misunderstood each other at every level. Is that when you determined to marry your younger sister to a fortune?''

She choked, and it was some moments before she could command her voice again. "Now you see that your hopes were optimistic, for we obviously cannot be in the same room for as much as five minutes without coming to blows. No, it was not. You might be even more surprised to learn that Diana fell in love with your stupid nephew even before she had any notion he possessed a fortune.''

"My nephew is not particularly stupid,'' he corrected her. "I am beginning to suspect he is less guilty of the conventional prejudices of our class than I am. Unfortunately, this changes nothing, for I still cannot countenance his marriage to your sister, for reasons that must be obvious to both of us. But if money is such a problem, as seems obvious from the style of this house and your brother's admissions to me yesterday, I might have a different solution for you.''

For a moment she seemed struck speechless. Then without a word she put aside her mending and rose to hobble with the aid of her cane to the door and open it. "And what do you expect in return?'' she demanded. "A promise that Diana will relinquish your precious nephew? Or perhaps I am underestimating you and you expect a more personal return for your money? I have not forgotten that kiss yesterday. But in either case the answer is no!''

He followed her and calmly shut the door again. "You shouldn't be walking on that ankle.''

"There are a great many things I shouldn't do, and chief among them is waste another moment with you. I have grown inured to men who assume that because my aunt was once an actress, my sister and I must be grateful for any offer, no matter how insulting. But at least I thought myself safe from you, if only because you made no bones about how much you despised me. But then I am well aware that that little matters to men of your type, does it?''

If he had had any further doubts, they were now laid to rest. He had been nearly as startled as she was to hear himself make such an offer for he had had no such intention when he came. But then he seemed to be capable of a great many things he had never before suspected.

But he said merely, ''And how many men have there been?''

Her lovely upper lip curled disdainfully. ''I have lost count over the years. Diana usually attracts most of them, because she is younger and prettier, but I have had my fair share as well. It is always those who hope to take advantage of what they see as our misfortune—and I need hardly add, I'm sure, that like you, they seldom have marriage in mind.''

''And yet Julian did,'' he pointed out oddly.

She flushed and then met his eyes defiantly. ''Yes, Julian did. Perhaps you will see now why I thought nothing too great a price to pay to ensure my sister's happiness. And despite all you think, she will make him an excellent wife, as he has had the sense to see. And I warn you that I won't let you destroy her future, whatever it takes to prevent you. And now I think indeed you had better go.''

''And if there are no strings to my offer?'' He was even more astonished to hear his own voice calmly making such a preposterous offer. Whatever he thought her now—and he was not at all certain in his own mind what that was any longer—he knew perfectly well that no woman would be foolish enough to spurn what was in effect an offer too good to be true. Certainly the woman he had believed her to be would have fluttered and protested, but wasted little time in closing with him for fear he would retract so foolish a statement.

Philippa Mayhew unmistakably bristled, her cheeks scarlet with rage. ''Get out,'' she cried. ''Did you think I would accept charity from you if I would not accept your bribes? Whether my sister marries Julian or not, I hope I need never see you again."

But he was no longer listening, for when she raised her arm to gesture dramatically, her sleeve fell back, revealing the ugly bruise on one slender wrist.

"Did I do that?" he demanded harshly, pushing her sleeve back even further, an unaccustomed flush on his lean cheeks.

She tried ineffectually to release herself, saying irritably. "What did you expect when you handled me so? Those are the least of the marks I bear from our last encounter, as you well know."

"Any other marks you bear were the result of your own folly," he countered curtly. "But if I caused this, I am sorry."

She raised her own eyes to his face, as if trying to read something there that eluded her. "I bruise easily," she said at last in a more normal tone. "It doesn't matter anyway."

For answer he shocked them both very much by abruptly raising her hand and pressing his lips against the soft bruised skin on her inner wrist.

She gasped and once more tried to pull her hand away, her eyes raising to his with a startled discovery in them.

His own brows were drawn harshly together, and he was breathing a little fast when, absurdly, they were interrupted. The door opened and a young blond tripped in, accompanied by a much younger child. "Pippa, Genia and I are going to do the marketing now. Is there anything else—"

Then she broke off, her eyes widening in astonishment as she took in the scene she had interrupted.

But Philippa had instantly snatched her hand back, her cheeks crimson. "No, nothing," she said a little breathlessly. "Have you asked Aunt?"

The blonde, as if realizing she had come in at an inopportune moment, was already retreating, but her sister, recovering her composure with an effort, added, "No, don't go yet, Diana. It is time you two met at last. Lord Roxbury, this is my sister, Diana, and my youngest sister, Iphigenia.''

The earl had already realized who she must be, of course, and though he was scowling a little at the untimely interruption, he was forced to acknowledge it had been fortunate, for he had been on the verge of making a complete fool of himself. But he was aware, among a great many more pressing sensations, of the slight challenge in Philippa's voice, and he made himself look the blonde over with an interest he was far from feeling at the moment.

He was obliged to admit the challenge was deserved, for Diana was very different from what he had been expecting. She looked, in fact, like a shy and slightly frightened child, and though she cast one anguished look at her eldest sister, she came forward to say hesitantly, "I . . . How do you d-do, Lord Roxbury?''

He frowned, successfully recalled to reality. She was indeed prettier than her elder sister, as he had been told, but in a pale, childlike way that did not appeal to him. Her figure was slender and undeveloped, and she was dressed becomingly, if not expensively, in a simple blue gown that matched her eyes. Her hair was fairer than her sister's, but lacked its luxuriance, and her shy eyes and soft mouth both betrayed her extreme youth.

But he was interrupted in this scrutiny by a childish voice asking with no hint of shyness, "Are you really the wicked earl?''

Startled, he looked down to find himself under the critical observation of the child with the absurd name. He was amused, despite himself, and answered willingly, if a touch dryly, "I can readily believe your sister thinks so, at least. And you must be Iphigenia?''

She ignored that. "I bet you don't really approve of the marriage, whatever Julian says," she said challengingly. "In all the novels it's always the wicked uncle who parts the lovers, usually because he wants their fortune for himself.''

Diana was looking mortified, but to her credit Philippa made no attempt to restrain her sister.

He said in amusement, "Yes, but have you ever looked at it from the wicked uncle's point of view? In those same books, as I recall, he usually has four wives all locked up in his cellar, and you can't blame him for finding them a trial to support."

She giggled unexpectedly. "Do you? Why do you keep them in the cellar?"

"Because if I didn't, they might expect me to squander some of my nephew's ill-gotten fortune on them, of course. Or didn't I explain that I am a miser and merely married each of them for the fortune she could bring me?"

Genia giggled again, but asked critically, "How do you keep your wives' relatives from complaining when they come to visit you, though?"

"Oh, I let that one out of the cellar then."

"Yes, but—"

Philippa, who knew her sister better than he did, interrupted then. "No, that's enough nonsense for one day, Genia. Go and wait for Diana downstairs."

The child evidently recognized the voice of authority, for she turned and began to drag her feet reluctantly toward the door. "Oh, all right," she said, but added in the innocent voice of a child merely seeking enlightenment, "But if he has four wives already, why was he kissing your hand when we came in?"

Philippa blushed becomingly and Diana said hurriedly, latching on to her youngest sister, "I must go too! I . . . It was a pleasure to meet you, sir."

Once they were gone, Philippa said defiantly, "Well, Lord Roxbury, what was it you once called us? Harpies? Was Diana the harpy you had been expecting?"

He shrugged, irritated once more. "If you must have it in words, she seems a shy, pretty child, if not your equal. Does that satisfy you?"

But she gasped at that, forgetting the larger issue for the moment. "Not my equal? Are you mad?"

"Not in the least," he retorted deliberately. "She may be conventionally prettier than you, but she lacks either your vivacity or your intelligence. I don't doubt most men would find her quite charming, but she is a touch insipid for my taste.''

She was still blushing, but recovered rapidly. ''Yes, but then we are not discussing your taste. Can you dare to tell me she will not make a fitting wife to your nephew?''

He said harshly, ''I am sorry to disappoint you, but however charming she may be, my original objection must stand. However much I seem to be in danger of forgetting it myself lately.''

17

LATER THAT afternoon, when Aunt Bella learned from Diana that Roxbury had been there, she hurried up to commiserate with her niece, fearing the mood she would find her in.

She found Philippa still seated on the sofa, her mending basket beside her and a stocking in her lap. But her fingers were idle and she was staring off into space, a strange, almost wounded look in her face.

Aunt Bella stared in alarm, and said pitiably, "Tell me the worst at once. Diana told me that wretched man had been back. He wishes his mortgage returned, doesn't he? I knew it was too good to be true."

Philippa looked up slowly, as if only then becoming aware of her aunt's presence. "No," she said oddly at last. "He can't anyway, for he tore it up."

Her aunt was by now quite alarmed by her odd behavior. "Don't try to spare me, my dear," she begged. "It always alarms me far more than the truth would have done in the first place. What did he want?"

Philippa seemed to be coming out of a fog, for she shook her head vaguely, then said, still on that odd note, "I think, but I can't be quite sure, that he came to offer me a carte blanche, ma'am."

Aunt Bella rolled back on her heels, thoroughly startled for it was the last thing she had expected. "What? He dared to, after all there has been between you? Now isn't

that just like a man?" But for all her outrage, she was
thinking rapidly, and added frankly, on a far-less-elevated
tone, "Not that it isn't a considerble feather in your cap,
my love, though I don't expect you to see it. He is a far
richer prize than Julian, and from what I have been able to
discover, by no means as inclined in that direction as his
father was. He seems in fact to prefer married women of
his own class, so of course they cannot parade jewels of
his bestowing, which to my mind merely shows how
closefisted he is. Which makes it all the more remarkable.
Are you sure he actually offered to set you up as his
mistress, my love?"

"No," said Philippa truthfully. "He certainly offered to
help us out of our present difficulties. But that may merely
have been another attempt to prevent Diana's marriage to
his nephew." She roused a little more and asked, as if
against her will, "Have there been many? Mistresses, I
mean?"

"Well, dear, all men must have some outlet in that
direction, you know," said her aunt frankly. "It is not fair
to hold that against him. Not, as I have just been telling
you that very many women he has been connected with
can boast expensive trinkets of his bestowing. If he has
indeed offered to set you up, it is the first of that nature I
have ever heard of. Not that I mean it is not a great
impertinence, of course, but you should be a little flattered, nonetheless. And then, I don't mean to make you
angry, my love, but you have scarcely, by your behavior,
given him any reason to doubt you would be open to such
a proposal."

"No," said Philippa again. "He has made his opinion
of me more than plain."

Her aunt, seeming to realize that she had gone too far, got
up and said more cheerfully, "Well, it does no good to discuss it. I know so-called virtuous women are supposed to be
insulted by such a proposal, but I have always thought that
absurd. There is no need to make such heavy work over what
is, after all, a compliment. And it *was* a compliment, my
dear, from such a source, for if you have managed to
captivate so notorious a skinflint, that is something indeed."

"I was not insulted, ma'am," said Philippa. "In fact, if you must know, I was strongly tempted to accept his offer." Then, as her aunt boggled at her, Philippa said wearily, "Never mind. I must go up and change for dinner."

But once in her room, she did not immediately change her dress, but sank slowly down on the bed, her thoughts chaotic. If Roxbury had been undergoing a period of unwanted revelations, the one Philippa had just experienced had been blinding in its unpleasant truths. And most blinding and unpleasant of all was the fact that she had indeed, for one heart-stopping moment, been tempted to accept Roxbury's offer, whatever dishonor it entailed, and despite all her responsibilities.

Or perhaps because of them. She loved her brother and sisters, but she had long ago realized that they did not fill her whole life and had wondered what was to become of her after they had gone, even before Roxbury had come to destroy her peace of mind. They needed her now, it was true, but they would soon grow up, and then what would she have left? She was fond of Aunt Bella, but the thought of spending the rest of her life with her was oddly depressing. For one thing, whatever her past, Aunt Bella had at least enjoyed her youth—far more than most, really—and had her memories to sustain her. But what memories would Philippa have, when she was old and faded?

The thought had shaken her to the core of her being. She had been sitting on the sofa downstairs for hours trying to convince herself that virtue was its own reward, as she had been taught. But she had discovered she was by no means convinced of that any longer. If the truth be faced, she had not even been particularly shocked at the sort of liaison Roxbury was proposing. He had not offered marriage, it was true, but she had long ago given up any hope of marriage for herself. But did that mean she must also give up any hope of loving or being loved? Surely even half a loaf was better than no loaf at all?

Well, certainly Roxbury did not love her; and her aunt had chosen happiness over virtue, at least in her youth. Was she really any happier? But that new, unknown side of Philippa had answered recklessly that perhaps Aunt Bella was no happier now, but at least she had had some experience of the world, and led a full and enjoyable existence. Philippa herself would end up equally alone, but without even any memories to sustain her. When she was eighty would it really matter to her that her one chance to know love and life had had no honorable proposal of marriage behind it, she wondered.

But she knew even that was not what was at the root of her most blinding revelation of all. Until Roxbury had come into her life, she had known what her future must be. She had vaguely regretted it, but the years had never stretched before her in a bleak and unending line of duty and joylessness that she would never escape.

The truth was, until this afternoon she had failed—or deliberately refused to acknowledge—the most unpalatable truth of all: that she was far from being as indifferent to the wicked earl as she pretended. He had insulted her, mistreated her, behaved in every way in a manner designed to give her a disgust of him, but that seemed not to matter. And from the first he had brought out a side of her she had not known existed, and one that frightened her a little. She had pretended to hate and despise him for his unreasonable prejudices, but in truth she wondered now if she had not reacted as much out of disappointment as anger. Her first impression of him had been more than favorable. She had thought, ludicrously as it turned out, that she had finally met a man she might like and respect. No, that was too mild a word. In that first shock of meeting it had seemed almost as if she had been confronted by the embodiment of a dream. It was not one she had even been aware of, for she had thought herself far too practical to engage in such folly; but she had recognized in him at a glimpse her most secret projections.

That had soon changed, of course, but she wondered now if all the time she had convinced herself she hated him, it had not been merely out of pique that the first man she had ever found to admire should be one who turned out to be her sworn enemy and who wholly despised her.

Well, it did no good to dwell on that, even as it did no

good to remember this afternoon. But it had come as a shock to realize that she had actually been tempted today, for one brief mad moment, to accept his offer. She, who had thought herself past such romantic folly, was in serious danger of falling in love with a man who despised her, and who was prepared to go to any lengths to prevent his nephew from ruining himself by marriage with her sister. One, moreover, who had made his opinion of her plain. He desired her, yes. His behavior the other day and this afternoon had made that plain. But he despised the desire even as she did her own, and obviously it changed nothing in his mind. If she had accepted his offer, he would have set her up in some discreet house until he grew tired of her; he might even have helped financially with the children, but he would still not have agreed to his nephew marrying her sister. He would in fact have no doubt considered he had even more excuse for his objections.

And that betrayed to her the worst of her folly. Not only had she fallen in love with a man she ought to hate, she had somehow been seduced into creating a romantic and highly improbable vision of his sweeping her out of her boring life—even of assuming all her burdens and responsibilities as well—with the easy strength he had used to carry her so effortlessly.

Unfortunately she did not live in a fairy-tale world, for that was the only place such things were likely to happen. And the very fact that she had longed, however subconsciously, to be relieved of her burdens frightened her a little, as if it were admitting for the first time they were beyond her. But perhaps it was true. She had mismanaged Diana's affairs from the beginning, for she should never have permitted her to fall in love with Julian, and once she had, she should have discouraged the romance instead of being so angered by Roxbury's prejudice that she had been led into foolishly furthering it.

Darius, too, seemed to be growing beyond her control, for she had been too preoccupied with Diana's problems to notice how much his youthful dependence weighed on him, and how much he resented her for treating him as a child. Nor had she known how serious he was about leaving school to earn some money. She had scrimped and saved and schemed for so long to make sure he got an education that she had dismissed his protests as unimportant. Humiliatingly, it had taken Roxbury only one brief meeting to recognize the problem and convince Darius of the need for an education, despite all the arguments and threats she had expended.

Well, she had known Darius needed a male influence in his life, which was perhaps another reason she had been tempted to envision Roxbury in the role. She had hoped Julian might be able to help, but that had never been more than a vague wish, for too few years stood between them, and Julian was far too easygoing and uncomplicated to understand the more difficult Darius. Julian was kind to him, but stood a little in awe of his scholarship, since he frankly confessed he had no head for books at all. But they were too different ever to develop a real friendship, and Darius needed someone he could respect and look up to.

Obviously the Earl of Roxbury could fill that role, and he had been carelessly kind to Darius on more than one occasion. But it was folly to encourage either him—or herself—to believe the earl would ever be willing to do it on more than a temporary basis.

And that was why she had ultimately rejected his offer, though it was doubtful if her thoughts had been so logical at the moment. Whatever she might foolishly wish for herself, and be prepared to give up in return for it, she was still burdened with the responsibility for her family, and she could not sacrifice their happiness as well. It was what she had long ago decided, after all.

She was aware that many would call that decision virtuous. At the moment she was only aware that she didn't feel virtuous at all, merely bitter and oddly empty.

18

BUT SHE at last shook off her uncharacteristic depression and changed and went down to dinner. There she behaved so normally that Aunt Bella, at first suspicious and inclined to watch her closely, soon relaxed.

At least she was spared having Julian there as well, for Diana had received a hurried note from him saying that he had been called unexpectedly out of town on business and would be gone for a few days.

Diana was far too low-spirited to be curious about what business could have taken him away, or even to remember to ask what Lord Roxbury had wanted. But Philippa, hearing the news, wondered unpleasantly if Roxbury wasn't behind this sudden journey. If so, he had wasted little time after leaving her this afternoon. But then, he had made it clear that he still meant to prevent the marriage at any cost.

She naturally saw no reason to point out these suspicions to Diana, but unfortunately Genia knew no such reticence. "I'll bet his uncle is behind this," she said with relish. "Although he's not nearly the snob I was expecting. Even so, it's nice to have a meal once in a while without Julian here, so I don't have to be on my best behavior all the time."

"I never noticed you being on your best behavior," pointed out Darius sarcastically.

She made a face at him but went on disastrously,

with a sly glance at her sister, "Why didn't you invite
Lord Roxbury to dine with us instead, Philippa? Despite my theory, which I'm convinced is right, I sort of
liked him."

Darius, too, spared a troubled glance at his elder
sister, but said snubbingly, "Because Philippa knows
he may object to eating his dinner at a table full of rude
children. At any rate, we are hardly in Lord Roxbury's
league."

"Why not?" asked Iphigenia, wide-eyed. "We're in
Julian's league, and he's his nephew."

"Julian is also in love with Diana, which means he
has to put up with us," retorted her brother. "And
anyway, I would prefer Lord Roxbury not to be given a
disgust of your table manners, since he has promised to
help me when I get out of school."

Philippa had ignored most of this, but she looked up
now to say abruptly, "Don't—try not to count too
much on Lord Roxbury helping you, Darius. A great
many things could happen between now and then, you
know."

"I'm not counting on it," insisted Darius with slightly
heightened color. "But he said he would."

"I know. But it would be a mistake to rely too much
upon that. He . . . Oh, never mind! Forget I said
anything. Do you still mean to drive out to visit your
friend tomorrow, Aunt Bella?"

Aunt Bella started and cast her a doubtful glance.
"Well, I had intended to, I know, but what with your
ankle and all, if you would rather not, I am sure I can
write and put it off."

"Don't be silly. I think the drive will do us all good,
and I for one will be delighted to get out into the
country for the day," answered Philippa briskly.

"Well, if you are sure. Although ten to one it will
come on to rain. I never yet planned a journey that it
didn't," she ended pessimistically.

It didn't rain, but as it happened, their journey was
marked by an even stranger occurrence, and one that Aunt
Bella was to regret far more than a little rain.

She still possessed a few old friends who had been on the stage with her and with whom she maintained sporadic contact. She occasionally drove out to visit one of them, who lived in a villa on the river just outside of Richmond.

Maria Beckford had been a rival beauty in both of their heydays, but unlike Aunt Bella, had soon retired to a progression of generous protectors who had not only been as tolerant as they were besotted, but had left her financially secure. Her villa was free and clear—a gift from her last admirer, a high-ranking member of government, though Philippa had never been able to discover who he was—and some shrewd investments over the years had relieved her of all worry when she at last chose to retire and live alone in the country.

She had kindly helped her old rival out of more than one financial crisis, over the years, and it was she who had extended the open invitation to come and live with her, if ever Aunt Bella decided to sell the house in Green Street. Aunt Bella was fond of her, but it had occurred to her when her young relations first came to live with her that she perhaps ought not to take her nieces along when she went to pay her old friend a visit.

Unfortunately she never liked traveling alone, and since Philippa had convinced her to give up her carriage, which was costing her a fortune to maintain, she was naturally forced to hire a coach for the journey, and she violently mistrusted all hired positions.

Aware of all this, Philippa had soon been able to persuade her to abandon her scruples on the subject. The children liked to get out into the country, and since Mrs. Beckford's villa possessed extensive gardens and fronted directly on the river, they were usually able to pass the day quite happily, Genia usually getting extremely dirty in the process, while the two old friends enjoyed a comfortable gossip about old times.

Since Julian was out of town, even Diana consented to come with them, though she had been half-inclined to remain at home and watch for the post, in the hope she would receive another letter from Julian. But Aunt Bella pointed out frankly that a letter would scarcely have had time to reach her, and at any rate everyone knew that anxiously watching for the postman only ensured your letter didn't arrive, so Diana was at last persuaded to join them.

The journey to Richmond was accomplished without mishap, despite Aunt Bella's dire prognostications of rain or at the very least footpads. And since Aunt Bella's old friend, through mysterious channels, had gotten wind of her niece's proposed marriage and was agog to hear the details, the two aging beauties occupied themselves quite happily for a number of hours in discussing the event.

Maria Beckford kept more abreast of the world than Aunt Bella did, and was thus not surprised to hear that Roxbury was not pleased with the match. She was, however, exceedingly surprised to hear, in the strictest of confidence—for Aunt Bella had not been able to resist boasting of it just a little—that he had offered a carte blanche to Philippa.

"Good God," exclaimed her friend, clearly impressed. "I don't suppose it would do, of course, but I would never have expected it, all the same. He has the reputation for being closefisted, and by no means the philanderer his father was. Is your niece also *éprise* in that direction, do you think?"

But that Aunt Bella couldn't answer. Until the day before, she would have said nothing was more unlikely, for Philippa had seemed to detest him. But it had uneasily occurred to her, too, to wonder if Philippa hadn't been protesting just a shade too much to mask a very different emotion. Certainly she had reacted from the outset toward him in a manner wholly unlike her usual calm self.

"Well, it doesn't matter anyway," said her friend, reluctantly dismissing the possibility. She adjusted the shade a trifle so the sun didn't shine too directly on her fading complexion, and added with the practicality of her former calling, "Your niece will never bring herself to abandon her responsibilities to her younger sisters and brother, and it is too much to expect any man to take them on as well. A pity, for I have always liked her. And I can say that of few other women of her class."

Aunt Bella was forced to agree with this gloomy assessment. Her friend, watching her, added bluntly, "It is even more foolish to expect him to marry her, of course. He is far too proud, from everything I have ever heard, and it is too much to expect him to overlook your somewhat unnatural connection with his father. Look what a fuss he is making about his nephew. A pity, as I said, for obviously the girl is in love with him. She would be a fool if she weren't, living the retired life she does. I am sorry, for she is a sensible, pretty-behaved girl with none of the snobbishness of her class. I like her. With her charm she might have done well on the stage, even though the younger sister is the prettier. But as we know, it is not always beauty that is the most captivating in the long run, and your Philippa has something that goes deeper than mere beauty. But never mind that. Roxbury shows unexpectedly good taste, nonetheless."

Aunt Bella might be gratified by such words, but she emerged from this visit more gloomily than was her usual habit, and kept a close eye on Philippa during the drive back to town. But if Philippa was nursing a broken heart, her aunt was obliged to own she was hiding it well, for she seemed in perfectly normal spirits and chatted quite cheerfully.

Aunt Bella allowed herself to be slightly reassured and soon closed her eyes, lulled to sleepiness by the sway of the coach. She had just persuaded herself that everything would work out for the best when she was startled to full wakefulness by an exclamation from her usually unflappable niece.

"Good God! What on earth—?"

Aunt Bella sat up with a jerk, convinced they were all in danger for their lives. "What? What is it? Robbers? I knew it was unsafe to drive out with no more than hired guards."

"No, of course not, Aunt Bella. I'm sorry to have startled you, only I've a suspicion . . . Pull the checkstring, Genia," said Philippa with sudden decision. "I'm sure that young girl shouldn't be out alone on such a road. Perhaps there's been an accident."

"Young girl? Accident? Good God, I was convinced we were all about to be murdered at the very least," exclaimed Aunt Bella, her fright making her irritable. "Pray don't frighten me like that, you wretched girl! And what on earth do we care if a girl is walking along the side of the road? If we are to stop for every pedestrian we meet, we shall never get back to town."

"Not every pedestrian, Aunt Bella. But you will soon see what I mean. I won't keep you but a moment, I promise."

The puzzled coachman had reined in, and Philippa did not wait for the steps to be let down, but hurriedly thrust open the door and jumped down, despite her stiff ankle. Aunt Bella stared after her in bewilderment, but Iphigenia, who was sitting on the same side of the coach as Philippa, perilously craned out the window, trying to see what her sister was doing.

After a moment she pulled her head back in to announce disgustedly, "It *is* only a girl! I thought it might at least be an overturned coach with dozens of people hurt and in need of rescue. Nothing exciting ever happens to me."

"Well, if you think it would be exciting to come across dozens of wounded people, all I can say is you have even odder tastes than I suspected," grumbled her aunt. "But what on earth can Philippa be thinking of? She can't mean to offer a perfect stranger a lift, for, aside from every other consideration, there is no room."

But Philippa did not seem to be concerned with that problem, for a very few minutes later she returned with a pretty, quite young female carrying a heavy carpetbag. "Aunt Bella, this is . . . oh, dear, I didn't discover your name. But never mind! She is on her way to London as well, and so I have offered her a lift. Come and sit with us, Genia, so that she may have your place."

Aunt Bella was far from pleased with this news, but short of flatly refusing to accept the stranger, she was forced to agree with the appearance, at least, of complaisance. Genia, regarding the newcomer with some interest, had already moved over, and the newcomer, after a rather searching look at the occupants of the coach, had unabashedly accepted the unusual invitation and was already climbing in.

Once she was settled, she said with what Aunt Bella considered unbecoming cheerfulness, "Thank you! I own it seems to be a great deal farther than I had expected, and I am excessively hot and thirsty. My feet hurt too, for I have discovered these sandals were never meant for walking any distance. And my name is Lucinda."

She offered no last name, and after only a moment's hesitation Philippa completed the introductions. Lucinda acknowledged these without a trace of self-consciousness, and Aunt Bella, who was looking her over with some astonishment, was only slightly mollified by her obvious gentility.

Whatever the reason for her being found alone, walking down a public road, she was dressed becomingly in a traveling dress and hat that, though dusty, betrayed their expensive origins, and she spoke in cultured tones. She looked to be about seventeen, and though she was not a beauty, possessed an animated little face and a great deal of vivacity that Aunt Bella, experienced in such matters, easily predicted would prove successful with the opposite sex when she was a little older. She possessed, as well, a considerable twinkle in her wide brown eyes that not only expressed no embarrassment, but made it obvious she was enjoying herself immensely.

But any mention of shoes was likely to appeal to Aunt Bella's sympathy, since she herself suffered constantly from swollen and aching feet, a legacy, or so she said, of her years on the stage. "Good gracious, so I should imagine," she said unwillingly. "Where have you walked from anyway, and on such a hot day?"

The twinkle in Lucinda's eyes grew even more pronounced. "Well, I think the driver said Brentford," she said mischievously. "But I was far too angry to be paying very much attention. Would you believe he put me off the stage when he found out I hadn't enough money to pay for my fare all the way to London? And so, when he told me it was only another five miles or so, I decided to walk, for it's very important I should get there by tomorrow."

"Five miles?" gasped Aunt Bella, exhausted just thinking about it. "And you don't seriously mean you traveled
on the common stage? What on earth are the times coming
to."

"I think it would be exciting," defended Iphigenia,
regarding the newcomer with considerable interest.

"Oh, it was," agreed Lucinda cheerfully. "Especially in
the beginning. There was a fat woman who kept eating
garlic sausages, and another man who kept staring uncomfortably at me, but aside from that, it was great fun. I had
no notion it could be so amusing riding on the stage. I
wanted to come on the mail, of course, but I hadn't enough
money. The man who kept staring offered to pay the rest
of my fare, as a matter of fact, when I was put off, but I
thought under the circumstances I would do better to walk,"
she added with unexpected good sense.

Aunt Bella almost shuddered at the thought. "Much
better! But what on earth can your parents be thinking of
to let you travel alone?"

Lucinda shot her a speculative look, brimful of mischief. But when she next glanced at Philippa, something
about her direct gaze seemed to change her mind, for she
said ingenuously, "Well, I have been telling everyone
that I have been at school and that my mother is very ill,
and all our money is gone, so I have been obliged to come
home on my own. But I just made that up. In truth, if you
must know, I have run away from home."

19

PHILIPPA DID not look to be very surprised, for she had already guessed as much. But Iphigenia said admiringly, "Have you really? What for?"

"I was under the vilest persecution at home," said Lucinda darkly. "And anyway, I warned them what would happen if they didn't take me seriously, so it's all their fault."

Divining from this that she had not really been seriously mistreated, Philippa said dryly, "Even so, don't you think your family will be worrying about you by now?"

Lucinda shot her another speculative glance, but said frankly, "I don't care if they are! And you needn't bother to lecture me, for I never mean to go home again. I only told you the truth at all because you have been so kind to me. I could have told you the other, and you would have believed me, because everyone else has. I got it from a book I once read. And even I was amazed at how well it answered, for the stationmaster where I bought my ticket was sorry for me and gave me something to eat, and the first driver we had was very kind. But evidently the second had heard the story before, or else didn't believe me, for he wouldn't even let me go on to London and send him the money later, which I thought excessively mean of him. Especially since I thought it such a brilliant story myself."

"Well, I think it is awfully exciting," said Iphigenia. "However did you dare?"

"Well, it didn't take any daring at all, if you must know, for I merely hid in the trap when one of the gardeners drove into the village. I had had it all figured out beforehand, you see. The only difficulty came in packing a bag without anyone catching me, but I was able to hide it under my bed. And it answered very well, even better than I had thought, for the maids never dust under the beds, as Mam—as I have always suspected," she hurriedly corrected her slip. "My only regret is that I couldn't be there when they discovered I was actually missing."

Aunt Bella thought she sounded unbecomingly heartless, but Iphigenia said admiringly, "I think it was very brave of you. Just like in a novel. What do you mean to do when you reach London?"

Lucinda dimpled up. "That is the most wonderful secret of all. But if I don't tell someone, I think I shall burst, for you wouldn't believe how clever I have been! Even Uncle . . . Well, never mind! But even he would be obliged to own that I didn't run away on an impulse, but thought it all out carefully beforehand and made all my plans. And *that* doesn't sound like I'm still a child, does it?" she demanded resentfully, as if recalling some unpleasant memory. "In fact, I wrote weeks ago to Malcom Bagshott, the theatrical producer, and got a reply back from him last week, inviting me to come in for an audition at my earliest convenience. For the truth is, I mean to become an actress and have all London at my feet."

Aunt Bella almost choked, but Iphigenia seemed to have no fault to find with this remarkable plan for she said approvingly, "Aunt Bella used to be an actress, you know. Maybe she can help you."

At once Lucinda clapped her hands and turned her bright gaze on the other. "No! Did you really! I've never met a real actress before. Tell me everything. Is it really as exciting as it seems?"

"If you consider dirty dressing rooms and uncomfortable inns exciting," said Aunt Bella depressingly, "which from the sound of it, I daresay you would. I toured the provinces for years playing bit parts and dodging the stage managers—and frequently the landlord when we couldn't pay our shot. But at least it was an education."

"But that was before you became an overnight sensation," objected Iphigenia. "Aunt Bella was the most famous actress of her day," she pointed out proudly to Lucinda. "The Prince Regent—before he grew so fat— used to come to see her in *The Merchant of Venice.*"

Lucinda glanced again at Aunt Bella, evidently having trouble in imagining her plump form transformed into a famous actress, but said instantly, "Really? What happened? Why did you give it up?"

"She gave it up when she married my uncle," said Iphigenia. "But he was unkind to her and later died."

Lucinda seemed to find the ending of the story a trifle flat, but she said with determination, "Well, I never mean to marry, so I needn't worry about that. I mean to become a fatal beauty and have all the men madly in love with me. Only I shall devote myself to my career and drive them all mad with jealousy and frustration."

To Philippa it sounded as if their guest, like her youngest sister, had indulged in too steady a diet of romantic novels, but Diana, her quick sympathy aroused, said pityingly, "Oh, no! You can't mean never to marry?"

Lucinda grinned and relented. "Well, perhaps, but only after a long and successful career, and only to a royal prince or someone equally romantic. Or perhaps I shall suffer from a hopeless passion and be obliged to bury myself in my art. What do you think? I lean toward the hopeless passion myself, for then I would remain aloof and mysterious, and eveyone would try to discover the unhappy secret in my past that has made me that way."

"Yes, and only after you are dead will they find a single, cryptic line pointing to his identity. No one else will guess, but he will have to suffer the rest of his life knowing the sacrifice you made for him," finished Genia raptly. She then added more prosaically, "Diana is in love and engaged to be married herself, and so can't understand why anyone should want to remain single."

Lucinda, who seemed to be Genia's psychological age, if not her chronological one, turned her head to regard the blushing Diana with her bright, interested eyes. "Are you? Are you very much in love, then?"

"She mopes around the house all the time when he's not there," supplied Genia in a disgusted voice. "But at least it has the advantage of being a star-crossed love affair. His family doesn't approve of her because our aunt was an actress. I thought his uncle meant to withhold his fortune as well, but now I'm not so sure. But it would make the story much more interesting, don't you think? In novels there's always a wicked uncle."

"Yes, or else a jealous stepmother." But Lucinda was evidently regarding Diana with new respect. "Do they really disapprove of the marriage? Are you going to elope? How exciting! I have a wicked uncle, as a matter of fact. It's his fault I have been obliged to run away, for he wouldn't believe me when I told him how unhappy I was. In fact, I warned him that I would do something desperate if he didn't let me come and live with my aunt, or even my grandmother, for at least they live in a town and not the country, so I might see a little excitement. But he would only say unfeelingly that he was sorry, but there was nothing he could do. I'll bet he's sorry now he didn't believe me. I'll bet they're all sorry."

"Does your aunt live in London?" inquired Philippa with apparent disinterest.

But Lucinda cast her a mischievous look and just shook her head. "I said she lived in *a* town, not London. You won't succeed in tricking me that way, you know. I don't mean to be rude, but if you knew who I was, you would only be obliged to write to my family and tell them where I was. And now that I have finally gotten away, I don't mean ever to go back."

"Even so, you're awfully young to be on your own, especially in so large a city as London," pointed out Philippa gently.

"No, for I have it all planned out, as I said. If I can't become an actress, I shall very likely become a governess, or even a milliner. Anything is preferable to going back to be buried alive again. I know you think I'm exaggerating, but if you had seen the way I have had to live, for years and years, you wouldn't think so anymore. Mama never does anything but lie on a sofa in a darkened room with her smelling salts conveniently to hand, and Grandmama and Grandpapa—*not* the grandmother I wanted to live with—are just as bad. I must always be quiet to keep from making Mama any worse or bringing on one of her tics, and they are so strict they won't even allow me to go with one of my friends to the local assemblies, even though we would be perfectly adequately chaperoned. And when I reminded them that I would be eighteen soon and it was time to think of my come-out, they would only say that Mama wouldn't dream of letting anyone else present me, but that her health was too frail this year even to consider it. And you may be sure it would be the same story, year after year, until I died an old maid. And so I made up my mind to run away, for anything is preferable to never having a bit of fun or dying without ever really having lived at all."

Philippa found herself, in her present mood, surprisingly sympathetic to this passionate speech, but thought it unwise to encourage her unconventional guest. Instead, she said practically, "And what do you intend to do when you reach London? Even supposing you are taken on as an actress right away, you must have a place to sleep and some money to live on until you receive your first wages, you know."

"Oh, I have thought of all that as well," answered Lucinda sunnily. "The allowance they give me is absurdly small, and I couldn't put this plan into action until I reached London, for too many people know me near where I live, which is why I was obliged to run away with so very little money and miscalculated what it would cost to get all the way to London. But I have several pieces of jewelry I can pawn as soon as I get to town, to live on until I can support myself. And you needn't think I stole them, for they were gifts to me and aren't even heirlooms or anything. So it is perfectly proper for me to sell them if I want to."

Philippa had to restrain a smile at this naïve utterance and thought that Lucinda was not as persecuted as she would like them to believe if she received such handsome gifts. But after a rueful glance at her resigned aunt, she said calmly, "None whatsoever. You have obviously thought of everything. But I would suggest you come home with us, at least until you can have time to sell your jewelry. We have plenty of room and you will be doing us a favor, for my aunt likes company. Don't you, Aunt Bella?"

Aunt Bella halfheartedly agreed, and after only the slightest hesitation Lucinda readily accepted this offer, though she found only one fault to find with it. "You're not just inviting me so you can try to talk me into going home again, are you?" she asked suspiciously.

"I think you should go home, but I can't make you, particularly since I don't know your full name," answered Philippa honestly. "But I would far rather have you under our eye than on your own in a city like London."

"Yes, that's what I thought, which is why I didn't tell you my whole name," responded Lucinda ingenuously, with the air of someone congratulating herself. "But I don't mind admitting I would rather stay with you, as it happens. For one thing, I've never lived in a big family before, and I've always thought I would like to have brothers and sisters; and for another thing, Mrs. Mayhew can tell me all about the theater, which will be a very good thing, don't you think? I have played in theatricals several times at school, and everyone thought I was very good, but I'm not so foolish I think that the same thing. And I am very anxious to make good, for everything depends upon it."

Philippa did not bother to point out to her that in the world of the theater her aunt had known, acting ability seemed to count for very little. The mere thought of this foolish child alone in that world was enough to make her shudder. She was sorry to foist her on to her long-suffering aunt, but could not have turned her loose once they reached London.

Once back in Green Street Geneia took Lucinda up to unpack her modest carpetbag, and Philippa said ruefully to her aunt, "I beg your pardon, Aunt Bella. I seem to have saddled you with still another unwanted guest, but I couldn't just turn her loose."

"Especially not if she actually has an appointment with Malcolm Bagshott, as she said," replied her aunt grimly. "He was notorious even in my day. At any rate, if I am to house all of London anyway, as seems likely, what difference does one more make? Not that I hope you mean to house her for more than one night, for if she won't tell you her name, she will have to be turned over to the authorities at once."

"Yes, I daresay you're right," said Philippa regretfully. "But I own I hate to do it. It's obvious her birth is respectable."

Her aunt sniffed. "If we don't, we may find ourselves accused of kidnapping her. Unless I much miss my guess, and it's not likely when it comes to jewels, those pearl drops in her ears are worth a pretty penny, let alone the other jewels she mentioned. It's a wonder she wasn't murdered for them long before she reached London."

"Yes, we must on all accounts keep her from trying to sell them. I agree something will have to be done, but not just yet. For one thing, from what I've seen she's quite capable of giving the authorities the slip or hoaxing them with some even more absurd tale, and for another, I can't deny I felt a certain sympathy for her plight."

Her aunt snorted. "You can't tell me you believed her tale of persecution?"

Philippa had to smile. "No. But, well, there are different kinds of persecutions, as I think you know. I own from the signs she has been spoiled—at least materially. But it does sound as if she had been kept too close and denied the normal outlets of a girl her age. For one of her obvious spirits, that is almost criminal. I can't help thinking her family deserves a little scare thrown into them."

Aunt Bella still looked unconvinced, but Philippa added thoughtfully, "At any rate, if she is returned now, nothing is more likely than that she will simply run away again. And at least she is in no danger here, as she would be out on the streets. I have hopes I may convince her to confide in me before we must do anything so drastic as turning her over to the police.''

Aunt Bella threw up her hands. ''As if we didn't have enough troubles around here already,'' she grumbled. ''But do what you wish. Lately even the thought of prison has begun to look peaceful to me.''

Philippa kissed her cheek, correctly divining that her aunt was resigned, if not happy, about Lucinda's continued presence in the house, and she went away to make sure their unexpected guest had everything she needed.

20

BUT IF Philippa had hoped to convince Lucinda to confide in her, Lucinda was obviously equally on her guard, and determined to let nothing slip.

Philippa stopped by her bedchamber later that evening to find Lucinda already in bed and yawning after her exausting day. Lucinda was quite happy to see her and grateful for her help, but whenever Philippa mentioned her home, or how much her family must be worrying, her piquant little face closed. "I know you mean well, but I won't go home again, at least until they realize that I am growing up and give me some freedom. You don't know what it was like, with Mama always ill and Grandmama and Grandpapa always blaming me if I said anything to upset her. And when even my uncle, whom Mama is afraid of, a little, refused to help me, I made up my mind then what I must do. And if you persist in questioning me, I will only run away again, for I am determined not to give in."

Something in her words rang a faint chord in Philippa's memory, but she thought it wisest to give up, at least for the moment. And since Lucinda yawned sleepily again, she merely blew out the candle and bid her young guest good night. She couldn't help feeling a great deal of sympathy for her, as she had told Aunt Bella, but she was wise enough to know something would have to be done soon if Lucinda didn't break down and tell her the truth.

Philippa soon went to bed herself with a faint frown between her eyes, troubled as well by Julian's continued absence.

She had solved neither problem by morning, but Lucinda, at least, seemed full of spirits and fully recovered from her adventure. Fortunately she was easily persuaded to delay selling any of her jewels, at least for the moment, but charged Philippa with keeping a strict accounting of what it cost them to keep her, for she meant to repay them every penny.

This did a great deal to further resign Aunt Bella to her presence, and she even added the weight of her arguments to convince the newcomer to abandon any plans to keep her appointment with the notorious Malcolm Bagshott.

This was less easy to do, for Lucinda held strong to her resolve to become an actress. Only by dint of Aunt Bella's promising vaguely to give some thought to the matter and introduce Lucinda to one or two directors of her acquaintance who might be able to help her, was Lucinda at last persuaded, reluctantly, to forgo her appointment.

That decided, she readily agreed to Philippa's suggestion that the first thing they must do was to augment her sketchy wardrobe. She had understandably been able to bring very little with her in her carpetbag, and aside from her night things and a few other essentials, possessed only the dress she stood up in, which was considerably the worse for her journey.

In fact, she thought it great fun to have several of Diana's outgrown gowns taken in for her, which Philippa thought dryly revealed just how wealthy was her background, for she had obviously never heard of such a practice. She stood patiently to be fitted, but once Philippa had settled down to the less-interesting task of taking in the seams, she was easily persuaded to go out sightseeing with Diana and Genia.

She hesitated only a moment, which made Philippa

suspect she possessed relatives or friends who lived in London. But when she realized they planned to take a cab into the City to view the Tower and the menagerie there, she relaxed, evidently feeling she ran no danger of meeting anyone she knew in such unfashionable spots.

Philippa stored the information away for future use, but short of placing an advertisement in the paper, or parading her up and down the more fashionable streets in hope someone recognized her, she could not immediately see how it could be put to good use.

When the sightseers returned much later that afternoon, it was obvious from Lucinda's pink cheeks and excited eyes that she had enjoyed the day's outing. Philippa thought it betrayed how young she was, despite her much-vaunted maturity, but it also showed just how starved she was for excitement and adventure. In fact, Philippa had conceived a strong dislike for Lucinda's family and was by no means eager to restore her to them.

That was foolish, of course, for aside from every other consideration, she could not foist her on Aunt Bella indefinitely. And so she delicately tried once more to draw Lucinda out over dinner that evening, without much success.

Lucinda said cheerfully, looking around the shabby dining room, "How fun this all is! I never had any brothers or sisters, you know, and you cannot imagine how dull dinner at home is. No one discusses anything in the least interesting, and we all maintain such a strict decorum, on account of the servants, you know, that I am tempted sometimes to throw down my napkin and scream. You don't know how lucky you all are."

Philippa thought it sad she should enjoy a dinner composed of a cold joint and only one remove, for Cook was down in her back again, but said calmly, "Don't you possess any cousins even? You spoke of an uncle, I believe?"

For once Lucinda did not seem to suspect a trap, or else thought the question harmless enough. "Oh, yes! I do have a cousin that I like well enough, but he's quite a few years older than me, so I don't know him very well. And the rest of my relations don't like each other. Except for Grandmama, of course—the one I *don't* live with—but she's special!"

Something again touched a chord in Philippa's memory, but she said merely, rather dryly, "Don't you think she at least deserves to know that you are safe? She must be nearly sick with worry by now."

But Lucinda was not to be caught that way. "No, for she won't have heard anything about it yet. And I do mean to write, once everything is settled."

"It would be kindest to write at once, regardless of whether you are settled," countered Philippa a little sternly. "I realize you look upon this as a huge lark, but however much you may resent your relations for their treatment of you, you must know they love you very much and don't deserve to be frightened this way."

Lucinda had the grace to look briefly chastened, but she bounced back quickly. "Yes, but if I write them they will know I am in London, which would give them too much of an advantage in trying to find me," she pointed out reasonably. "And anyway, they deserve to be made to worry, for I warned them what would happen."

Philippa once more gave it up, but said, as if thoughtfully, "Yes, but I have been thinking, and it occurs to me you will have to have a last name of some kind. If you are not successful in your ambition to go upon the stage, you will have to find other employment, and I fear employers are notoriously wary of hiring young women with no names and no references and no family backgrounds."

But unfortunately that merely prompted Lucinda to try to think of a good last name for herself, preferably one that would look good on a playbill. In this she was ably abetted by the irrepressible Genia, much to Aunt Bella's disgust.

At last that lady broke in tartly. "Good God, you talk as if the theater were a fairy-tale place, full of princes and handsome, wealthy heroes waiting to carry you off. I fear it is far otherwise, as I should know. Even if you should manage to become a hit, the hours are long, the pay frequently miserly, and in the long run you will find even success oddly hard to hold on to. Beauty fades, helped along by the ravages of stage makeup and so many late nights, and there is always another actress waiting in the wings, hoping to succeed you in the public's fickle fancy. And then there are the snubs and cuts you receive, for however glamorous, acting is hardly a respectable profession. Anyone who didn't have to would be a fool to go into it.''

Lucinda indeed looked thoughtful at these dampening words, but she was too intelligent not to guess Aunt Bella was being deliberately discouraging, and said, ''Well, I don't have my heart set upon being an actress, although it does seem like the easiest way to have a great many adventures and I would far prefer it to being a dressmaker, or a chambermaid. Unless, of course, I were employed in a house where there is a handsome young duke, made lonely by his rank and the exaggerated way everyone treats him. He would naturally fall in love with me, and only after he had married me would he discover that I was really eligible, after all, and not at all the penniless orphan he thought me.''

Aunt Bella also gave it up, merely remarking dampingly, ''You can be quite sure no woman would hire you as a chambermaid in any household where there was an impressionable young man. And if you think you would find it so romantic to be a chambermaid, you might follow Betty around for a day or two. That should cure you.''

She said waspishly to Philippa later, however, that she was beginning to fear they would be stuck with Lucinda for the rest of their days, for if her relatives had any sense, they wouldn't want her back. ''Lonely dukes indeed! If you ask me, her only problem is not that she has been persecuted, but that she has been spoiled unmercifully. If she had even a taste of any of the absurd things she talks of, she would soon be crying for home again, you may be sure.''

''Yes, of course she would. But I own I am beginning to be worried,'' said Philippa unwillingly. ''I could not have left her on her own in the city, for you know better than anyone what can befall a girl alone and penniless in such a place. I shudder even to think of it. But you're right that as long as she is with us, she will be even less inclined to return home. I wish I knew what to do. In the end I suppose I shall have to notify the authorities, but once that's done, there is little hope of avoiding a scandal. I hope her reputation may not be ruined by this absurd escapade, but if it should become publicly known, I don't know how she is to avoid it.''

"You had far better turn your mind to a more-pressing problem,'' retorted her aunt. "I didn't care to say anything, with Diana already moping about as if Julian had been gone two months instead of two days, but unless I miss my guess, his uncle is behind this sudden disappearance. If we're not careful, we shall find ourselves balked on that suit as well. Not that I ever approved of encouraging the marriage, under the circumstances, for heaven knows we have enough troubles already without adding one more mouth to feed, especially if we are to have that absurd child on our hands now as well. But I just thought I had better warn you.''

Philippa flushed, but said shortly, "Yes, that had occurred to me as well. If so, there is nothing I can do about it, though. I never meant to do more than ensure Julian's fortune so that he could make a choice unhampered by his uncle's blackmail. And I have failed even in that! If he has been made to reconsider or fallen out of love with Diana, I am sorry for it, but Diana would do better to discover it now rather than later. And surely even Roxbury would not dare to kidnap a grown man, just to prevent him from marrying against his wishes.''

Aunt Bella was by no means so sure. But as it happened Roxbury had far more pressing matters than his nephew's marriage on his mind at the moment.

Even so, the earl found himself thinking about the Mayhews—or at least one of them—with annoying frequency, and did his best to banish her image from his mind.

With indifferent success. He was forced to admit that Philippa Mayhew was fast becoming something of an obsession with him. It was absurd, for he had known far more beautiful women. If he no longer believed her the temptress he had once thought her, he yet had every reason to know that any sort of relationship between them was out of the question. And yet none of that seemed to matter.

He told himself that he would soon forget her, that he was fortunate she had rejected his rash offer and saved him from himself. She might have a vitality and spirit, and even a courage, that he had never expected to find in a woman other than his mother, but she was only a woman, after all, and he had always before found them easily expendable. He should know by now that the best of them were heartless and wholly immoral when it came to something they wanted. Even Philippa, despite what he now thought her, had not hesitated to resort to blackmail to achieve her sister's happiness. In fact, to call women the weaker sex was to vastly understate the matter.

However, he could no longer completely condemn her as he would once have done. In fact, he found himself with the wholly uncharacteristic desire not to blame her, but to lift some of her burdens from shoulders too slight to bear them. If she had behaved unscrupulously, it was in defense of her sister, and she seemed to have little thought for anything but her family.

He recognized he was behaving wholly irrationally, and that he was in danger of allowing a beautiful face to make him reject everything he had ever believed in.

And yet, that was not entirely true: even without his unexpected attraction to Philippa, he had to own that young Darius interested him strongly, for some reason. It was obvious he was in need of some male influence, and equally as obvious that Philippa, preoccupied as she was with her sister and with making ends meet, had had little time to recognize that need.

And then, if he were being honest, that scamp Iphigenia of the absurd name had amused him, despite her nonsense. He had never had any particular desire for a family, and aside from Julian and his mother, had paid very little attention to his own, but the impossible Mayhews seemed somehow to have aroused his interest, and even his compassion, and made him question his determination never to marry.

Well, if his life, previously so satisfying, had begun to seem unexpectedly boring and lonely the answer was simple. He had only to marry one of the females his sister was always pushing at him. He would no doubt find any one of them, picked at random, as satisfactory as any other.

But the sneaking suspicion that any woman without Philippa's luxurious hair and flashing eyes and combative personality would soon bore him to distraction would not be wholly dismissed, however much he tried.

Perhaps it was that that made him ask abruptly, one day when out riding with his nephew, "Tell me, are you still determined to wed your Diana?"

They had had a long, frustrating day in the saddle, and even Julian was looking far from his usual cheerful self, while his uncle's temper was frankly savage. He looked somewhat startled at the unexpected subject, but said, flushing a little, "Yes, of course. Good God, Marcus, you've met her now. You must have seen that she is totally unlike what Mama suspects. I know that she is the only wife for me."

"She is still the niece of a notorious actress," his uncle pointed out rather shortly. "Never mind! I have no doubt she is a pearl past price. But you are engaging in foolish optimism if you believe your mother will ever agree or accept such a marriage. And I hope you are prepared to take on responsibility for her entire family as well, for you will be responsible, you know."

"Of course I am prepared to help them if necessary," said Julian rather stiffly. "If . . . . Once I am in possession of my principal I think I should certainly help with Darius' fees, for I know from Diana that is their biggest worry. But if you think they will hang on my sleeve, you are mistaken. Diana says that her sister is very proud and has no intention of accepting any help from us. I—we hope that once the other children are grown and off her hands, she may care to come and live with us, but even that is by no means certain, for she seems to have some odd idea of traveling, once she is free.''

The earl frowned abruptly. ''What nonsense is this?'' he demanded impatiently. ''Surely she will have married herself long before that time?''

''Oh, I wouldn't think so. I mean, she is already quite old, and with the added liability of the children, I would be surprised if she did,'' Julian answered naïvely.

Roxbury, who had just decided that all women were interchangeable, found himself irrationally irritated by this absurd assumption. ''Old? Good God, you talk as if she were five-and-fifty instead of five-and-twenty.''

''No, of course I don't mean that,'' said Julian quickly. ''But there are the children to think of, as you pointed out, and you know yourself few men are willing to take on a woman with such liabilities. At least Diana fears her older sister will never marry, and I must say I think she's right. It would be different if she were a particular beauty, of course. But situated as she is, I doubt she will ever meet anyone likely to appreciate her good qualities.''

The earl, far from pleased by this bleak picture, bit back his instinctive harsh response and abruptly abandoned the subject.

21

BUT AT least one of Philippa's immediate worries was soon relieved, for Diana received a letter from Julian the next day.

He seemed to have little time to spare for writing, nor did he give any indication of when he might be returning to town. But his letter evidently gave no hint that his affections were shifting or he was indulging in any second thoughts, for Diana, whose spirits had been increasingly affected by his absence, positively glowed after she read it, and sat throughout breakfast in a happy fog.

Aunt Bella, sourly observing this remarkable transformation, remarked afterward to Philippa, "I suppose I should be grateful, but I wouldn't have thought that short scrawl worthy of such a look. You'd think she'd received news of a fortune. In my day love letters were at least . . ." Then she remembered her audience, which included the highly curious and perceptive Lucinda, and apparently thought better of what she had been about to say. "Never mind," she amended hastily. "I've forgotten what I was about to say."

Lucinda had been taking all this in with her usual bright curiosity, but she said surprisingly now, "Julian? Is that the name of her fiancé? I wonder . . . . ?" Then she, too, seemed to think better of what she had been about to say and broke off, looking oddly mischievous.

Aunt Bella, who was fast coming to regret the generous

impulse that had prompted her to admit one she was coming to regard as a permanent liability, was far too wrapped up in her own thoughts to pay any attention to this. "Even so, according to Diana, he says nothing of when he means to return or what urgent matter has taken him out of town at such a time. I hope I haven't been fooled in him and he isn't playing fast and loose with her, after all."

Lucinda started to say something else, then clapped a hand over her mouth, her eyes beginning to dance, and soon found an excuse to leave the room.

Aunt Bella was frankly glad to see her go. "As for your latest protégée, the less said, the better. Has she let slip anything at all about her home or family?"

Philippa shook her head guiltily. "She's obviously very much on her guard. If I don't learn something soon, I shall have to turn her over to the authorities, I fear. But it's only been a few days, after all. I am convinced I shall get her to confide in me soon."

But in truth she was no longer nearly as optimistic on that subject as she had led her aunt to believe. So far Lucinda had proven exceedingly wily, as a matter of fact, more than once clapping a hand over her mouth as she had come close to revealing something about her past and obviously enjoying her stolen holiday to the fullest. If she were troubled by any twinge of inconvenient conscience about the trouble she was causing, she did not reveal it, nor did she display any trace of homesickness, as Philippa had hoped.

Philippa at last gave up the annoying problem for the moment to wrestle with her accounts instead. Lucinda and Genia were to go to Astley's Amphitheater in Darius' company that afternoon, for Philippa saw no point in not letting Lucinda enjoy herself as much as possible while in London. Darius did not much approve of their flighty young guest, but had nobly volunteered to take them, since Genia had so enjoyed it the last time.

That problem off her mind, at least for the moment, Philippa tried instead to juggle a particularly annoying column of figures, an exercise that proved hardly any more satisfying. They represented their minimum expenses and totaled to a gloomy sum, which she was determined to reduce, if possible. Darius' fees must be found somewhere, and she had resolved to cut costs, but Aunt Bella was right that money just seemed to slip through one's fingers, however careful you tried to be. And there could be all the expense of Diana's bride clothes to be met—presuming, of course, that the marriage ever took place.

But that, at least, she refused to think about for the moment, deciding she had enough problems already. She was frowning heavily over her depressing figures when Roxbury was unexpectedly announced.

Philippa's pen spluttered annoyingly across the page, spoiling an hour's work, and she looked up, unaccountably shy to see him after their last encounter. She felt herself blushing foolishly in fact, but made herself put down her pen and rise with a pretense of calm, at least.

She saw, to her surprise, that he was looking tired and drawn, and by no means in a pleasant temper, but he said curtly, "No, don't get up. How is your ankle, by the way?"

"My ankle? Good God, I had forgotten it already," she answered, relieved to have a neutral topic to discuss. "Surely you did not call again just to ask me that?"

"No. But you are looking pale still."

She flushed again, having no need to be reminded that she was looking washed out. "I certainly hope you have not come merely to inform me I am looking hagged," she complained. "My mirror has been confirming the fact to me for some time now. It is the heat, no doubt. I cannot get used to London in the summer."

His quick frown showed at that. "Surely you don't mean to stay in town all summer?"

This was turning into a ridiculous conversation, and she could not imagine why he had come. It seemed he had said everything there was to be said between them the last time, beyond hope of mistake. "It might surprise you to learn there are any number of people who live in London year round. At any rate, if it comes to that, you are hardly looking your best, either, I must say."

"No, I have had a damnable week," he said still more curtly. "And you don't look hagged. Merely not in your usual blooming health. Is it your sister's future that is worrying you?" he asked still more unexpectedly. "I see you are trying to make your accounts balance. Not very successfully, by the looks of it."

She was even more surprised, but answered truthfully, "No. At least, not entirely. If you must know, Darius' fees are bothering me more at the moment, but I don't doubt I will find them somewhere. I did fear for a while, when Julian went away so unexpectedly, that you had managed to convince him at last, or even abducted him to remove him from my sister's dangerous influence," she added provocatively. "But if so, he is still able to get letters out, for Diana had one from him a few days ago."

He turned away rather abruptly. "No, I have not done that. In fact, that's what I've come to discuss with you, when I could ill spare the time. I know you have thought me unreasonable on the subject."

"That is indeed a handsome admission, coming from you," she answered.

To her surprise he smiled faintly and turned back. "Perhaps. My reasons must be obvious, but I have no intention of going over them again. But I have decided, been forced to conclude, that the attachment between them is genuine. I have therefore decided— "

But it seemed they were never to have an uninterrupted conversation again, for at that most inopportune moment the door burst open to admit Lucinda, who said in her usual impetuous fashion, "Philippa, I just came to tell you that we are off now . . . Oh, I beg your pardon. I didn't know you had compan—*oh*!"

Roxbury had turned impatiently at her entrance, and he now stiffened and stared at her almost as if he were seeing a ghost. "You . . . *here*?" he demanded incredulously.

Lucinda was looking by no means her confident self, either, for she backed a little before him and squeaked, "Un-uncle Marcus! How—how did you find me?"

Philippa looked between the two of them in growing astonishment. "Uncle? Oh, good God," she exclaimed in disgust. "I don't believe it. You don't mean all this time . . . . ?"

She got no further, for Roxbury's face had frozen, his black brows drawn harshly together and a dark uncustomary flush on his lean cheeks. "I suppose I should have expected this," he said contemptuously at last. "After all, you did warn me that you meant to make me sorry if it was the last thing you ever did."

It took a moment even for her to take in the enormity of his accusation, and when she did, she flinched as if he had struck her. Then a rage, more icy than any she had ever known came to her rescue. "You think—you *dare* to think—"

He gave a savage laugh. "I seem to have given up thinking where you are concerned, Miss Mayhew. I had actually come here today, when I could ill spare the time from looking for my missing niece, or so I thought, to tell you I was withdrawing all opposition to my nephew's marriage. Does that amuse you? It should. Even I was capable of being taken in by your beautiful, treacherous face, and I have every reason to despise women of your kind, God knows."

Lucinda was taking all this in with rounded eyes, but at that she said urgently, "What are you talking about? Philippa didn't— "

He turned a face of such savage fury on her that she was, for once, effectively silenced. "As for you, I will deal with you later! Go and get your things."

Lucinda flushed and shrank back toward the door, biting her lip, plainly torn.

Philippa said curtly, "It doesn't matter, Lucinda. Do as he asks."

Once Lucinda was out of the room, however, she said icily, "You need not take out your foul temper on her, at least."

He laughed again. "Since I have just spent the last three days searching for her, along with my nephew and any number of men on the estate, and even set the Bow Street runners to looking for her, while her mother has imagined her dead, or kidnapped or worse, that is rich, even coming from you. She will be lucky if I don't beat her.''

''That is exactly what I might expect from you,'' she retorted contemptuously. ''She had my sympathy from the first, but knowing now that you are her uncle, I begin to understand why she was forced to run away.''

''I am grateful for your advice. I would be even more grateful if you had not tried to ruin her by importing her into so notorious a house.''

She paled at the unforgiveable insult. ''Out!'' she cried in a trembling voice. ''Get out! I hope never to have the misfortune to see you again!''

''That, at least, I can guarantee, Miss Mayhew,'' he said curtly, and left her without another word.

22

WHEN A wide-eyed Betty reported to Aunt Bella that her young guest had been dragged out by an obviously furious Roxbury, that much-tried lady gaped, and wasted no time in finding Philippa.

"Good God, what is this Betty has been telling me now?" she demanded, bursting in on her niece. "Can Lucinda really have been related to Roxbury all this time?" Then she saw her niece's expression and her face fell ludicrously. "No, don't tell me! You've quarrelled with Roxbury again and he means to have us up on kidnapping charges. I swear if it's not one disaster it's another, these days."

Philippa gave a contemptuous laugh that sounded perilously like a sob. "Lucinda is Roxbury's niece, Aunt Bella. It appears he and Julian have been searching for her all this time. As for quarreling with him, I warn you I never want to see him again, or even so much as hear his name spoken in this house for as long as I live. As for Diana marrying Julian, I doubt there is any longer much fear of that happening now, but if she does, I tell you now theirs is one house I will never set foot in so long as Julian retains any ties with his uncle. I have never hated anyone as I hate him."

Aunt Bella, feeling a little as if she had stumbled into a madhouse, wisely said no more, but tottered away, her head reeling.

*   *   *

Roxbury, in the throes of an equal if not greater fury, had almost dragged his niece out of the house and ungently thrust her up into his waiting curricle.

Lucinda was looking more than a little scared by now, for she had never seen her uncle in such a mood, but she said again, urgently, "Uncle Marcus, Philippa didn't know—"

He turned on her with such fury that she shrank from him, her eyes huge and her mouth a little agape. "Never dare to mention her name to me again," he thundered, just as Philippa had done. "And if you are wise, you will not attempt to say anything more to me at the moment, for my temper is none too pleasant and I haven't forgotten I've yet to deal with you."

Lucinda, humiliatingly aware of her uncle's groom up behind, and more frightened of her uncle than she liked to admit, cowered in her seat and wisely said no more.

Once arrived in Grosvenor Place, however, Roxbury pulled up and flung his reins to his groom, then lifted his niece down without ceremony and almost dragged her into the house, with little regard for the startled and then highly curious stares of his staff.

Lucinda, very aware of them and by now thoroughly frightened and humiliated, tried to pull away from him crying furiously, "You don't have to drag me in. I'll come willingly."

He laughed unkindly and at last released her. "You are lucky I don't lock you in your room and throw away the key, as you so richly deserve. And spare me your tears, for I am wholly unmoved by them. In fact, I am tempted to take my whip to you, for you have proven yourself by this escapade a spoiled, unprincipled little brat without a scrap of feeling for anyone but yourself. Now go to your room and remain there. And I would advise you not to make the mistake of trying to run away from me, my girl," he added savagely, "for you will not like the methods I use to retrieve you. In addition, I have every intention of setting a guard outside your door."

"Marcus," cried a startled voice behind him.

Both turned at the dowager's voice, Roxbury with an uncharactertistic dull flush in his cheeks and Lucinda to throw herself into her grandmother's arms. The dowager received her in bewilderment and demanded, "*Lucinda!* What on earth is the meaning of this? Where did you find her?"

"She was with Miss Mayhew," he said, more curtly than she had ever yet heard him speak to her. "I am leaving instructions that a guard is to be posted outside her door until we set out for Featherby tomorrow. In the meantime, don't wait dinner for me, for I won't be home." He turned and walked out without another word.

The dowager, bewildered, turned toward her granddaughter, but Lucinda completed her confusion by bursting into overwrought tears.

The earl not only did not return for dinner, he didn't come in all night. His valet, torn between duty and fear for his employer's safety, had long since fallen into an uneasy doze when his lordship at last strode in at half-past seven the next morning.

Wilcox woke with a start and said foolishly, "My lord! Thank God you are safe."

Far from appearing to be gratified by this devotion, Roxbury rounded on him. "If you know what's good for you, you will confine your attention—and your remarks—to your duty," he said savagely. "But so long as you have chosen to play the martyr all night, you may send for some hot water so I can shave, and set out some fresh clothes for me."

The valet scrambled up, his eyes almost starting from his head, for he had never seen his master in such a mood. "But my lord, surely you mean to get some sleep?"

He was instantly sorry for his temerity, and afterward confined himself strictly to his duty. It was obvious to him that his lordship had been drinking, but he was no longer drunk now, if he had ever been. But his clothes were disheveled and his eyes bloodshot, and he looked like a man who had been up all night.

Worse, his lordship's face was set into such bitter lines that Wilcox scarcely recognized him. In fact, if he had not known better, he would have said his lordship bore all the signs of a man crossed in love. Which was ridiculous, of course.

The dowager, nearly as startled to see her son stride into the breakfast room half an hour later, his face a harsh mask, was not so quick to dismiss that particular suspicion. "Good God," she said, looking him over with a mother's critical eye. "You look as if you ought to be in bed, my dear. But never mind that. What on earth has been going on? I am about to die of curiosity."

She was obliged to sustain her curiosity some minutes longer, however, for Firth chose that moment to sail in to serve his lordship's breakfast. The earl rejected any suggestion of food with every appearance of loathing, but accepted a cup of black coffee, and once that was poured, unceremoniously ordered his butler to get out and not come back.

Once Firth had sailed out again, his dignity evidently unimpaired, his lordship's mother remarked blandly, "Your manners are always so charming, my dear. It is hardly Firth's fault you have a hangover this morning. But I am wholly uninterested in your health at the moment. Tell me at once before I burst, what is all this nonsense about Miss Mayhew?"

It was the last subject he wanted to discuss, but he laughed unpleasantly. "It's hardly nonsense. I can only assume Lucinda has spent the past few days in her company. Yes, I found the fact nearly as startling and a great deal more unpleasant when I discovered her there, I can promise you. But then I knew Miss Mayhew would stop at nothing to secure Julian's fortune for her sister. I just hadn't realized exactly how far she was prepared to go."

His mother was indeed looking startled. "But—this is incredible! You can't honestly be suggesting . . . No, I won't believe it," she said with finality. "If you are suggesting, as I think you are, that Miss Mayhew somehow managed to learn of Lucinda's existence and then kidnapped her or lured her away from her home for her own ends, I have never heard anything so absurd."

"No, I have no doubt the chit ran away from home on her own," he retorted impatiently. "But Miss Mayhew certainly managed to latch on to her somehow and made no attempt to inform me or even Lucinda's mother of her whereabouts. And I warn you I am in no mood to discuss it, Mama."

But the dowager was frowning and made no attempt to comply with this prohibition. "I still can't believe it. I am going to send for Lucinda at once and have the whole story from her."

"Send for her? I would have thought you'd had the whole from her long ago."

"No, for the wretched child refused to discuss it. I tell you I have seldom been so frustrated between the pair of you."

He thrust back his chair with suppressed violence and rose. "Do as you wish," he said harshly. "It is a matter of complete indifference to me. But kindly inform Lucinda that I mean to set out within the hour. The sooner I return her to her mother's care and wash my hands of the whole affair, the happier I'll be."

"But, dearest, you can't mean to set out without any sleep," protested the dowager. "Surely tomorrow will do as well as today? I have sent a message already to Louisa that Lucinda has been found, so there can be no need for this haste."

He ignored her and strode toward the door, but as he reached it, it opened unexpectedly under his hand. He drew back, saying furiously, "I thought I told you not to come back until you were sent for, Firth."

But it was not his butler who stood in the open doorway, but an uncharacteristically chastened if determined Lucinda. "It's not Firth, Uncle Marcus," she said bravely. "But I have to talk to you."

He recoiled with something very like loathing, but the dowager said soothingly, "Yes, dear, I was just going to send for you. Come in and don't be afraid. But I think you had better tell us everything, don't you?"

Lucinda stole a timid glance at her uncle, but came gratefully on into the room. "Yes. I tried to yesterday, but

. . . Is Mama very worried about me?'' she asked shame-facedly. ''I never meant to cause everyone so much trouble.''

Her uncle gave a bitter laugh, but the dowager quelled him with one look. ''Well, it is only natural, my dear, but we will discuss that later. For the moment I want you to tell us exactly what happened after you ran away from home.''

Lucinda glanced again at the earl, but launched reluctantly into her story. The earl had gone to stand by the window, as if divorcing himself from the proceedings, but his grim expression deepened as she hesitantly told of her escape from home, and how she had hidden her suitcase, and her intention of selling her jewels when she reached London.

Even the dowager paled a little when Lucinda reached the part about not having enough money to travel on the stage and the man who had offered to pay for her ticket. But Lucinda said a little defiantly, glancing again toward her uncle, ''But you needn't worry, for I knew better than to accept such an offer from a stranger, which shows that I am far from being the child everyone thinks me. In fact, I planned the whole for weeks beforehand, so you needn't think it was a spur-of-the-moment temptation or that I acted out of pique. I knew exactly what I was going to do, and except for miscalculating about the fare, everything went just as I had planned it. I even knew what I was going to do when I reached London, and if I hadn't met Miss Mayhew, I would have, too.''

''Yes, dear,'' said the dowager. ''But you have now come to the part that interests us exceedingly. How did you meet Miss Mayhew?''

So Lucinda told her of deciding to walk the rest of the way to London, and of Philippa stopping to offer her a ride. ''And she was very kind, for she wouldn't let me sell my jewels or pay her for anything, and if you must know, I had meant to become an actress when I came to town and had an appointment with an actual theatrical director,'' she said even more defiantly. ''But she and her aunt convinced me he was not at all respectable, and so I didn't go, after all, so you have a great deal to be grateful to her for if you but knew it. And as for knowing who I was, I tried to explain to Uncle Marcus yesterday that I never told her my whole name, and even when she tried to pump me, I was always very careful not to let anything slip, even though I began to suspect it was Julian Diana meant to marry. And I w-won't have her blamed for my folly, for she tried from the beginning to make me go home, or even to write to Mama and tell her I was safe, for she disapproved as much as you did of my running away."

"What?" demanded Roxbury, no longer feigning indifference to her story. "Are you seriously expecting me to believe the whole time she never knew who you were?"

"Yes. I knew if I told her she would have no choice but to tell Mama, or y-you, and I would be forced home in disgrace. And I'm not sorry I did it, either, for I have never had so much fun or enjoyed myself more. And I don't care if her aunt used to be an actress, or if I will never get to leave home again for as long as I live, for at least I have had one adventure to look back on. Only I couldn't allow you to blame Philippa," said Lucinda, and burst into tears once more.

As her grandmother soothed her, Roxbury stood as if turned to stone. Then at last he put his head in his hands and cried harshly, "Oh, my God! What have I done, Mama? What have I done?"

23

WHEN THE Earl of Roxbury presented himself in Green Street for the second time in as many days, the maid Betty first gaped at him and then blushed.

"I'm sorry, my lord," she said in some embarrassment. "But Miss said if you was to da—if you was to come back, I was to say she wasn't at home."

He pushed past her without a moment's hesitation. "Very well, you have done so. Now where is she?" he demanded curtly. "Upstairs?"

When she nodded in wide-eyed wonder, he waited for no more, but took the stairs two at a time.

He found Philippa and her aunt in the small drawing room. Mrs. Mayhew frankly goggled at him and the obese pug asleep in her lap woke and began to growl menacingly. The earl ignored both and said abruptly, "Miss Mayhew—Philippa, I must speak to you."

Philippa had risen at his abrupt entrance, nearly as white as her aunt was red, but said now, with frigid disdain, "There is nothing we have to say to each other, as I thought I told my maid to make clear."

"Yes, she told me," he said impatiently. "Philippa!"

Her disdain deepened. "I should have expected you to have no more respect than to force your way past my maid. But whatever you may think of me, this is my aunt's house and you are unwelcome here. Be so good as to leave at once."

"Philippa!" gasped her aunt, a little shocked despite herself. "Oh, hush, Caesar, or I'll put you out. As a matter of fact, you don't need me, either," she added with a shrewd glance at his lordship and beginning to haul herself to her feet.

"Aunt Bella, don't you dare to desert me," cried Philippa a little shrilly. "I am not in the least interested in hearing anything Lord Roxbury may have to say to me."

Aunt Bella looked uncertain and sank back again.

Roxbury said harshly, "Then I will say what I have to say in her presence. You must know why I have come. My niece has disclosed the whole, and it seems clear I am considerably in your debt. If I misjudged you, I beg your pardon."

She replied frigidly, "Your opinion is a matter of complete indifference to me. Now, if that is all you wished to say, pray go."

He bit his lip in frustration. He was operating under all the handicaps of an autocratic man faced with the evidence of his own willful blindness and for once unsure of his ground, and he was even further hampered by the presence of her aunt. Worse, despite everything he knew, he still was convinced no relationship between them was possible because of his mother. To marry the niece of a woman his father had once made a fool of his mother with, was out of the question. It had been bad enough when Julian wished to marry her sister. But how could he, who had spent his life protecting his mother, deal her such a humiliating blow?

After a moment he said stiffly, "No, it is not all, as you very well know. I have no excuse for my conduct, except that I had endured an exhausting week searching for the little—searching for my niece. I misjudged you and I beg your pardon. But Lucinda has told me how very much I must be in your debt, as well as your aunt's, and I had to come and tell you so. I can only apologize for my niece's conduct as well, and offer to reimburse you for any expense you may have been put to during her stay with you."

Philippa turned in an instant from a disdainful goddess

to an avenging fury. "If you *dare* to offer me money, I shall throw it back in your face," she cried pantingly. "That's your answer to everything, isn't it? As for misjudging me, from the first you have delighted in believing the worst of me."

"If I have, you must be aware of my reasons," he said still more stiffly. Then his stiffness dissolved, and despite himself he took a hasty step toward her. "Philippa—!"

She recoiled as if she could not bear him to touch her. "But then I suppose I should hardly have been surprised you believed me capable of using an innocent young girl to be revenged upon you," she cried violently. "I am, after all, guilty of trapping an innocent boy for his fortune, as well as confronting an elderly and harmless woman with the proof of a twenty-year-old affair merely out of spite! It is no wonder you believed I would not stop at so little a thing as kidnapping to achieve my own ends."

He halted, a slight flush staining his cheeks. "You must know I have long since stopped believing you guilty of any of those things. And in my defense, I think even in my first white-hot rage I never believed you had done it out of spite. But I haven't forgotten, if you have, that you once told me you would do almost anything to secure your sister's happiness. Or that my own inexcusable conduct may have forced you into it."

Far from being appeased, she nearly gasped with rage. "I should be grateful to you, I suppose. At least you believed I had some justification, however immoral, for ruining your niece."

Once more he flushed darkly. "I didn't mean that, and you know it. It is clear you are determined to think the worst of me—as determined as I once was, I will admit, to think the worst of you. But it has been a long time since I have been able to do so—or to remember with any consistency why it would be madness to become involved with you."

"I take it that is supposed to be a compliment?" she demanded icily. "I find it somewhat difficult to tell your compliments from your insults. But I feel certain that, with your determination, you have managed to overcome any such madness.''

He gave a harsh laugh. "No. That is the damnable part. Even when I believed you the harpy you spared no effort to make me believe you, you little spitfire, you haunted me to a degree I could not explain—or forgive in myself. Even this conversation shows how very far I have sunk, for I have vowed to say none of this to you. And don't look so outraged, for you know exactly why I am in danger of betraying everything I had believed in.''

She was indeed looking outraged. "The only thing I know is that I have never met anyone I dislike as I dislike you.''

"And I have come to love you, against all honor or reason or will," he said harshly. "If you wished to be revenged upon me, you could not have chosen a better way.''

"You! You don't even understand the meaning of the word 'love.' And if you *dare* to ask me to become your mistress again, I shall—I shall—I don't know what I'll do, but it will make everything that has gone between us before look innocent, believe me!''

Both of them had completely forgotten Aunt Bella's presence by then. "No," he said curtly. "I have no intention of asking you to become my mistress. I had sworn to give you up, but it begins to seem as if I can't live without you. I am asking you to become my wife, God help me. It is the one thing I have no right—no moral right—to do, but it seems I can't help myself. And that is your fault as well, for before I met you, I was a rational man, with no intention whatsoever of getting married, let alone to the one woman in the world I should hold at arm's length.''

As a proposal it was hardly fortunate, but he sounded like a man goaded beyond endurance, as he was. Philippa, unfortunately, heard only the harshness in his tone, which she took for contempt. "How dare you?" she cried again, in a voice that shook with the force of her emotions. "I should no doubt be honored that the great Earl of Roxbury would stoop to wed the niece of a notorious actress, however unwillingly, but I think I would rather die first.''

He realized his mistake, too late, and he put out a hand to her, an odd laugh escaping him. ''Oh, God, I must be mad. Philippa, my darling shrew, I don't give a damn about your aunt. It's you I've discovered I can't live without, God help me.''

But the laugh settled it. ''I thought you had insulted me in every conceivable way, my lord,'' she said in a low, throbbing voice. ''But it seems I was mistaken! If you could believe me capable of marrying you, after all that has passed between us, that is by far the worst insult of all.''

He flushed abruptly, the laugh dying on his lips and his hand dropping slowly to his side again. ''Forgive me. You may believe no insult was intended,'' he said at last. ''I may have spoken clumsily, but in fact I offered you what I have never offered to any other woman before.''

When she still showed no signs of unbending, he hesitated, then bowed once and added ironically, ''But forgive me. I will not insult you any longer with my presence.'' He bowed and walked out.

Aunt Bella, who had been sitting throughout this remarkable exchange with her mouth agape, bounced up as soon as he was gone, tumbling the unprepared Caesar on the ground and crying wrathfully, ''Philippa! Have you gone mad? Good God, he actually proposed! I wouldn't have believed it if I hadn't heard it with my own ears. And to think he was ready to ruin us over his nephew marrying Diana.''

Philippa had not moved since he walked out, but at that she seemed to recover a little, for she flushed and said in a strangled voice, ''If he proposed, you may be sure it was only to insult me. Oh, I have never hated anyone as I hate him. How dare he think that he had only to dangle his handkerchief, despite all the things he has accused me of, and I would leap into his arms like the—the light-skirts he believed me.''

''Philippa!'' cried her scandalized aunt. ''That is a term I won't have in this house. At any rate,'' she added, descending rapidly from such Olympian heights, "no proposal from a man with his fortune is an insult, believe me, you wretched girl. When I think . . . Julian's fortune is paltry compared with his. And what with Darius' fees, and Genia's future to think of, not to mention your own, I could just scream with vexation."

"I would rather all of us starved than be beholden to him for so much as a penny, Aunt Bella. At any rate, you may be sure he didn't mean it. He regretted it almost as soon as the words were out of his mouth."

"Good God, there's nothing new in that," said her experienced aunt. "No man likes to give up his freedom, and with you acting the ice princess and shrieking at him whatever he said, I'm sure it's no wonder. But you may be sure he won't be back, after the way you treated him. Oh, it's enough to make me tear my hair."

"I don't want him back," cried Philippa. "And if he dares to show his face here again, I shall have him arrested, I swear I will." Then she proved it by bursting violently into tears and abruptly running from the room.

24

LORD ROXBURY returned home in a bitter
mood that was not helped by finding his mother impatiently awaiting him, eager to hear the outcome of his
visit. He had, as a matter of fact, seldom been less in
charity with her, and had to make himself go up to see her.

"Well?" she said eagerly. "Did you see Miss Mayhew
and apologize? From what that scamp Lucinda has been
telling me, we have even more reason than I thought to be
grateful to her. I shudder to think what might not have
become of her if they hadn't taken her in. Incidentally, we
have had a reply from Louisa—or rather from Lady Minton, for it seems Louisa is still too prostrated to write
yet." Her eyes began to twinkle. "She fears that Louisa's
shattered nerves are unequal to facing the return of Lucinda just yet, and so has agreed to let her remain in
London with Theresa, at least for the time being."

Roxbury was glad to find a legitimate outlet for his
temper, and exploded, "Good God, I might have expected
it. The only thing Louisa suffers from is a fatal tendency
to quack herself. I can almost forgive Lucinda for running
away. But the result is that she is now to be rewarded,
instead of punished for her outrageous conduct."

"Yes, dear, I'm afraid it will seem so to Lucinda, but
we both know she will be far better off with Theresa,
whatever we may think of the methods she used to achieve
her end," replied his mother blandly. "And I think, after

183

all, that she is quite chastened—if not for the reasons we might wish. She is very concerned that Miss Mayhew not be blamed for her conduct, which I hope you will own shows her heart is in the right place. Which brings me back to the subject at hand. I hope you were able to atone to her for your dreadful suspicions?''

He laughed rather harshly. ''Not with any noticeable degree of success. But then it seems I have wasted few opportunities either to insult her or to abuse her, or worse. She hardly has any reason to love me, I fear.''

His mother looked at him with a faint frown in her eyes, for it was unlike her son to be humble. ''Good God. I know you disapproved of Julian's marriage to her sister, but surely that was just a misunderstanding that can be cleared up?''

''I fear you are optimistic, Mama. But then you don't yet know the whole. I have threatened Miss Mayhew, tried to ruin her, and even offered her bodily harm,'' he said bluntly, an expression in his eyes she had never seen there before. ''I thought I was doing it to protect Julian, but now I am no longer so sure. I seem not to know myself any longer.'' He looked up and gave another harsh laugh. ''You should be pleased, in fact, for if nothing else she has done her best to point out my arrogance to me. I fear I have indeed grown as xenophobic and unbearable as you have often accused me of being.''

She smiled at him. ''Not if you can say that, dearest. You love her, don't you?''

He again buried his head in his hands. ''Oh, God! Is it so obvious? I must be mad, for I had thought myself the last man to be taken in by a beautiful face. And God knows I have fought against it.''

''Then stop fighting against it and give in and marry the girl,'' recommended his mother strongly. ''Forget who her aunt is.''

He raised his head at that. ''Do you really believe me such a snot I give a damn what her aunt used to be?'' he cried violently.

Then, as she frowned, he seemed to recover himself slightly and turned abruptly away. ''At any rate, your advice is too late. I am so lost to all sanity, God help me, that I proposed to her, when it was the one thing I had vowed never to do. But I have made her hate me and I have no one but myself to blame.'' He laughed again without humor. ''It's almost poetic justice, wouldn't you say?''

''No, for I have no taste for that sort of thing. And why on earth was marrying Miss Mayhew the one thing you vowed never to do?''

But he had had time now to remember exactly who he was talking to, and possessed just enough remaining decency to pull himself up short. ''No!'' he said with obvious self-loathing. ''I have not fallen quite that low yet. Let us talk of something else—anything else, Mama. I had no right to trouble you with any of this anyway.''

The dowager ignored that completely. ''I hope it is not because you are protecting me, my dearest?'' she asked, troubled. ''Because if so, I fear I am the one at fault, for not telling you long ago that I am perfectly aware your father once tried to elope with her aunt.''

He stiffened and drew up his head to look at her as if he had never seen her before. ''No! I don't believe it. You can't have known all these years.''

''Dearest, of course I knew. A woman always knows those things,'' she said calmly. ''I've no doubt it upset me at the time, but I have had over twenty years to get over it, after all. Good heavens, is that why you have opposed poor Julian's marriage all this time? Poor boy, it is hardly fair to make him suffer for the sins of his elders.''

He still seemed unable to take it in. ''You have known . . . Oh, God, that makes it even more exquisitely humorous. And all these years, I never guessed. It seems I am far less observant than I have prided myself on being.''

''My dear, I learned long ago not to wear my heart on my sleeve. But of course I knew, as I knew about all the other affairs your father engaged in. For obvious reasons I saw no need to discuss it with you, but perhaps I should have. Perhaps it would have made a great many things different, for you mustn't think I ever blamed your father. He was what he was, and he couldn't help that any more than you can help being what you are. And I fear I was a most unsatisfactory wife, you know.''

"*I* blame him," he said harshly. "I always resented him for his treatment of you, but at least I knew nothing about that side of him until *that* particular affair. But once I did—and after I knew—it was impossible to close my eyes to it, for he was hardly discreet about his affairs, I fear. I met the evidence of them everywhere. I think I actually hated him.''

"Yes, I should have known it was something like that," she said sadly. "My poor darling, I fear you have lately been hating yourself even more, for falling in love with the one woman you thought you couldn't have. That is my fault as well, I fear. But it needn't be final, surely? If you were to explain to her—''

He gave a ghost of a laugh. "It is far too late for that, Mama, and it has nothing to do with you. I have no one to blame but myself. I met the one woman capable of being unswayed by my title and possessions, when I didn't believe such a woman existed, and then lost no opportunity to make her hate and despise me. You should be proud of me indeed.''

In the meantime, Philippa came downstairs the next morning to breakfast, heavy-eyed, but composed, her unusual bout of weeping over.

She came to kiss her aunt's cheek and said steadily, "I beg your pardon for making such a fuss, Aunt Bella. Lord Roxbury is not even worth our notice. Where are the children?''

"I sent them off to the park," answered her bewildered aunt. "They were nearly as overcome with curiosity as I am, I must confess. Fortunately Julian came last night and told us all about it, or I think I would have gone completely mad. It seems he and his uncle had been searching all over for Lucinda, as you said. He could scarcely get over the coincidence of her being here all the time.''

Philippa ignored that and poured herself a cup of coffee. "What will happen to Lucinda now, did he know?''

"Yes, but I should have known that one would land on her feet like a cat," retorted her aunt a little bitterly. "It seems her mama is too upset to have her back, so she is to

remain in London after all, with Julian's mother. Julian
said she is already talking of her come-out ball and the
need to order a whole new wardrobe. He thought it amusing, obviously, but I must confess I had begun to wonder
if it wasn't what she intended from the beginning, and all
her talk of the stage so much hot air.''

"Yes," said Philippa, "I long ago suspected as much.
But you mustn't blame her, and I'm glad if she is to be
happy now."

"I would be even gladder if someone a great deal closer
to me were happy now," retorted her aunt bluntly. "As
you might have been if you weren't so pigheaded. To
think of letting Roxbury slip through your fingers . . ."

But Philippa had stiffened, looking suddenly so unlike
herself that even her aunt was a little shaken, and broke off
unwillingly. "I warn you, Aunt, that I don't want to
discuss it—ever," she said hardly.

Her aunt hesitated, then reluctantly gave in. "Oh, very
well, though why—" Then she caught Philippa's eyes and
relented completely. "Oh, never mind, I've done! I'm far
from understanding any of it anyway. Though if Diana
weds Julian you may have trouble maintaining that pose.
But then I daresay she won't, for I always knew it was too
good to be true," she ended pessimistically. "You will
all end your days old maids, scraping and pinching exactly
like I have always done, which is a great shame, if you ask
me. But then if you are resigned to it, who am I to
complain?"

When Philippa remained unsoftened, she finally gave it
up and went away, shaking her head.

She might have been encouraged by the fact that the
Dowager Countess of Roxbury called in Green Street unexpectedly that same afternoon, but unfortunately she had
gone out and didn't know of it.

For her part, Philippa's first panicked inclination was to
refuse to see the dowager. Then belated dignity stiffened
her spine and she went downstairs to receive her, ashamed
of her cowardice.

If the dowager noticed her shadowed eyes and rapidly
fluctuating color, she was too tactful to remark on it. She

herself was leaning very heavily on her sticks, which she explained cheerfully always happened when the wind was in a certain quarter. Even so, she still managed to look remarkably elegant and made Philippa, in her homemade dress, feel even more awkward and foolish.

"But I have not come to talk of that, of course, my dear," said the dowager in her charming way, "but to thank you for your care of my naughty granddaughter."

Philippa blushed and felt even more wretched. "There— believe me there was no need, ma'am," she said with a lamentable lack of poise, which was unlike her.

"On the contrary, there is every need. I shudder to think what would have happened to her if it hadn't been for you. I hope I need hardly tell you that she had no notion either, which hardly excuses her, of course. I fear she has been kept far too sheltered and is something of a hoyden as well."

"Oh, no, pray don't apologize for her," said Philippa in some agitation. "And you must believe that I did no more than any other responsible person would have done in the same circumstances. It is *I* who should apologize, for I knew—knew how concerned her family must be. I tried to make her tell me where she lived, or at least write to you herself, even if without revealing where she was. You must believe that! I would never—"

"My dear, no one blames you," said the dowager kindly. "I won't deny we were all frightened, but no great harm has come of it, after all, thanks to you, apart from my daughter's taking to her bed, which she always does in any emergency. I could never have advocated such a violent method of getting our attention, but I won't deny even some good may have come of it, for Lucinda is to live with her aunt, my other daughter, at least for the present. So perhaps we may be spared any more adventures of that particular kind, at least."

"Yes, so Julian told us," said Philippa inadequately. "I'm glad, for I liked her very much."

"And she enjoyed her stay with you far more than she should have, I fear," confessed the dowager with an engaging twinkle. "But now that we have disposed of my naughty granddaughter, I must confess I had another reason for wishing to speak to you, my dear. What is this you have been doing to my usually sensible son?''

Philippa paled and then flushed hotly and said desperately, losing what little poise she still possessed, ''N-nothing! Ma'am—please, I must beg of you—if he s-sent you, there is nothing more to discuss. I th-thought I had made that very clear to him.''

''Yes, he said he had made you hate him,'' said the dowager frankly, looking her over with a good deal of shrewd interest. ''But from our last conversation together—which, incidentally, I enjoyed very much—I hoped that might not be wholly true. You see, I had given up on ever having a daughter-in-law, and certainly one I could enjoy, so my interest is a very personal one. I was hoping to persuade you my son is not so very bad, after all.''

Philippa was wringing her hands by now. ''Ma'am, you cannot know the whole,'' she said wretchedly. ''If you did, you would despise me, not wish me for your daughter-in-law. For one thing, my aunt was used to be a notorious actress. Have you forgotten that?''

''Not in the least. And if I minded, I fail to see what that has to do with you, my dear.''

This remarkable large-mindedness shocked Philippa a little, but she said desperately, ''For another, your son was right about me from the beginning. I schemed and plotted to get your grandson's fortune for my sister.''

''Yes, and quite rightly too,'' said the dowager approvingly and even more surprisingly. ''What else were you to do with two sisters on your hands, and a brother to educate as well? I'm sure I would have done exactly the same thing.''

''Ma'am! You don't . . . Thank you! I know you are trying to be kind. But there is still worse to come. I tried to—to—blackmail your son!''

''Yes, dear, I know,'' said the dowager calmly. ''I can't remember when I have been so diverted, as a matter of fact.''

25

"YOU—YOU *know?*" cried Philippa in disbelief. "And still you came?"

"My son told me all about it," said the dowager calmly, drawing off her gloves in a gesture that indicated she had no intention of leaving any time soon. "I found it very brave of you, in fact, for I suspect my son can be very formidable."

"I—I was trying to force him into releasing your grandson's fortune so Diana could marry him," cried Philippa, as if convinced the other could not have fully grasped the enormity of her crimes.

The dowager's twinkle grew even more pronounced. "Yes, but according to Marcus, the provocation was very great."

"He said that?" demanded Philippa in astonishment. Then she made an attempt to recover herself. "If—if so, he was being kind, ma'am. No provocation could have justified what I did, and he was certainly furious enough himself at the time."

"That, at least, I can believe," said the dowager in amusement. "But before we go any further, perhaps I should clear the air at once by admitting that I also know all about your aunt's affair with my husband, so long ago. I knew about it at the time, as a matter of fact."

Philippa groped for a chair and sat down, because her knees would no longer support her. "You knew that too?"

she whispered in shame, her hands to her blazing cheeks. "Oh, what must you think of me?"

"You might be very much surprised," said the dowager. "And if I had admitted it long ago, instead of clinging to my foolish pride, a great deal of unhappiness might have been avoided, I fear. Has my son told you anything about his childhood, by the way, my dear?" she added in an apparent non sequitur.

"No. No, of course not. But believe me, there is no need!"

The dowager smiled a little sadly and ignored that. "No, I thought not. But there is every need, for it explains much that may not be readily apparent to you. As you may have gathered, he is some years younger than his sisters, and was born long after we—and particularly his father—had given up any hope of achieving a son. My health had already begun to deteriorate, I fear, after my accident, and in fact my doctors warned me point-blank against having any more children. But my husband was insistent and—who knows? Perhaps I hoped that if I gave him a son, it would bind him to me. You see, I make no attempt to excuse myself in what happened. But at any rate, that is neither here nor there. After some time Marcus was born. I won't bore you with the details, but the birth was a difficult one, as foreseen, and I regret to say that my health was never the same afterward."

Philippa's hands were still to her burning cheeks, and she asked painfully, "Why are you telling me this, ma'am?"

"Bear with me, my dear. I will try to be as brief as possible. But as a result of my ill health, I foolishly chose to remain in the country after that, and so perhaps I am to blame for my husband's philandering as well. Naturally my son remained with me, and since both my daughters were grown by that time, I fear I clung to him more than I perhaps should have. My husband was bored in the country and had an unfortunate and quite genuine dislike of any physical infirmity, so as a consequence we saw very little of him."

"Oh, no," cried Philippa in genuine horror.

Lady Roxbury smiled more naturally. "I'm not trying to arouse your sympathy, my dear, but only to explain, a little bit, why my son is—as he is. He and his father were not close, and he had come to blame him for his own birth, which is absurd, of course, except that he was convinced my health had been sacrificed for the sake of an heir. Under the circumstances he soon began to resent it when my husband shrank from me and neglected me, or so he thought. I don't make light of my part in this, Miss Mayhew, for I should have seen what was happening and put a stop to it. But . . . Well, it is easy to be wise after the fact, and I was not very wise then, I fear."

When Philippa said nothing, but sat as if rooted to the spot, her eyes alive with pain and pity, the dowager went on calmly, "As a result, he grew up rather absurdly protective of me, as you might imagine. Even so, he should have outgrown it, and no doubt would have, had he not learned, at a particularly impressionable age, of his father's affair with your aunt."

"Oh, no," whispered Philippa again, feeling sick.

"I won't go into details, my dear. In fact, I only began to suspect he knew just recently, when he behaved so oddly over Julian. It seems we were both foolishly protecting the other, for he, in turn, never dreamed that I knew. Well, the long and the sort of it is that his relationship with his father deteriorated even further, to the point that they were barely speaking at his death, and I fear he became far too cynical, at too early an age. He naturally blamed his father most, but he developed an obsession against—forgive me!—women like your aunt, whom he perceived as heartless and immoral. I had no idea what was the cause, but I knew something must have happened, of course. In fact, until recently I had given up all hope of his ever marrying."

Philippa had flushed again violently at that, but she said, in a voice she tried without much success to keep steady, "I repeat, ma'am, why are you telling me this?"

"Because it has a great deal of bearing on you, I suspect, and because, as I said, it has all been bottled up for too long. Perhaps you can see, now, why when you and your sister crossed his path, he was prepared to be-

lieve the worst. He would have, in any case, for I have
said he is far too cynical, but your aunt being who she was
only made it worse, of course. I am not trying to excuse
him, my dear, but only to explain to you why he behaved
as he did, however inexcusably.''

Philippa rose abruptly and took an agitated turn away.
''It is unnecessary, I assure you, ma'am,'' she said jerkily.
''At any rate, it does not concern me. Whatever you may
think, Lord Roxbury does not really desire to marry me.''

The dowager was regarding her with disconcerting sympathy. ''Doesn't he, my dear? He said he had met the one
woman capable of being unswayed by his title and possessions, and then he had ruined it all by making you despise
him, which I must confess I have never heard him say
about any other woman.''

Philippa's cheeks were now flying hot color and she
could no longer meet the dowager's eyes. ''Ma'am,
please! I beg of you!'' She made an effort to control her
voice and went on more strongly, ''I don't know what
Lord Roxbury may have told you, but I fear you must have
mis-misunderstood. If he proposed, he regretted it almost
instantly. Whatever he may have said, d-deep down he
despises me as well as my aunt. If you could have heard
. . . But it makes no difference. Be assured that such a
m-marriage is the last thing either of us desires.''

''Yes, I fear he bungled his proposal badly, my dear,
but I have discovered most men do, when it comes to
something that really matters to them.''

''E-even so, ma'am, there is no possibility of my agreeing to such a match. My own responsibilities make any
marriage impossible at the moment, and for a good
many years to come. My brother and sister are still
very young, and much as I love my aunt, I could not
ask or expect her to take over the responsibility for
them. I had, in fact, m-made up my mind not to marry
until they were grown.''

''I'm sure that is very noble of you, my dear, but I
wonder if it is not unnecessary? And I think you are
underestimating my son,'' said the dowager frankly. ''Are
you so very sure he would be unwilling to take responsibil-

ity for your brother and sister as well? Keep in mind he has stood much in the position of father for his nephew Julian for nearly ten years, despite the slight difference in their ages. I have always thought, in fact, that he would make an excellent father.''

Philippa was thrown to her last defense. "That—that may be, ma'am, but Ju—Lord Holyoke is a blood relation, after all, and he must have known him all his life. This situation is quite otherwise—in fact, it is impossible. Aside from my brother and sisters, there is my aunt. She has been far too kind to us for me to abandon her now, nor can I expect your family to accept such a relationship. In fact, everything you have told me this morning has only made me more determined. There is too much bitterness and pain between us ever to be forgotten, I fear. Lord Roxbury may desire me, but it goes no deeper than that, believe me, ma'am," she said a little bitterly. "If—if he l—loved me or I him, it might be different, but as it is, there can be no hope of lasting happiness for either of us. I beg you to accept that.''

The dowager looked troubled and said very gently, "For my son I can only assure you I think you are mistaken, my dear. But forgive me, I think you are not quite as indifferent to him as you would have me believe. In fact, I think you are very much in love with him, aren't you?''

"Too much to risk seeing him come to hate me, as my uncle did my aunt, ma'am," said Philippa in a low voice, her eyes on her tightly clasped hands.

The dowager sighed and pulled on her gloves at last. "How little we realize, when we are young, how long our sins will continue to haunt others. My dear, I am sorry. I don't mean to press you anymore, for only you know what is in your own heart, after all. I will only say that I let my own pride stand in the way of competing for my husband for a great many years, and I have come to bitterly regret it. I hope you won't make the same mistake I did. Now I am going, but I hope we shall see each other again—whatever you decide. No, don't come with me. My maid is just outside and knows ex-

actly how to help me. Good-bye, my dear, and I am
sorry if I've upset you."

She was gone on the words, leaving Philippa a prey to a
great many emotions, chief among which was a despair
blacker than any she had ever known before.

26

IF PHILIPPA enjoyed a second bout of bitter tears after the dowager's departure, at least this time no one knew of it. And she was still convinced she had done the right, indeed the only, thing. Roxbury could not love her. Even his proposal had been couched in such terms as to make his opinions of her clear. And if he had been prepared to go to such lengths to prevent her sister's marriage to his nephew, how much more reason would he have to come to despise a wife who possessed undesirable relatives and who could only serve to remind his adored mother of an unhappy time in her life?

That sensibly decided, she determined to put the whole out of her mind and succeeded so well she lost all her appetite and had to make herself show an interest in the normal household events. At the same time she was disgusted by her own folly. She had long ago determined to give up all hope of marriage, at least until the two youngest children were off her hands. And certainly, despite what his mother had said, she could not imagine Roxbury living with her brother and sister, nor would she ever abandon them to Aunt Bella.

In fact, everything supported her decision, she told herself, and tried to draw herself out of her uncharacteristic depression.

But if she were looking for proof of the wisdom of her decision, it gave her surprisingly little pleasure to be proved right about Roxbury. If he were not already regretting his proposal, he certainly made no further attempt to see her or convince her to change her mind, and she heard no more from the dowager.

She had determined not to weaken if he did, but she could not suppress a bitter stab of disappointment that her noble resolve was not even put to the test. Very likely he was congratulating himself already on his narrow escape, which only proved how right she had been to refuse him.

Unfortunately Aunt Bella was far from being reconciled to such a loss. She did not directly refer to the subject again, in reluctant obedience to Philippa's unexpectedly harsh fiat, but she could scarcely contain her disappointment. She was pessimistically convinced, as well, that Julian would somehow slip through their fingers, for she could not believe that, after everything, Roxbury would not keep his promise to withhold his nephew's fortune.

But in that she was proven wrong, for Julian soon reported, quite unconscious of the bombshell he was dropping, that his uncle had already put the legal paperwork in train to put him in full possession of his fortune, so that he and Diana could be married almost immediately.

Aunt Bella almost choked, her hope reviving dramatically, especially when Julian also reported that his uncle had at last brought his mama around and convinced her, if not to welcome his marriage, at least to accept it with an appearance of complaisance. But Philippa soon deflated her hopes again by saying shortly that no doubt he had merely at last given in to the inevitable, as she had always known he must. At any rate, it was far more likely the dowager had been behind this sudden turnaround, not Roxbury.

Aunt Bella was grateful to have that small crumb at least, when she had been convinced they were likely to lose the whole cake, and afterward threw herself into plans for Diana's wedding with enthusiasm, eager to have it safely over. If Philippa could not be as enthusiastic, she was determined that no one would guess how little her heart was now in something she had gone to such lengths to try to achieve.

They had heard nothing beyond a brief note from Lucinda, repeating the gratitude she feared she had not adequately expressed and apologizing for any trouble she may have caused them. She also reported that her uncle was returning her to her home, after all, but only briefly, to see her mama and pick up her baggage.

She was obviously happy, and the rest of the short note was full of her plans for the future. She promised to come and see them as soon as she returned, and hoped they would see one another frequently, especially now that Diana was to be her cousin. In the meantime, she remained, etc., their Incorrigible Lucinda.

Aunt Bella read through this missive a second time and humphed over it, but it was obvious it had done much to soften her opinion of the flighty Lucinda. But Philippa could read a lively curiosity between the lines about what had happened between Philippa and her uncle, and was not sorry not to see her and be obliged to fend off her questions. But then she doubted whether either Roxbury or Lady Holyoke would encourage her to keep up so unlikely a friendship.

And for once she was fortunate, for she was out with Diana helping to choose a length of silk for her bridal gown a few days later when Lucinda at last called, freshly returned from her visit into the country and full of all her old mischief.

Lucinda was thus obliged to make do with Aunt Bella, who reported vaguely to Philippa afterward that she had been full of talk of the wedding and her own come-out next year. She had promised to come again as soon as she was able, and had seemed delighted that Diana was to be her cousin, but had said very little more and in fact only stopped by on her way to do some shopping.

So comfortable was Aunt Bella's report that when Roxbury burst in upon her late in the afternoon some two days later, Lucinda was the last thing on Philippa's mind.

She stiffened at sight of him, angry with herself for feeling a first, betraying joy. But any faint, clinging hope that he might have come to make her change her mind was killed by the harsh expression on his face. From the look of him it was clearly not as a lover he had come, but a man operating under some strong and much more unpleasant emotion.

Her heart sank, but before she could speak he said curtly, "I am sorry to intrude, but my business will admit of no delay. In fact, I am hoping you have tried to reach me already. Unfortunately, I was out until half an hour ago. Is Lucinda with you?"

It was the last thing she had expected, and she stiffened even more, unable to believe he could insult her in the same way so soon again. "No, she is not," she said furiously. "And if that is what you have come bursting in here to ask me—"

But he was frowning harshly and said almost blankly, "Good God! I made sure you would have her safe. In fact, I have just spent half an hour I could ill spare convincing my sister of the fact. Are you sure there is no chance that one of your sisters might be deceived into hiding her?"

She should have been annoyed by that further insulting suggestion, but something in his face made her suddenly abandon her high horse and say urgently, "No, of course not! What is it? I cannot believe she has run away again."

He hesitated, then laughed harshly. "If she is not with you, then I can only assume so. And in that case I am sorry to have disturbed you."

He bowed and would have left her, had she not cried out in considerable frustration. "No, wait! You can't be serious. In the note she wrote us Lucinda sounded exceedingly happy, and my aunt said when she saw her two days ago that she was full of her come-out. I can't believe it."

He hesitated, but remained, if obviously against his will. "Nor could I," he responded harshly. "But I am left in little doubt of the matter, for she left a damned preposterous note for my sister's delectation. Unfortunately, my sister was out most of the day, and I myself only returned home half an hour ago, so she has had any number of hours' head start. Which is also why I cannot delay any longer. I had hoped—indeed counted on your having her safe. But if not, I again beg your pardon for disturbing you."

"But what are you going to do?" she demanded urgently, mistrusting the look on his face.

"Find her," he said grimly. "And when I do, she will be lucky if I don't murder her."

"No! Wait! Let me think," she said in some agitation. "This is absurd, for I tell you she had no intention of running away two days ago. Has anything happened since then to upset her?"

He was plainly impatient to be off, but answered shortly, "Nothing, according to my sister. She is convinced she meant all the time to trick us, but if so, she belongs on the stage, for she is a better actress than I gave her credit for." Then he laughed harshly. "But apparently that is her conclusion as well, for she informed us of the fact in her remarkable note."

"Informed you of . . . But that is more ridiculous than all the rest. I would swear, in fact, that she has no such ambitions. When she ran away the first time, it was because she was unhappy and you had refused to intercede for her. She has no more desire of becoming an actress than I do."

He flushed a little at the implied rebuke. "If I refused to intercede for her, it was because I had no legal standing to do so," he said unwillingly. "I am not her guardian, nor in any way responsible for her. But this is all wasting time. If I am to catch up with her tonight, I must set out at once."

"To do what?" she demanded. "You had no luck the last time, remember. And I tell you none of this makes sense. Oh, let me see her note."

He shrugged, but after a moment pulled it from an inner pocket and handed it to her. "I warn you you will find it as nauseating as I did, Miss Mayhew. As an epistle it is remarkable only for its misspellings and the remarkable pap she chose to regale us with. It certainly betrays no clues as to her destination."

But Philippa was already rapidly scanning it, a frown between her own brows. It was addressed, not to Roxbury, but to Lucinda's Aunt Theresa, and was indeed full of misspellings and a great deal of nonsense. But as she read on in growing horror, she paled and once exclaimed aloud. She could see now why Roxbury had thought immediately of her, for Lucinda said quite frankly that she had decided to become an actress, after all, despite being allowed to live in London and promised her come-out. She was sorry for all the trouble she had caused, but her aunt wasn't to worry, for she had an introduction to a reputable manager this time, who had agreed to take her on for a tryout while they toured outside London. If she succeeded, as she had every hope she would, she would be given a part when they returned to London, and then very likely she would soon become as famous as Mrs. Mayhew had been. In the meantime she sent her love to her mother and grandparents and was sorry she would miss Julian's wedding, but she hoped everyone would understand. She remained her aunt's obedient Lucinda.

Philippa looked at up last, her cheeks very white. "But I don't understand," she cried helplessly. "In fact, I don't believe a word of this. She had given up any ambition to become an actress, I *know* she had. As for an introduction to a reputable manager, you can't think that I would—"

"I think nothing of the kind," he interrupted shortly. "This is merely another of her tricks. But this discussion is getting us nowhere, I'm afraid."

But she had paled even more and said now, almost afraid even to express her doubts, "No! Aunt Bella could never have . . . I won't believe it."

"Calm yourself, Miss Mayhew. I don't suspect either you or your aunt is behind it. As I said, I only came because I hoped—was convinced, in fact—that she would come to you and you would have her safe."

But she was scarcely listening. "Wait here," she cried abruptly and almost ran from the room.

She was aware that he had not obeyed her and was close on her heels, but she was too upset to care. She almost burst in on her aunt, napping in her dressing room, and said urgently, "Aunt Bella, I am sorry for disturbing you, but it's very important. Earlier this week when Lucinda was here, did she give you any hint that she was unhappy or still thinking of becoming an actress? Please tell me."

Aunt Bella was naturally startled, and Caesar awoke, rising to shake himself and glare at the intruders. But it was not the dog that commanded Philippa's attention, for to her horror Aunt Bella had flushed up with every appearance of guilt.

It took some time to drag the whole story out of her aunt, and by the time she had, Philippa could scarcely hold her head up. Aunt Bella had been feeling a little low the day Lucinda had called, and had been encouraged by Lucinda to engage in reminiscences of her successful days on the stage.

Lucinda had been flatteringly interested, and now that she had returned to her family, Aunt Bella had seen no harm in regaling her with a few of the more amusing stories of her youth—or at least those suitable for a seventeen-year-old to hear. Lucinda had been fascinated, saying she had been to the theater with her aunt the night before and had never enjoyed herself so much, and wondering who of those still famous Mrs. Mayhew knew.

Aunt Bella had seen no harm in dropping a few names, either, and it was only in retrospect that she had wondered if Lucinda hadn't been a bit too insistent for one interested only in the vicarious thrill of the theater. "But I never guessed she meant to do anything about it," she cried unhappily. "In fact, she was full of her come-out ball, as I told you."

"Oh, Aunt Bella," said Philippa, alive with shame. "At least try to remember what you told her. She talks of a company going on tour. Did you tell her of such a company?"

Aunt Bella succumbed to a few easy tears, but at length confessed that she had just received a note from an old friend, telling her about a company they had once both belonged to that was setting out on tour. It was that that had made her nostalgic for the old days, and it was just possible she might have mentioned it to Lucinda. Well, more than possible, for she remembered discussing the manager, who was still the same after all these years, and mentioning that they were setting out almost at once. Lucinda had been very attentive, but Aunt Bella had meant no harm and had never guessed that she might be noting it all down for future reference.

"Oh, Aunt," said Philippa again, sick at heart. "Where were they going? Do you know that at least?"

But Aunt Bella, pulling herself together, certainly knew. They were to tour the south, starting with Brighton, and to remain for some weeks playing there, if they were well-received. But she didn't know why Philippa was making such a fuss about it, for the whole thing was absurd. Manning, the manager, was a seasoned professional and would hardly take on a child of Lucinda's age, particularly with no experience.

"Even if she used your name and said you had recommended her?" asked Roxbury bluntly. "Believe me, she is perfectly capable of it."

Aunt Bella flushed tellingly again and reluctantly subsided.

Philippa made herself meet his eyes, almost overcome with shame and fear. "It is just possible, but you must believe I—we would never have aided her in such a step," she managed in a voice very unlike her own. "It was wrong of Aunt Bella, but she never guessed—and she knows their itinerary, or can find it out. Please, you must let us help."

He took a hasty step toward her and seemed momentarily to have forgotten her aunt—or even his niece for that matter. "My deares—my dear Miss Mayhew, I don't blame you. Calm yourself. You can't be blamed if my niece chose to take advantage of information your aunt let fall." His expression hardened. "In fact, I know exactly where to lay the blame."

But Philippa was beyond hearing him. "No, I fear it is my fault, for she met my aunt through me. B-but I'm sure you will be able to overtake them before she can come to any real harm. My aunt says—says he is an honorable man, and we must believe that."

Roxbury took her hand and held it warmly. "You may be sure I will find her, but whether she will be safe once I do is another question. Don't upset yourself needlessly. Now, I must go. I have stayed too long already."

She had no idea why he was being so kind to her, but it only made it worse. She clung to his hand and said foolishly, "You cannot go alone. She will need a woman—someone she knows—to be with her."

"Unfortunately my mother is visiting friends out of town, nor would I subject her to such a journey, and my sister is so angry with Lucinda she would hardly be a comfort to her. At any rate, I doubt it will be a comfortable journey."

But she had straightened, seeing something she could do, at least. "Then I am coming with you," she said determinedly.

He looked thunderstruck. "Don't be absurd. It will be a far-from-comfortable journey, and thanks to my aunt's social obligations, the note was not found until very late. They have many hours' head start on me. I am by no means certain I will even overtake them tonight."

He sounded so grim, she said urgently, "Oh, what does that matter? What does any of it matter so long as we find her safe—and in time. I am coming with you if I have to hire my own chaise to do it. Oh, why do you stand there arguing when every moment may be vital?"

He looked down at her for a moment longer, a frown deep in his eyes, then gave in without another word.

27

ROXBURY INSISTED upon her bringing a warm cloak with her, however, for he had no idea what time they might return, then escorted her out to his waiting curricle with little delay.

Philippa, nearly as anxious as he and almost overcome with shame and guilt, was surprised when he chose to waste what she considered valuable time in searching out the offices of the theatrical company to discover their exact route. Once he had disappeared inside, she sat impatiently waiting for him to return, trying to calm her terrified nerves, which insisted that every second's delay might be important. She did not think Lucinda would come to any harm, but she dared not take that chance, particularly given her Aunt Bella's guilt in the affair.

Roxbury seemed to take an inordinate time and she was almost ready to scream by the time he at last returned, escorted by a stout, red-faced man. They seemed to be on excellent terms, which relieved one of her fears, at least, for the man shook his hand warmly and watched him swing up into his curricle again, before going back inside.

Philippa said impatiently, "Oh, what have you been doing? You have been an age."

"It has been time well spent," he retorted with grim satisfaction. "As I suspected, they are hardly traveling light, for they set out with no fewer than five post chaises and as many wagons. Even better, they did not start until after noon, due to some confusion with the baggage, which I gather is their normal mode of travel. We should catch them up along before they reach Brighton.''

She felt a little cheered by this news and so held her tongue while he necessarily maintained what seemed like a snail's pace in the busy city streets, frequently held up entirely by traffic and obliged to weave his way between carts and pedestrians.

But once Westminster Bridge was crossed, she could not resist saying urgently, ''Oh, thank God! Now we can make some time.''

He glanced at her, but merely urged his chestnuts into a brisk trot. ''I am sorry to disappoint you, but we have some miles to travel before the first change, and not even for Lucinda do I have any intention of ruining my horses' knees,'' he said dryly. ''It would end up wasting even more time, anyway, if I have to bring them in dead lame,'' he said shortly.

She was reluctantly forced to recognize the truth of his words and said no more. But within the first few miles she had to admit that he knew what he was doing and that he was quite as grimly determined as she was to find Lucinda. He maintained a steady pace that ate up the miles, his chestnuts apparently indefatigable, and only by the harshness of his expression and his concentration did he reveal his own urgency. Even so, he communicated none of that urgency to his horses, and she soon acknowledged him an excellent whip.

He was forced to check briefly at the Kennington turnpike gate, but his groom had the yard of tin ready and blew up for the pike in good time. As they drove through, Fobbing warned in a low voice, ''Mind Brixton Hill, my lord. No point in taking the heart out of them so soon.''

Roxbury didn't bother to answer, nor did he need the advice, as circumstances fell out. It was past five o'clock by then, and they had mercilessly met little traffic once they left London behind. But at Brixton Church they drew up behind a mail coach, which obstinately held the center of the road and refused to let them pass.

Roxbury was forced to pull to a crawl, cursing softly

under his breath. His groom said pessimistically, "You'll not get past before Streatham, my lord."

"You are mistaken," returned his lordship grimly. They had approached a sharp bend in the road and the mail-coach driver, evidently secure in the conviction they would not try to pass him on so sharp a turn, pulled fractionally back to his side of the road, in case there might be any oncoming traffic.

Roxbury did not hesitate, but abruptly gave his chest-nuts their heads. His groom gasped and Philippa hung on tightly, aware of a small thrill of fear. But the next moment they flashed past the mail with seemingly only inches to spare.

"Oh, well done," cried Philippa spontaneously, and surprised a laugh out of Roxbury.

"Yes, you have been wanting me to spring them since we set out, haven't you?" he inquired. "Well, you are about to have your wish."

He took the four miles remaining at a gallop, while his groom hung on for dear life and shook his head at both of them.

In Croydon he was obliged to slow down again, but even she could tell his chestnuts were nearly spent. "Let's hope you haven't lamed them," said his groom grimly, and blew for the change.

They drew up in the courtyard of the posting house where the ostlers and postboys already stood ready. Philippa nervily declined any offer of refreshment and waited in a fever of impatience for the new team to be put to and arrangements to be made for the return of Roxbury's own team.

The next moment Roxbury swung up beside her again and said shortly, "They passed through here scarcely three hours ago. It is fortunate they are so remarkable a party. The postboys easily remembered them."

She was slightly reassured, but still kept her gloved hands gripped rather tightly in her lap as they set off once more.

At any other time she would have enjoyed the scenery they were passing through, but she was too keyed up to

notice it. It was evident at once that the new team was by
no means the equal of his chestnuts, but he kept them well
up, and they encountered no more mishaps. By the end of
the long stage they were obviously laboring, however, and
his groom said encouragingly, "No more than a couple of
miles on, now, sir, and downhill all the way."

Roxbury merely grunted. When they reached Horley
and waited for the next change, he insisted upon Philippa
getting down and stretching her legs, however. He also
sent for a glass of lemonade and some macaroons for her,
over her protests, and insisted she eat them, saying shortly
that it would do no one any good if she were to make
herself ill.

She flushed, but was forced to agree and indeed drank
the lemonade, at least, very gratefully, for she was exceedingly thirsty by then. But she was unused to his uncharacteristic solicitude, however gruffly administered.

He himself had gone to question the ostlers again and
soon returned to report with satisfaction that they were
gaining on the theatrical troupe. "We should catch them
up by Cuckfield, if we're lucky. Are you ready to go on?"

"Yes, of course," she answered quickly, allowing him
to help her into his curricle again. "They are still on this
road, then?"

"Oh, yes! Even if they suspected they were being followed, they had no hope of any speed with such an
assorted cavalcade. It would hardly seem an ideal way to
make off with inexperienced young fools like my niece,"
he said contemptuously.

She flushed again, thus reminded of her guilt in the
matter, and said no more.

The new team was worse than either of the previous
ones, and even Roxbury was unable to hold them up to
their bits. It was almost dark by then and growing quite
chilly, and Roxbury made Philippa pull her cloak around
her, his expression growing even grimmer as the miles
wore on.

At the next stop he went briefly to confer with his groom,
then came back to say abruptly, "I am sending you home,
Miss Mayhew. It was folly to have permitted you to come

along on such a journey, and you are obviously exhausted. I have engaged a post chaise to take you back. It will leave as soon as you have had some dinner and are a little rested."

She nearly gaped at him, furious that he could think her so weak as to be prostrated by a simple journey, however nerve-racking. "I have no intention of going back on my own. I said I was coming with you, and I meant it. And since my purpose in coming in the first place was to protect Lucinda, I have every intention of continuing on. If you won't take me with you, I will follow in the post chaise instead."

He looked annoyed, but after a rather searching look at her face in the light spilling out from the open door of the inn, he gave in. "Very well! I am agreeing only because we should overtake them within the hour. But I should insist upon sending you back."

She made no answer, and they did not delay much longer but were soon on the road again.

She was indeed very tired by then and beginning to feel the chill wind, but the news that they should find Lucinda within the hour heartened her considerably. The newly poled team was a vast improvement on the last, and she sat up a little straighter, consumed by a renewed urgency now that they were so close. She wanted to beg him to hurry, but wisely held her tongue and betrayed her anxiety only by the way her eyes strained to see in the darkness before them and by the tension in her posture.

Roxbury, too, seemed to feel a little of her urgency, for he was taking the road very fast, no longer bothering to nurse his team or make allowances for the limited visibility.

Once his groom said sharply, "It will do none of us any good if we land in the ditch, my lord."

"Leave the driving to me," retorted the earl, and made no attempt to slacken his pace. "I know this road like the back of my hand, and there is a straight run to Hand Cross."

The groom looked unconvinced, but subsided, once more shaking his head. Philippa sympathized with him, but could not but be grateful, despite the obvious danger of barreling through the dark at such a pace. She had long since placed complete confidence in Roxbury's driving, and now that they were so close, she would have liked to have gone even faster.

But in the event, the groom was soon proved right, for in another couple of miles there was an ominous crack, and the next thing Philippa knew she was thrown heavily forward, only Roxbury's hard arm preventing her from being thrown out completely.

Then Roxbury snapped harshly to his groom, his hands full calming his team, "Go to their heads! Are you all right? I should be whipped for not sending you back before."

She straightened gingerly, aware the vehicle was resting at an ominous angle. "Yes, of course," she said automatically, straightening her hat. "But how are we to go on? We must catch Lucinda tonight."

Fobbing had gone to the horses' heads by then, and Roxbury was able to climb down and help her out. "Obviously we can't. We will have to wait here until Fobbing can ride into the next village and send a vehicle back for us."

She bit her lip, aware it would do no good to protest, but absurdly near to tears for some reason. "It can't be helped," she said at last. "How—how far is the next village?"

It proved to be no more than a couple of miles, but they were obliged to cool their heels while Fobbing rode in and sent a vehicle back for them. Roxbury insisted upon wrapping her in his coat, despite her protests, and she sank onto a stone beside the road, suddenly enormously weary now that all hope of catching Lucinda anytime soon had been lost.

They were required to wait nearly half an hour before Fobbing at last returned for them. "You won't get that wheel fixed tonight, my lord, at least not without sending into Cuckfield for the parts," he reported gloomily. "But I've hired this vehicle and a sturdy-enough pair, and if I remain behind to see to the repair of the curricle, you should not lose much more than an hour and a half, all told."

Roxbury made no reply to that, but merely inquired shortly, "Is there an inn in this village?"

Upon being assured that there was, he lifted Philippa into the hired vehicle as if she were no longer able to help herself, then climbed in after her and took the reins from his groom.

Once they reached the village, he made straight for the inn and said even more shortly, "We are staying here for the night. No arguments! My mind is made up. I should never have brought you along in the first place on such a wild-goose chase."

She started to protest; then, realizing he would not be stopping if it weren't for her, she said insistently, "You go on. I will be perfectly all right here, and you may catch them even yet."

"Don't be absurd! I am fast losing all desire to catch up with them, and I have no intention of dragging you any farther—nor of leaving you alone here," he answered harshly. "From their dilatory progress so far, it seems obvious they won't reach Brighton tonight, and if today's evidence is anything to go on, they will scarcely set off again before noon tomorrow. We should reach them long before that."

She opened her mouth impetuously, foolishly unable to accept that they would not rescue Lucinda before morning, after all, then closed it again, seeing it would do no good to argue any further. Her tired brain told her he was right, and it would make no real difference, but her heart was insistent on the necessity of overtaking Lucinda before she had spent a night away from home. She did not believe any real harm would come to her—she could not allow herself to believe it—but if such an escapade should ever become known, it would effectively ruin Lucinda's reputation.

She must pray it would never become known, and at worst she could always claim Lucinda had been in her company all the time. But given her aunt's reputation, that was hardly likely to prove any particular help or lessen the scandal if any whispers should start.

In her weariness, she could only feel wholly to blame

and knew she would never be able to forgive herself if Lucinda should be ruined, or worse.

But as if aware of her thoughts, Roxbury put an unexpectedly warm hand on her cold and twisting fingers. "Stop it," he said. "You are not to blame, so stop torturing yourself. Now come inside and warm up. You will be the better for some dinner, believe me."

She was by no means as convinced, but he was proved right, for after they had been served with a surprisingly adequate meal, given the lateness of the hour, she was obliged to own a slight improvement in her spirits.

But then Roxbury, at his most autocratic, had also insisted upon her drinking a glass of wine with her dinner, and perhaps it had done as much as the food to raise her spirits.

She was certainly exhausted and had trouble keeping her eyes open by the time he escorted her up to her allotted bedchamber and stood holding a candle for her. But then it was past midnight, after a long and exhausting day, so perhaps it was little wonder.

She stood a little shyly before him at the door, suddenly remembering all that lay between them, and could not quite meet his eyes. "I feel much better now, as you said. What time do you wish to leave in the morning?"

"I will have you called at seven. And thank you! I fear it is not a word I often use, but I do thank you, and apologize." He started to say something more, then, as once before, abruptly raised one of her hands to his lips before turning away and striding down the hall.

28

PHILIPPA THOUGHT she would be too keyed-up to sleep, but in fact she knew nothing more from the time her head hit the pillow to being awakened the next morning by the chambermaid bringing her morning tea.

She was instantly awake, surprised and a little ashamed she had slept so well. She washed and dressed hastily, having to make do with yesterday's crumpled gown and a borrowed comb, then hurried down, once more impatient to be on their way.

She found Roxbury already in the coffee room before her, but he insisted she eat some breakfast before they set out. When she impatiently declined, he made her drink a cup of coffee and peeled a peach for her himself.

She was embarrassed by his ministrations and did not know him in this softer mood. But then it occurred to her that that was not the only difference in him this morning. It was almost as if the fury that had driven him yesterday had gone, for some reason. It might merely be that she was unused to his solicitude on her behalf, for certainly she was far more used to his insults, but she did not think it was only that. It was almost as if the urgency of their mission had gone as well, as far as he was concerned. He seemed merely preoccupied, as a matter of fact, as if his thoughts were elsewhere, and did not rush her over breakfast.

He did not protest, however, when she finished her

peach and insisted she was ready to set out, but rose and led the way outside.

She discovered that Fobbing had been busy that morning, for he had already arranged for his lordship's wheel to be taken into Cuckfield to be repaired and had the horses for the hired vehicle already put to. He would plainly have preferred to supervise these repairs himself, but Roxbury said shortly, with an odd frown, "No, I may need you. You had better come with us."

The groom looked rather curious, but obediently swung himself up and they set out once more.

They were only five miles from Cuckfield and reached it in less than an hour. It proved to be a thriving little town, with two inns on the main street, one a coaching inn, its yard bustling with traffic even at that early hour, and another, far more modest inn at the far end of town. Without hesitation Roxbury passed the first and drove on to the second.

They were rewarded almost at once by the sight of several gentlemen and colorfully dressed ladies lounging or sitting about the yard, and a number of shabby vehicles still standing with their shafts empty. Several of them eyed the newcomers with some interest, making Philippa aware of what she must look like after a long day in an open vehicle and no baggage the night before, but one readily volunteered, when asked, that they were with the theatrical company.

Now that the moment had arrived, Philippa's heart was beating a little fast, half-afraid of what they might find. Roxbury, too, was looking slightly more grim again, but he climbed down without a word and handed her out.

At the door she restrained him with a hand on his arm, saying in a low voice, "Please, what do you intend to do? Perhaps it would be better if I saw her first."

He looked down at her for a moment. "I am not, as you so obviously envision, planning to lay violent hands on the manager, or even Lucinda, much as I might like to," he said dryly at last. "In fact, I have the oddest suspicion . . ." Then he broke off and shrugged. "Never mind! Let's get this over."

He led the way inside and was directed by a chamber-maid up the stairs. Philippa followed him, wondering what he had been about to say. But there was no time for that, for he had already reached the door indicated, and hesitated only a moment before thrusting it open without warning. Then he froze on the threshold, an expression of the blankest astonishment on his face. "Good God! I was beginning to suspect a trick of some kind, but . . . *you!*"

It took Philippa, close at his heels, a moment longer to take in the extraordinary scene that met her eyes. The room seemed to be a private parlor of some sort, and Lucinda was seated at a small table, calmly eating raspberries and cream for a late breakfast, while the Dowager Countess of Roxbury was seated by the window, leafing through a newspaper.

Both looked up as the door opened, but betrayed no astonishment at sight of them. The dowager, in fact, smiled and said calmly, "Come in, dear, and close the door. I expected you last night, in fact."

"We had a slight accident," returned her son grimly. "I should no longer be surprised by anything you might do, Mama, but I must confess you have astonished me. Perhaps someone will be kind enough to tell me what the devil is going on."

He made no apology for his language, and his mother had seldom been treated to the harsher aspects of his temper, but she merely smiled and said blandly, "All in good time, my dear. But you said you had begun to suspect a trick. I'm curious. What gave us away?"

He laughed briefly, without humor. "The trail was far too easy to follow, if you must know! I began to suspect yesterday when we gained on you so rapidly. A great deal might have been explained by the dilatoriness of your progress, but not all. It was almost as if the company took care to keep just ahead of me and make themselves conspicuous, which I began to find very curious indeed."

"Oh, dear! I am not very good at this, I fear. And you have no idea how difficult it is to dawdle along the road when it is important you do so. I'm sure I never had a journey when I was in a hurry that was so free of delay and bad fortune. As I said, I expected you to catch up with us yesterday. Really, I was almost annoyed with you, my dear.''

"I apologize. You must blame it on my delayed start. Unfortunately Theresa did not return home to find Lucinda's letter until late in the afternoon, and it took me a while to follow the careful clues you left for me," he returned sardonically.

"Yes, but you did, in the end," put in Lucinda admiringly, obviously enjoying herself. "I think it was dreadfully clever of you."

"Yes, Mrs. Mayhew played her part very well. I can see she used to be a talented actress. I take it she was also in on the plot?"

Lucinda admitted it unabashedly, but Philippa seemed unable to take any of it in. "Aunt Bella was in on this? But why?" she demanded in bewilderment. "That is what I can't understand."

"I can tell you that," said Roxbury harshly. "My mother and my niece, in a misguided and wholly inexcusable wish to meddle in my affairs, hoped to bring us back together again. I had at least expected better from you, Mama, than to lend yourself to such an inexcusable charade."

"Oh, no!" cried Philippa, her hands to her suddenly hot cheeks.

Lucinda bounced up out of her chair. "Yes, but now it is even better than we thought, for you came to save me from being ruined, but it is Philippa who has been ruined instead. Now she will have to marry you to save her reputation," she pointed out irrepressibly.

"Oh, no," choked Philippa again in an agony of embarrassment and humiliation. "Oh, no, how could you?"

Roxbury's face was as harsh as she had ever seen it, but he said curtly, "Calm yourself, Miss Mayhew. That fate at least need not befall you."

"No," said the dowager still calmly. "If Philippa does not wish to marry my son, then of course she doesn't have to. I have only to say she was in my company all night, and I will be believed. But I must confess I hope very much you will reconsider, my dear.''

"That is indeed noble of you, Mama," interrupted her son savagely. "It would have been even more noble if you had refrained from meddling in what doesn't concern you, and incidentally saved Miss Mayhew, not to mention yourself, a long and needless journey. It is scarcely a fitting reward for her concern about Lucinda, I would have thought."

"Nonsense, I at least enjoyed the journey very much," insisted the dowager. "I hope I am not so old and decrepit I still cannot enjoy an adventure or two in my life. And you had made such a muddle of things, my dear, with your harsh temper and clumsy proposal, it seemed to me something drastic was called for. I will say only one thing more, before I leave you to sort out your differences, for I despise women who become managing in-laws," she added with an infectious twinkle in her eye. "Philippa—very naturally, given your behavior, I must say—dared not marry you for fear you would come to hate her as her uncle came to hate her aunt. But since the cases are in no way similar—and I knew that was nonsense, for it is clear she is the only woman likely to save you from yourself—I felt justified in interfering, just this once. Now we are going. Come on, Lucinda. We must bid our new acquaintances good-bye, for they have wasted enough time in helping us.''

But neither Roxbury nor Philippa was paying any attention any longer, or even noticed when she whisked Lucinda out, with only a minimum of protest from that highly curious damsel.

"Is that true?" he demanded at last incredulously. "Good God, you little fool! I thought I had made you hate me."

She blushed, but found she could not let him go on thinking that, for some reason. "Surely you must know how long it has been since I have been able to hate you as I thought I should?" she inquired in a low voice, unable to meet his eyes. "But please, I beg of you, say no more. You must—you can't—''

But he wholly ignored her prohibition to sweep her

abruptly into his arms. "You little fool," he said again.
"And it has been even longer since I have been able to
remember anything other than that I want you more than I
had thought it possible to want a woman. My mother will
tell you that, for even when everything in me rebelled at
what I thought was a betrayal of her, I still could not fight
your damnable attraction for me. I told you once that if
you wished to be revenged upon me, you could not have
chosen a better method. I meant to use every means at my
disposal to prevent Julian's marriage with your sister, and
instead, I found myself falling hopelessly in love with
you."

She was very pale by now, but continued to hold him at
arm's length, with some difficulty. "Don't!" she whispered. "Oh, can't you see? Whatever I—we feel, it is not
fair to your family."

"To hell with my family," he retorted roundly. "At
any rate, it must be obvious by this elaborate and ridiculous charade that my mother at least is more than delighted
with the match. Obviously she knows she will get grandchildren from me no other way."

"No," cried Philippa pitifully, trying to cling to what
she knew was right, against growing odds. "You cannot—
you don't know what you're saying. Have you forgotten
my aunt was once a notorious actress and tried to run off
with your father?"

"I have neither forgotten, nor particularly care what she
was once, my foolish darling. I am far more interested in
the fact that she was kind to you at a moment when you
needed her, and that is all that matters to me."

She thought she must be dreaming, for she had never
expected to hear such words from him. But still she re-
sisted the lure of weakly giving in to him. "Even so, there
is still my brother and sisters. And I will not abandon them
to Aunt Bella."

"Unlike your late and never-to-be-sufficiently unlamented
fiancé, I not only don't expect you to, but I would strongly
resist leaving them in your aunt's care. I have no wish to
insult you, my poor darling, but it has been obvious to me
for some time that they could use a man's hand in their

upbringing. Not only am I quite prepared to accept them into my household—at least until Diana marries Julian, which, incidentally, I think should come after, not before, our own marriage—but I like both of them, surprisingly. I haven't much experience with children, but I think I can make a good brother-in-law to them.''

"As for that, they both like you already,'' she said foolishly, scarcely knowing what she was saying. "But you don't really wish to marry me, I know you don't. You proposed the first time against your will, and this time you have been forced into it by your well-meaning mother.''

He calmly tipped up her chin and ruthlessly kissed her. When she at last recovered from this embrace, a great deal of her resolve had been shaken, but she said in a breathless voice, "You—you want me, I know that, but that is a very different thing. Please, I beg of you, don't make this any harder than it is already.''

"I not only want you, you have become a total obsession with me, my darling. I don't yet know myself whether I was actually asking you to become my mistress, so long ago, but I think I knew even then that that would never satisfy me. I hate to admit it, but I think I clung to my misconceptions about you for so long for the simple reason that I was afraid of you, and the power you might have over me, from the moment we first met. I do know that I was jealous of the thought of you with my nephew, however much I might despise the sort of woman I believed you to be.''

She weakly leaned her cheek against his shoulder because her neck seemed too weak to support it any longer. "This is ridiculous. You can't wish to wed the niece of a woman you have despised for so long, you know you can't.''

"Shut up!'' he retorted, kissing her violently again. "I not only wish to wed her, I have begun to discover in the last week that I cannot live without her. I have thought you a great many things, but I had never before suspected you of being stupid, my love.''

As if finally convinced by these unloverlike words, Philippa abruptly abandoned the argument and threw her arms around his neck, lifting her face again to his. "And I—I have long realized that I never hated you at all, much as I tried to. I should despise myself, for you have treated me abominably, but it doesn't seem to matter anymore. I only know that without you the future had never seemed so bleak."

When Lucinda at last tentatively stuck her head around the door, some time later, it was to find them seated side by side on the settee, her uncle's arm tightly around Philippa and her bright head against his shoulder. She observed these unmistakable signs of reconciliation with some interest, but said, "I'm sorry to interrupt, but I just came to tell you that Grandmama and I are leaving now. Fobbing has hired a post chaise for us, but Grandmama says you need not come with us, for he will be all the escort we need." She grinned and added irrepressibly, "Are you going to be married? I'm glad. Now you will be doubly related to me, for Diana will be my cousin and you will be my aunt."

"That is hardly the reason we are marrying," pointed out her uncle dryly. "And you are a scamp. If I weren't—reluctantly—obliged to be grateful to you, I would send you straight back to your mother."

She grinned. "Yes, but then I would only be obliged to run away again," she retorted incorrigibly. "I'm going! I'm going! But don't you mean to see us off?" she demanded mischievously.

She correctly read the answer on his face and closed the door again, wondering how to tell her grandmama that she had been supplanted in her son's affections at long last.

About the Author

Dawn Lindsey was born and grew up in Oklahoma, where her ancestors were early pioneers, so she came by her fascination with history naturally. After graduating from college she pursued several careers, the strangest and most interesting of which (aside from writing romance novels) was doing public relations for several zoos. She and her attorney husband now make their home in the San Francisco area.

ROMANTIC INTERLUDES